ST. MARTIN'S

MINOTAUR

MYSTERIES

PRAISE FOR THE SISTER MARY HELEN MYSTERY SERIES:

"O'Marie twines the strands of these disparate lives with humor and sympathy."
> —*Publishers Weekly* on *Requiem at the Refuge*

"Another first-rate installment in an unfailingly entertaining series."
> —*Booklist* on *Requiem at the Refuge*

"Enlivened by its series of incisive character studies—and sure to please the Sister's legion of fans."
> —*Kirkus Reviews* on *Death Takes Up a Collection*

"O'Marie delivers compelling characters and sophisticated plotting in her best effort to date."
> —*Publishers Weekly* on *Death of an Angel*

"[An] excellent mystery series . . . hard to put down."
> —*Booklist* on *Death of an Angel*

"The author's handy mix of humor and suspense again proves irresistible."
> —*Publishers Weekly* on *The Missing Madonna*

Also by Sister Carol Anne O'Marie

DEATH TAKES UP A COLLECTION

DEATH OF AN ANGEL

ADVENT OF DYING

Available from
St. Martin's/Minotaur Paperbacks

The
Corporal Works
of Murder

❧❧❧

Sister Carol Anne O'Marie

St. Martin's Paperbacks

THE CORPORAL WORKS OF MURDER

Copyright © 2002 by Sister Carol Anne O'Marie.

All rights reserved. No part of this book may be used or reproduced in any manner whatsoever without written permission except in the case of brief quotations embodied in critical articles or reviews. For information address St. Martin's Press, 175 Fifth Avenue, New York, NY 10010.

Library of Congress Catalog Card Number: 2001059795

ISBN: 0-312-98466-9

Printed in the United States of America

St. Martin's Press hardcover edition / August 2002
St. Martin's Paperbacks edition / June 2003

St. Martin's Paperbacks are published by St. Martin's Press, 175 Fifth Avenue, New York, NY 10010.

10 9 8 7 6 5 4 3 2 1

Congratulations to
my sister, Kathleen O'Marie,
on her sixtieth birthday!

And to
my nephew, John Benson,
and his new bride, Denise!

With special love to my nieces,
Caroline and Noelle Benson!

The
Corporal Works
of Murder

Sunday, June 3

❧❧❧

Feast of Pentecost

The early-morning knock on her bedroom door startled Sister Mary Helen out of a deep sleep. "What is it?" she called, fighting down the dread that immediately began gripping her stomach.

"Telephone," Sister Anne whispered hoarsely. "It's Sister Eileen."

"What's wrong?" Mary Helen quickly slipped on her robe and slippers. In her experience, anything good rarely came in an early-morning or a late-night telephone call. She hoped this call from her old friend was an exception to the rule.

"Nothing's wrong. I think she just wants to talk," Anne said reassuringly.

"At this hour?" Mary Helen grumbled. Putting on her bifocals, she checked her bedside clock. Good night, nurse! It was six o'clock in the morning! What could be so important?

"Hello," Mary Helen said.

"Hello, yourself, old dear," Sister Eileen called cheerfully.

At the sound of her good friend's voice, any grumpiness Mary Helen felt melted away. As it turned out, all that was wrong with Eileen was a little loneliness and a big desire to chat.

No wonder, Mary Helen thought. Eileen had been in Ireland for over a year caring for her sister Molly, who was slowly dying of cancer. It was a very difficult task that she was doing remarkably well.

During that same time, Sister Mary Helen had been with Sister Anne, one of the young nuns, ministering to homeless women at the Refuge, a daytime drop-in shelter in downtown San Francisco. After more than fifty plus years in education, it was all new to her. Much to everyone's surprise, including her own, she loved the work, proving that some old dogs can learn new tricks.

Although Eileen and she spoke and wrote frequently, there was still a lot to catch up on. The time slipped away. "If we talk much longer, it'll be cheaper to fly over," Mary Helen said finally.

Reluctantly Eileen agreed. "Regardless of cost, I feel a hundred percent better," she said before she hung up. Mary Helen did, too.

Running a little late, Mary Helen hurried across the campus of Mount St. Francis College, where she lived, toward the chapel. The thick fog made her face tingle and her nose drip. The sides of the college hill were so banked in that, if she didn't know better, she'd think the city below had disappeared.

Sister Mary Helen slipped into her pew just as Father Adams, wearing bright red vestments, entered the sanctuary to begin the liturgy for Pentecost. Mary Helen loved Pentecost Sunday. She never tired of hearing the Scriptural account of the first Pentecost with the disciples of Jesus cowering in the upper room, afraid that they, too, would suffer His fate.

Suddenly, a driving wind had filled the room and tongues of

fire rested above each of them as the Holy Spirit infused them with courage and wisdom, commanding them to go forth and teach all nations. *It must have been something to see,* Mary Helen thought, imagining the group bursting from the room, all speaking at once. Amazingly, when they spoke, everyone, regardless of the language, was able to understand.

That's hard to do even when everyone speaks the same language, Mary Helen thought as Father Adams continued on with the Mass.

When it was over, Mary Helen joined the other nuns for breakfast in the Sisters' dining room. Sister Therese, who liked her name pronounced "trays," had the floor. "Since the Holy Spirit came in tongues of fire," she announced with a silly grin, "I suggest we have a barbecue for supper."

Sister Mary Helen noticed Sister Patricia's gazing out the dining room window. She knew exactly what the college president must have been thinking. The whole hill was shrouded in a thick June fog. The foggiest month in San Francisco and Therese wants to have a barbecue! She could imagine what the kitchen crew would have to say when they were told. Fortunately, most of them spoke only Spanish.

For a moment Mary Helen thought of all those tourists who must be downtown shivering in short sleeves. No amount of vacation write-ups about the city's strange microclimates ever seemed to convince them that San Francisco in the summer is cold. She thought, too, of the women who dropped into the Refuge during the week for warmth and comfort. She wondered how "the refugees," as they were affectionately called, were faring today. No doubt they were wearing everything they owned.

"You think it's quite the weather for a barbecue?" Sister Ursula asked tactfully. Apparently the question fell on Therese's deaf ear.

"Since red is the order of the day," Therese announced, "we can have red meat done on red coals, red wine, and tomatoes!"

She looked so pleased that no one, not even old Donata, who usually could be counted on to call a spade a spade, had the heart to dampen her spirit.

The day passed quietly. Mary Helen even had time for a short nap and a long read of her latest Marcia Muller mystery. "A murder mystery is the normal recreation of the noble mind," some sage had once said. Mary Helen believed it, although she still covered her paperback whodunits with an ornate prayer book cover. No sense scandalizing the ignoble.

At supper time, Sister Mary Helen stood shivering with the other Sisters near the large black barbecue grill. She tried her best to look pleasant, but between the fog and the smoke, it was difficult.

"This is nuts!" old Donata complained loudly as Therese, undeterred by smoking coals, flipped over the tritips. "I'm taking mine inside," Donata grumbled. "The rest of you can freeze to death if you don't have any better sense."

Mary Helen noticed several faces brighten at Donata's suggestion. She was so preoccupied with her frozen fingers that she didn't hear Sister Anne sidle up to her.

"Are you all set for tomorrow?" Anne asked through chattering teeth.

"Child's play after this." Mary Helen closed her eyes against a billow of black smoke. "Why do you ask?"

"I just remembered that I have a dentist appointment in the morning at ten," Anne said. "I'm wondering if you'll be all right alone at the Refuge. Ruth Davis is the volunteer. It's just a check-up. I won't be long."

"All right alone?" Mary Helen felt a sharp jab of annoyance. "First of all, I'll hardly be alone. Secondly, why wouldn't I be all right?" she asked, feeling sure that Anne was harking back to last year when Mary Helen had discovered the battered body of a young prostitute at the side door of the Refuge. It had been unnerving, surely, but how often does a thing like that happen?

She marveled at how much more at home she was with the refugees now than she had been then. She was even beginning to understand their special language—"street talk," as they called it. Crazily she imagined a little flame hovering above her head ready to impart courage and wisdom and the gift of a street-talking tongue.

"Of course I'll be all right. What could possibly go wrong?" she asked crisply, and then wished she hadn't. She didn't like the wary look that flickered for a moment in Anne's big hazel eyes.

Monday, June 4

❧❧❧

Feast of St. Francis Caracciolo, Confessor

Sister Mary Helen woke to the sound of foghorns outside the Golden Gate. Their melancholy wail warned all who could hear that it was going to be another damp, dreary summer day.

Slowly she opened her eyes to check the time. In five minutes her alarm clock would begin its jarring ring. Happy to be saved from that annoying noise, she pressed the off button. Then she wrestled down the temptation to turn over and go back to sleep.

She heard the convent's central heating system snap on. Ten minutes more, she thought, and her bedroom would be just warm enough to make getting up bearable.

When she woke again, forty-five minutes later, she scarcely had time to dress and hurry across the campus to the college chapel. Father Adams, notorious for his quick Masses, was already at the homily. She arrived to hear him making reference to the saint of the day, Francis Caracciolo, who, with a group of fellow clerics, had begun an order dedicated to practicing the corporal works of mercy.

He began to list them in the same rote manner that Mary Helen had taught them to generations of schoolchildren. "To feed the hungry, give drink to the thirsty, clothe the naked, visit the imprisoned, shelter the homeless, visit the sick, and bury the dead."

Listening, Mary Helen was strangely moved. Now that she was actually "feeding the hungry" and "sheltering the homeless," these phrases took on a deeper meaning. More than that, they took on human faces.

When Sister Anne and Sister Mary Helen drove up to the Refuge, a group of women were already waiting at the front door. Wordlessly they huddled together for warmth. Most were covered with layers of clothing. One woman was wrapped in a faded green, ragged blanket. As Mary Helen approached the group, she instinctively held her breath. The odor of dirt and sweat, mingled with damp wool, was overpowering.

"Good morning, ladies," Anne said, quickly unlocking the door. "And how are you all this morning?" she asked cheerfully.

A woman standing beside a shopping cart full of black garbage bags answered for the group. "I be blessed," she said simply.

Mary Helen felt as if someone had squeezed her heart.

Once inside, the two nuns snapped into action making fresh coffee, serving doughnuts, and, above all, turning on the heat. Before long the women seemed to literally thaw and the Refuge took on its usual comfortable feel.

Ruth Davis, the morning volunteer, arrived a little early. Mary Helen was glad to see her. Ruth, a retired nurse, was a no-nonsense kind of woman. Tall and big boned, she was willing to take on any task. Instinctively the women knew to go to Ruth to have a wound cleaned and bandaged or to complain about an ailment. More times than not, she suggested a cup of hot tea and a little rest. Amazingly, that usually did the trick.

As the morning wore on, the "regulars" drifted in, one by one. Venus was the first to arrive. She looked as if she hadn't slept all weekend. Maybe she hadn't, since the welfare checks were distributed last Friday, June 1. Her restless eyes darted around the room.

"I be hungry," Venus declared.

"Help yourself to a doughnut," Mary Helen held out a tray.

"It be freezing out there!" she said accusingly.

"There's hot coffee," Mary Helen added, feeling that she was somehow being held responsible for the weather.

"Why you hungry? What you do with your check?" Peanuts had slipped in quietly. The tiny woman's dark eyes searched the doughnut tray until she found an old-fashioned buttermilk.

"I had to take care of my business," Venus snapped, but Peanuts had lost interest.

"How you be, girlfriend?" Miss Bobbie greeted Mary Helen with a happy grin.

Mary Helen, who had never been called "girlfriend" in her life until she came to the Refuge, marveled at how good it made her feel. Walking across the gathering room, she noticed that Crazy Alice was unusually quiet. Most days she carried on an animated conversation with imaginary companions at her table.

"Is everything all right?" Mary Helen asked.

Crazy Alice looked puzzled.

"You're so quiet," she added to clear up her question.

The woman smiled sweetly and explained as if she were talking to a backward child. "Today, honey," she said, "is Monday. On Mondays I listen."

"I'm about ready to go," Sister Anne said softly.

Mary Helen checked her watch and was surprised that it was nearly ten o'clock. Although, now that she thought about it, her legs did feel as if they could use a time-out.

"You're sure you'll be all right?" Anne asked. She sounded a little too concerned for Mary Helen's liking.

"Of course," Mary Helen tried to keep the annoyance out of her voice. After all, Anne was just trying to be sensitive to her feelings. At least, she knew that's what Anne would say.

"Great!" Anne called and hurried out the door.

After making sure that the snack table was amply supplied, Mary Helen and Ruth fixed their own coffees. Mary Helen found a table. Ruth brought over two glazed doughnuts. Resolved to eat only a small piece of one, Mary Helen cut the doughnut in quarters, then licked her fingers. *Why does everything that is bad for you taste so good?* she wondered, cutting another small piece of the doughnut.

She had just popped it into her mouth, when she heard a tinny bang at the entrance.

"Sounds like a shopping cart hitting the front door," Ruth said. And Ruth was right.

The door opened and a woman Mary Helen had never seen before came into the gathering room. She was pulling a rusty wire grocery cart—the kind women used to use when they walked to and from the grocery store. It must be an antique.

The cart bulged with plastic bags full of who knows what. A dirty quilt was folded on the top to keep everything secure. The woman pulling the cart was tall and probably very thin. The layers of clothes she wore made it hard to tell. Her top garment was a tattered brown woolen cape with a hood. She had wrapped her entire head with white sheeting until it resembled the coif of a medieval nun's habit.

Her face was the only thing visible. The beauty of it struck Mary Helen. Although the woman's features were finely cut and her cheekbones high, the thing that really drew Mary Helen's attention was her radiant pink skin. Clear and smooth as any baby's in an Ivory Soap commercial, the dampness outside had given it a glow that made her look almost angelic.

Purposefully the woman strode across the room to where Mary

Helen sat. "I need a shower," she said in a pleasant voice. "May I take one?"

Mary Helen looked up into piercing blue eyes, deep with intelligence. Guilelessly they studied her. "My name is Sarah," the woman said. "What's yours?"

When Sarah was safely in the shower and clearly out of earshot, Ruth leaned toward Mary Helen and asked the question that was on both their minds. "What do you think her problem is?

Mary Helen shrugged. "Beats me," she said.

"She has such a pretty face and is so well spoken," Ruth said, clearly thinking aloud, "and her eyes are sharp."

Mary Helen toyed with the edge of her napkin. "It's hard to tell, but something has to be amiss. Why else would anyone walk around in that getup? At first glance, she reminds me of an old-fashioned holy card of Saint Teresa of Avila."

Ruth looked blank. Obviously she had never seen the picture of the saint in her brown habit and white wimple. Mary Helen was wondering just how to explain it to her, when Geraldine came through the front door. Happily, she changed the subject. "Now there's the gal that will know about Sarah if anyone does," Mary Helen said, smiling at the older woman. "Geraldine knows everything there is to know."

As soon as she was inside, Geraldine removed the scarf from her newly fixed hair. Her soft brown skin shone from the damp fog. She was a pleasant woman and, at fifty, still good-looking. Her graying hair gave her a distinguished air. In her youth, Geraldine had been a prostitute. Fortunately, one of her steady clients had left her a small but adequate retirement fund. She had jumped at the chance to do just that—retire! Her good fortune made her a kind of celebrity among the women. That, and the fact that she was the auntie of Junior Johnson, who, Mary Helen was told, was "the man." Whatever that meant.

The thing about Geraldine that genuinely amazed Mary Helen was her ability to know the news of the neighborhood. She was an inexhaustible font of knowledge about what was going on.

"Hi, Sister," Geraldine greeted Mary Helen warmly. "I can't stay long," she said, sitting down with her cup of coffee.

Geraldine began every visit with that proclamation. Mary Helen suspected that it was an insurance policy of sorts. If the conversation at the table was too hot or too boring, she could leave without hurting feelings.

No sense wasting time, Mary Helen thought, coming right to the point. "Do you know a young woman named Sarah?" she asked. "She wears a long brown cape and wraps her head with white material."

Geraldine nodded. "I seen her around the neighborhood. Comes from Oakland, I thinks. Been here—maybe two weeks."

"What is her problem?" Ruth asked. She was as tenacious as a bloodhound on a scent.

In an effort not to be overheard, Geraldine bent forward and shook her head. "I don't know what be her problem. What I does know is she gives me a awful funny feeling."

Mary Helen frowned. "A funny feeling? What kind of a funny feeling?" she asked.

"Just a funny feeling, like ants crawling up my arms." Geraldine said. "Makes me think something be wrong." She took a sip of her coffee. "One thing I knows for sure is that girl ain't been on the streets long."

"What makes you say that?" Mary Helen pressed.

Geraldine stopped for another drink from her cup. "Good," she said, smacking her lips.

"About Sarah?" Mary Helen urged.

Geraldine blinked as though she wasn't quite sure what they were talking about. *Maddening*, Mary Helen thought. "Why don't you think she's been on the streets long?"

"Well, for one thing, her teeth," Geraldine said finally.

"Teeth?" What in heaven's name do the woman's teeth have to do with anything? Mary Helen wondered.

Geraldine raised her head quickly. "You notice anything special about them teeth?"

Mary Helen tried to picture them. "As far as I can remember, they were just perfectly ordinary straight teeth," she said.

"You be right, Sister," Geraldine's eyes caught hers. "But them teeth be too good, too ordinary. Nobody been on the streets for very long has them kind of good teeth." She pointed to her own upper plate.

Mary Helen had to admit that what Geraldine was saying was shockingly true. Now that she thought about it, most women who dropped by the Refuge had missing teeth, cracked teeth, and stained teeth. A dentist was not readily available to homeless women. Even if a woman did go to the clinic for care, it was generally to have a painful tooth extracted.

"You know what I'm saying?" Geraldine asked.

Mary Helen did.

"What do you think is her problem?" Ruth seemed determined to get an answer.

Geraldine's eyes darted toward the shower room, checking that Sarah was still in it. "I don't know," she admitted. "Maybe somebody after her and she be trying to get hid."

"Like the Mafia?" Ruth said, her dark eyes enormous. "Or maybe she knows something she shouldn't and she's in danger."

"Or maybe you've been watching too much television," Mary Helen said and all three women laughed.

Sarah came out of the shower still wrapped up like Saint Teresa. Her pink face glowed from the steam in the room and, if anything, she looked more angelic. When she smiled, Mary Helen couldn't help studying her mouth full of white teeth. Geraldine was right. Someone had spent a fortune on an orthodontist. Maybe Sarah had taken some bad drugs during college, which left her psychotic. Poor parents, Mary Helen thought, wondering if they were out there somewhere searching for this lost child.

"Girlfriend, we need some more sugar, please," Miss Bobbie called.

"And napkins, too," Venus said.

Suddenly Mary Helen was so busy that she had no time to think about Sarah and her problem. She and Ruth were still running when Sister Anne came back from the dentist.

"Look, Ma. No cavities," was all that Anne had time to say before she jumped back into the routine.

All morning long, women came in and out of the Refuge. Many showered or washed their filthy clothes. Several napped or read. The telephone rang continually. The refreshment table needed to be replenished innumerable times. Ruth cleaned and bandaged some cuts and scrapes. Anne made pot after pot of fresh coffee. Mary Helen took time to chitchat with a donor who stopped by with things she thought the center could use. The afternoon volunteer called in sick. Much to Mary Helen's relief, Ruth offered to stay on.

The three women were so busy keeping up with the demands that none of them saw Sarah and her cart leave.

"Isn't it time for another break?" Anne asked finally. "It's after two o'clock and we haven't even stopped for lunch."

By now, Mary Helen's legs were numb. She expected that Ruth's weren't too far behind. She had staved off her hunger with small bites of doughnut. If she didn't watch out, soon she'd be unable to button her skirt. In fact, she probably should think about getting skirts with elastic waistbands.

Or think about not taking bites of doughnut, a nasty inner voice suggested. Mary Helen chose to ignore it.

The three had just sat down to tuna sandwiches when Sonia burst into the room. "Something going down out there," she said. "Something bad! Somebody be hurt."

No one spoke. Tension pressed down on the group like a lid.

"What's happened?" Anne asked, her voice loud in the silence, but Sonia had already ducked out of the Refuge.

"It ain't nothing good," Peanuts said.

The smell of fear permeated the gathering room. Instinctively, Mary Helen rose and headed for the door.

"Where are you going?" Anne asked nervously.

"To find out what happened," Mary Helen said. "Someone might be hurt."

"Be careful it ain't you," Geraldine called.

The quiet was shattered by Crazy Alice's high-pitched giggle. "Stop that noise," Venus hollered.

"Get off her back!" Peanuts piped up. Without warning the room exploded into an argument with Crazy Alice giggling above the fracas.

"You better stay here," Mary Helen whispered to Anne. "Ruth is a nurse. She can come with me."

Outside Mary Helen smelled the distinct odor of scorched metal—a gunshot. There was no mistaking it for anything else. She stood on the deserted sidewalk trying to get her bearings. Cars sped by on their way to the freeway. Halfway down the block she spotted Sarah's wire cart. It seemed to be abandoned in front of a tattoo parlor. For an instant she thought she saw a man in the shadow of the doorway, but when she looked again it was empty.

Beside the cart was a mound of discarded clothes. Had someone draped a brown cape over it? Mary Helen's stomach lurched. *It can't be*, she thought, racing down the block with Ruth right behind her.

Sarah lay on her back, her rosy skin ashen now. Great spots of blood grew like flowers from her chest. The brown cape was quickly darkening and blood began to run in rivulets toward the curb. Her eyelids fluttered.

"She's alive," Mary Helen whispered, looking around for help.

Ruth felt for a pulse. "Just barely," she said. "You stay here and I'll call 911."

Mary Helen knelt beside the dying woman and reached for her hand. "Dear Lord, please," she prayed, rocking back and forth, straining to hear the scream of an ambulance.

"Hold on, Sarah," she coaxed, unable to stop the tears running down her cheeks. "God loves you," she whispered in the woman's ear. "God loves you."

All at once, Sarah's eyelids fluttered again. Her lips moved.

Mary Helen bent to hear the words above the sound of passing cars. They were too faint. She bent still closer, until she felt the woman's breath on her ear. At first, she couldn't make out the word.

"Pity," she thought she heard Sarah whisper. "Pity."

Helplessly, Mary Helen watched the last blush of the color fade from Sarah's angelic face. Her ear was still near the woman's mouth when she heard the final rattle of death.

❧❧❧

Eyes closed, he clutched the steering wheel of his parked car, waiting for the shaking to stop. His mind replayed every detail, refusing to shut off. And her eyes kept staring. As hard as he tried, he couldn't make them stop.

How much does she know? he had wondered, walking up behind her, the sweat beginning to form on the palms of his hands. She had been unaware of him as he snuck up to her. Unaware that he was checking out her getup—the old, baggy, secondhand clothes, the brown blanket thing draped around her, the white dishtowel concealing her hair. Nice touch, he had thought, pleased with her disguise. Even her own mother wouldn't recognize her. At first, he had felt like laughing out loud but he hadn't wanted to startle her. It was obvious that she hadn't heard him yet. He had moved closer and stuck his hand

15

in the right pocket of his windbreaker. He had felt the cold steel of his gun with its silencer.

How much does she *really* know? he had wondered, feeling a little sick to his stomach. He had tried his best to keep her in the dark, feeding her half-truths. But she was a sharp one—too sharp for her own good, an insistent voice nagged at him. She's got to go before she blows everything. But not if she doesn't know anything, he had reasoned, struggling to put down his fear.

The phone call he'd received just about twenty minutes before he'd left had spooked him. "Do you think that girl is onto us?" the familiar voice had asked. A simple question whose answer could destroy their lives.

Anxiously he had checked out the street. Very little foot traffic. Good! Cars whizzed by intent on getting out of the city—not noticing or caring about any action on the sidewalk.

Shifting from one foot to the other, he had been uncertain exactly what to do. "Sarah," he had said her name quietly.

She had spun around, her beautiful young face clear and unblemished. Her cheeks were flushed and a half smile played on her lips. But when her blue eyes met his, he knew. It wasn't so much the fear in them as it was the hurt and the disbelief that made him realize that she knew the truth.

Fighting to steady his right hand, he gripped the gun in his pocket. At first she didn't seem to notice.

"You!" she had said, instantly looking older. "Why?" Her eyes shifted to his pocket and she watched, almost mesmerized, as he pulled out his weapon.

"But, why?" she had asked, forgetting even to run.

"I'm sorry," he had whispered. "I don't want to do this, but I can't let you ruin my life."

Sarah had studied him as if she didn't believe it was he. Well, she'd believe it soon, he had thought. With marksman precision, he had put one bullet through her chest and watched her crumple to the ground, her eyes still on him.

The shaking had started as he walked swiftly toward his parked car. Gripping the wheel, her eyes still haunted him. Would he ever forget those open blue eyes? he wondered, turning the key in the ignition, those eyes studying him, admonishing him, pitying him.

Pulling out into the traffic, sweat breaking out on his forehead, he knew with certainty that he would never rid himself of them, never.

⁂

Homicide Inspectors Kate Murphy and Dennis Gallagher were both at their desks completing some paperwork when the call came in. Gallagher reached for the telephone. "Anything, even murder, is better than writing up this damn report," he muttered, picking up the receiver.

Kate glanced up at her partner's pudgy face, frowning now as he listened, then jotted down an address. For an instant he looked—well—old. That was the only word for it. Although Gallagher constantly talked about retiring, he had never really looked "old" to her. Not that sixty-five was old. But this afternoon he did.

How had it happened? Kate wondered. *The same way that her son John had gone from his little blue layette to getting ready to enter kindergarten this fall*, she thought, gazing out the Detail window at the cars speeding along the James Lick Freeway. Time flies, life is so short.

"Geez, Katie-girl," Gallagher's voice startled her. She turned to find him staring at the paper in his hand as if it were hazardous.

"What is it?" she asked, trying to keep her imagination from running wild.

"This address," he said. "They said a young bag lady was shot. Happened on Eighth Street in front of a tattoo parlor, but I could swear it's awful close to where that nun friend of yours hangs out—that Refuge." His face was beginning to redden.

"She's *our* friend," Kate said calmly, "and she doesn't hang out. She ministers to homeless women."

"I'm not sure just what the hell she does," Gallagher grumbled and took his wrinkled jacket from the back of his chair, "but she does it too often for my liking, right in the middle of our homicide cases. Swear to God, if she's involved in this one, I'll pull her in!" Huffing, he turned on his heel and started toward the door.

"On what charge?" Kate asked, running behind him, trying to put on her trench coat. "What charge would you use to pull in an elderly nun?"

"Being a general nuisance," Gallagher grumbled, pushing the down button for the elevator.

"On being generally very helpful, would be more like it." Kate waited beside him. "You are an ungrateful son-of-a-gun, you know that?"

"Ungrateful? Me?" His watery blue eyes opened wide.

He was beginning to annoy her. "Do you remember how many cases she's helped us close?"

"Do you remember how many times she's got right in the middle of things?" Gallagher ran his hand across his bald crown. "All I'm asking, Kate, is that she stay in the convent where she belongs. Is that too much to expect? Huh? That she just does whatever it is that old nuns are supposed to do? Maybe retire. However that works. I'd give my eye teeth to retire to a nice, quiet convent."

Kate stared at him, imagining the cigar-smoking, tough-talking Gallagher in a peaceful convent garden surrounded by elderly nuns. "You'd be quite a novelty, if nothing else," she said.

"Besides, you don't know for sure if that address is near Sister Mary Helen's Refuge."

"Want to bet? Five bucks?" Gallagher challenged.

For a moment, Kate considered it. Later she was happy that the elevator came before she had a chance to say yes.

By the time the two homicide inspectors arrived at the scene, the paramedics and the uniformed officers responding to the call had covered the body and cordoned off the sidewalk immediately in front of the tattoo parlor. One of the uniforms was talking to a bearded man in his mid-forties. His biceps, bulging below the rolled sleeves of his T-shirt, were crisscrossed with an intricate web of tattoo. A blue dragon curled around the back of his neck, and across the fingers of one hand ornate letters spelled MOTHER. *He is either the owner or a very good customer,* Kate thought.

The afternoon sun had burned off nearly all the fog, leaving the pavement hot. Kate unbuttoned her trench coat and scanned the curious crowd gathered behind the yellow tape. The younger patrolman was trying with limited success to move them. Even the motorists on Eighth Street were slowing down for a quick peek at what was causing all the commotion. At the sight of the mound and the blood on the sidewalk, most turned away quickly, but not all. Before long there was bound to be a fender-bender.

Out of the corner of her eye, Kate caught sight of a cluster of women huddling around a short, solid figure in a navy blue suit and flat shoes. Her heart fell. Gallagher was right. Mary Helen was near—very near, in fact.

Quickly Kate walked toward the group. Several women drew back as though they were afraid. Kate recognized some of their faces from the murder case nearly a year ago involving the Refuge, but she was only able to remember a few names—Geraldine, Miss Bobbie, and Peanuts, a tiny woman hovering protectively next to the old nun.

"Sister, are you all right?" Kate asked softly. Thankfully, her partner had not yet noticed this group.

"I am as well as can be expected under the circumstances," Mary Helen said in a thin voice. Her face had lost all its color and she looked close to tears.

"Did you know the woman?" Kate asked gently.

Mary Helen shook her head. "I saw her for the first time today. Her name was Sarah. Or at least, that's what she told us."

"Any of you ladies know her?" Kate eyed the group.

Geraldine sighed. "Far as I knows, she only be on the streets for a couple of weeks," she said.

"Nobody know her," Miss Bobbie smiled sadly. "She must come from out of town."

"If nobody know her, why somebody kill her?" Peanuts asked. It was the same question Kate had.

"What are you doing here?" a familiar voice bellowed.

Mary Helen jumped. Gallagher had startled her. For a tense moment, she glared at him, her hazel eyes blazing. "I minister here!" she said, pointing toward the corner. Her tone was crisp, but controlled. "This woman, God rest her, was in our place taking a shower. After she had left, one of the other women alerted us that something was amiss on the street, that someone was hurt. The volunteer, who happens to be a nurse, and I came out to see if there was anything we could do to help."

"Came out to see?" Gallagher strained the words between clenched teeth. "Are you out of your mind, Sister? When you hear that something bad has happened on the streets, that someone is hurt, the best thing to do is stay inside and call the police. If you aren't careful"—he yanked at his tie as if it were a noose—"you could be the one getting hurt."

Mary Helen raised her chin. "But I didn't, did I, Inspector?" she said.

"Sister," Kate jumped in before Gallagher had a chance to explode, "did you happen to see anyone?"

Kate was relieved when her partner moved to another group. She shifted her attention back to Mary Helen, who appeared to be thinking over her answer.

"Any cars? Anyone running down the street? Anything suspicious at all? Think."

"No," Mary Helen said. "When I got here she was clearly dying."

Kate was surprised. "She was still alive?"

Mary Helen nodded. "The poor dear had just enough strength left to utter one word."

Kate's heart raced. She knew better than to hope. That kind of thing only happens in the movies. But maybe, just maybe, the victim had named the perp. "What word?" she asked.

Mary Helen frowned. "She was difficult to hear, but I think she said *pity*."

"Pity? Like 'have pity on me'?" Kate tried not to show her disappointment. "Like praying, pity?"

She must not have succeeded. Mary Helen looked a little hurt. "Yes, Kate," she said gently. "Like praying. And really, dear, you can't blame her. It seems to me rather like the natural thing to do when you are dying."

Embarrassed, Kate walked over to the body, careful to avoid the sticky blood covering the sidewalk. She picked up one corner of the covering and stared down at the woman.

She felt the hot, clammy sensation she always experienced when she viewed a murder victim. *At least I don't gag anymore*, she thought, taking a deep breath.

"Are you all right?" Mary Helen sounded concerned. "You look so pale."

"I'm fine, thank you, Sister," Kate smiled. Mary Helen squeezed her arm and Kate turned back to the body. A white cloth wound around the woman's entire head, exposing only her face, a lovely face with fine features and prominent cheekbones. Her skin, almost translucent now, was flawless. Someone had closed her eyes as if she were sleeping. Except for her blood-soaked chest, Sarah looked as if, at any minute, she was going to awaken, push herself up off the ground and join the crowd.

Kate couldn't take her eyes off the woman's face. There was something vaguely familiar about it. At the moment, she could not put her finger on what. Had she seen Sarah at the grocery store? The bank? Church? Had she worked at the cleaners? Used the library? It would come. Even with her mind a blank, this time Kate would gladly have bet five bucks that she knew this woman from somewhere.

Imagine anyone hearing that someone was hurt and staying inside! Mary Helen thought, still smarting from Inspector Gallagher's remarks. *That's part of the trouble with the world today,* she fumed. *No one wants to get involved. No one is willing to help a neighbor in need.*

This time he had really nettled her and she couldn't seem to let go of it. She intended to tell him so, too, once the dark scowl left his face. No sense teasing an angry bull, and that's what he'd sounded like, bellowing at her, "What are you doing here?"

What in heaven's name did he think I was doing? She sniffed. *I was comforting a dying woman, that's what.* Mary Helen sighed. It was at a time like this that she really missed Eileen. If her friend were here, she could get this off her chest and stop stewing about it.

Standing behind the yellow plastic tape, Mary Helen bit her bottom lip and watched several automobiles pull up along the curb. Car doors slammed. Men and women began milling around the crime scene. She watched as someone uncovered the body and cameras flashed. Her heart ached at the sight of the lifeless brown mound on the pavement. Minutes before it had been a beautiful, if troubled, young woman.

Meanwhile Inspectors Gallagher and Murphy, notebooks in hand, questioned members of the small crowd still gathered on the sidewalk. Mary Helen noted that they seemed to be writing down little. Like her, most of the onlookers probably saw or heard nothing.

When the coroner's van arrived, Mary Helen decided she'd had enough. She checked her wristwatch. Although it was only three o'clock, it was time to make her way back to the Refuge. She was tired and hot. Predictably, now that the fog had finally burned off, the summer sun was intense. The refugees, bundled in all they owned, must be melting. She'd fix a couple of pitchers of iced tea.

Inspector Gallagher, with his flushed face, looked as if he could use some, too, she thought, softening a bit. Happily, Kate Murphy, who had been the color of cement, was beginning to get a little pinkness back.

"Yoo-hoo, Kate!" Mary Helen called.

Frowning, Kate walked toward her. "What is it, Sister?" she asked.

"I'm on my way back to the Refuge," she said. "It's much cooler in there, I'm sure. If you're interested, I don't think Sister Anne will mind if you use that small sleep room to talk to witnesses. And," she added with a wink, "I make a pretty mean glass of iced tea, which is yours for the taking."

Very few women were in the Refuge when Mary Helen entered. The place had an uneasy quiet. She was surprised to find Anne at the kitchen sink emptying ice trays. From the look of things, she had already begun brewing tea. "Great minds!" Mary Helen said.

All she got in response was a sniff. When Anne finally turned to face her, it was obvious that the young nun had been crying.

"What is it?" Mary Helen asked.

"Nothing." Anne's voice was thick.

"You don't cry about nothing. I know you better than that."

As Mary Helen watched, a fresh tear ran down Anne's cheek. "I'm just upset, that's all," she said.

"That's understandable," Mary Helen said lamely.

"When I went outside I couldn't even look at the body. The very sight of the covered mound got to me. I felt as if I wanted to faint or throw up or something."

"That's only normal," Mary Helen said. She adjusted her bifocals and studied Anne's face. The young nun's hazel eyes were wide.

"What else is bothering you?" she asked, hoping she wasn't stepping onto a land mine.

Anne sucked in her breath. "If you really want to know, I'm afraid that some crazy person like the one who shot that Sarah will come in here and murder us. And that we can't do a thing about it!" As soon as the words were out, she started to sob.

Gently Mary Helen took Anne in her arms. "There, there," she crooned, knowing that there was really no way to assure Anne that she was wrong.

"And don't tell me about Divine Providence or about the very hairs on my head being numbered," Anne mumbled into Mary Helen's damp shoulder. "I've told myself all that and frankly, at this moment, it doesn't help."

Mary Helen had no intention of bringing up any such things. But she felt she ought to say something that would help Anne pull herself together. She was sure Kate and Inspector Gallagher would be there any moment and more refugees would be wandering into the center. Surely Anne wouldn't want them to see her dissolved. She played a long shot.

"You know, Anne, Sister Eileen had an old saying from back home that might fit this occasion." She felt Anne stiffen. Had she said the wrong thing? Anne always enjoyed Eileen, or so she'd thought.

"Eileen's sayings! I think she makes them up," Anne muttered, not unkindly.

Often Mary Helen had suspected the same thing, but now was not the time to quibble. "Humor me," she said.

"If I must." Anne was starting to regain some of her usual good humor. Hooray!

"If I remember correctly, Eileen says, 'If you're born to be hanged, there's no need to fear water.'"

Anne hiccupped and pushed herself away. "Is that supposed to make me feel better?" she asked.

Mary Helen studied the young nun's face. She was actually smiling. *Mission accomplished!* Mary Helen thought. "And on the off chance that Eileen is wrong," she said, "I've invited Kate and Inspector Gallagher for iced tea and to use our sleep room to interview witnesses. I hope you don't mind."

"Mind?" Anne ran a towel under the faucet, and then covered her puffy face with it. "I'm delighted." Her voice was muffled. "At least we're safe for the day. No one would dare harm us with two homicide detectives in the place." She lowered the towel and sniffed. "Who in his right mind would risk killing a policeman?"

❧❧❧

Watching Sister Mary Helen walk the short half block to the Refuge, Kate realized how hot and thirsty she really was. Iced tea sounded pretty tempting to her. Gallagher and she were nearly done at the crime scene. The coroner had taken the body. They would only be in the way of the technical team. Actually, they should drop by the Refuge for more than a cold drink. If anybody had any idea why this woman had been shot, that's probably where they'd hear it.

She scanned the crowd for her partner and spotted him standing over a wire cart. It was stuffed to overflowing with plastic bags. "This looks like something my mother had," Kate said, joining him beside the cart.

"This looks like what every housewife in the good old days used to carry her groceries home in." Gallagher ran his finger around his shirt collar. "Geez, it's hot out here."

"Whose is it, anyway?" Kate used the pencil in her hand to move the quilt, stuffed like a lid over the top.

"A couple of women I talked to said they thought it belonged to the victim."

Kate let the quilt fall back in place. "I'll go through it," she said. "It might give us some idea who this woman is—was," she corrected herself. "There must be a next-of-kin to notify."

"Be my guest," Gallagher said with a slight bow toward the rickety cart.

Repelled by the thought of what might be in all those bags, Kate pulled a pair of rubber gloves from her trench coat pocket and slipped them on. Squaring her shoulders, she gingerly peeled off the quilt. Instantly she wished she'd held her breath. The grimy, musty smell was overpowering.

"You never know what you'll find," Gallagher said, watching Kate open the first plastic bag.

"I don't need to be reminded," Kate said, a shiver running up her spine.

The bag was filled with other plastic bags. She found another that was full of dirty clothes. Another contained soap, shampoo, and some partially used hand lotion. So far nothing interesting.

Kate was about halfway through them when she discovered a worn tennis shoe that seemed unusually heavy. The moment she pulled it out of the cart, she saw the reason. The black handle of a 40 caliber, semiautomatic Beretta was wedged into the heel of the shoe. The barrel pointed toward the toe.

"Denny," she called, trying to keep her voice even, "look what I found." Carefully she removed the gun from its hiding place. It was SFPD issue, exactly like her own.

All at once her heart dropped and she felt the bile rising in her throat. She knew exactly where she had seen that lovely face before, that smooth pink skin. In the elevator of the Hall of Justice. The victim was another cop!

"What the hell? Gallagher was at her side.

"She's on the force," Kate whispered, showing him the gun. "I've seen her at the Hall. She's Vice."

"Are you sure?" Gallagher's face was solemn.

"Almost positive," Kate said. "And I think I know why she dressed like that," she said softly.

"If she was undercover she probably wanted to look like her elevator didn't go all the way up," her partner guessed.

Kate shook her head. "It's her hair," she said. "She had a head of wild auburn curls. Anyone who had ever seen her hair would recognize her immediately, so she had to cover it with that white cloth. Although her skin was a dead giveaway. I should have realized that she had redhead skin."

"I thought redheads had freckles." Gallagher studied Kate's face.

She felt her cheeks flush. "That's just some redheads, like me," she said. "Other redheads like Sarah have that delicate, white skin that burns easily."

"Yeah, I guess." Gallagher didn't seem too impressed.

"I wonder if she was successful," Kate mused.

"Successful at what?" Gallagher sounded genuinely puzzled.

"At not being recognized."

"You didn't recognize her," Gallagher said.

"But I would have eventually," Kate said. "Given enough time I would have remembered where I had seen that face. I wonder if someone else recognized her."

"You're assuming that she stumbled into something and that's what got her killed. Maybe it was a random drive-by shooting. Or a crazy on the street who isn't pretending." Gallagher stared at her over the tops of his horn-rimmed glasses.

"I'm not ruling anything in or out," Kate said. "I'm just thinking out loud."

"And you could be wrong about who she is." Gallagher swallowed hard, then wagged his head like a weary hound. "I sure hope to God you're wrong."

"Me, too," Kate said, rummaging through the remaining plastic bags, hoping to find some positive identification. She was scarcely aware of the cars whizzing by on Eighth Street or the indelibly marked man studying her from the doorway of the tattoo parlor. "Nothing," she said finally.

"So we don't even know for sure she was Vice." Gallagher wasn't going to give up easily.

"Why don't I call Jack? Maybe he knows whether or not they've got a woman undercover."

Jack Bassetti, Kate's husband, worked the Vice Squad of the San Francisco Police Department. It was one of the reasons she used her maiden name—to avoid confusion. Two Inspector Bassettis was one too many. After Jack had been shot on duty, he was reassigned, but not for long. His heart was in Vice.

Quickly Kate stuffed the plastic bags back into the cart so a technician could take it downtown. "Why don't we use the phone in the Refuge? Their office would be private enough."

Gallagher scowled. "The Refuge?" he groaned. "That's just inviting trouble. There must be another phone in this area."

Kate shrugged. "Maybe, but I'm going to ask to use theirs. At least I know that no one will overhear me."

"No one but that old nun," Gallagher grumbled, "and who could be worse?"

"They have iced tea," Kate tempted him.

Still grousing, her partner followed her down the block. His thirst must have outweighed his objections.

The minute they opened the front door, a tense silence filled the room. Anxious faces studied them. "Good morning, ladies," Kate said pleasantly.

"That's what you think," tiny, black Peanuts sneered.

"It ain't a good day at all when one of us be dead!" Miss Bobbie, her hair tightly braided, spoke up.

"Ding, dong, the witch is dead. Which old witch?" a woman sang out.

There was no forgetting Crazy Alice. Although she was singing softer than Kate remembered, she looked as if she was going for the second line.

Before she had the chance, Mary Helen emerged from the kitchen. "Come in, Inspectors," she called, holding a large pitcher of iced tea. "Why don't you sit down for a few minutes to cool off?"

Sister Anne followed her with the stack of plastic glasses. A third woman, the volunteer who gave her name as Ruth Davis, carried an enormous tray of oatmeal cookies.

"We need to use your office phone first, if you don't mind," Kate said, grabbing a cookie. She noticed that her partner was unusually quiet, almost sheepish. *Good*, she thought, following Sister Anne, who unlocked the office door. He should feel shame-faced. While he had been outside complaining about Mary Helen, she had been inside doing something thoughtful for him. He had been so churlish with her and she, so gracious in return. Serves him right!

The Vice Squad telephone was answered on the second ring. Luckily, it was Jack who picked up the receiver. "Hi, pal. Do you have a woman named Sarah Something in Vice?" she asked without any preamble.

"Hi, hon. I'm fine, thanks. How are you?" Jack joked. "And, yes, we do. Sarah Spencer. Why?"

Quickly Kate told him of finding a homicide on the street and feeling that she recognized the woman's face, then discovering the Beretta and thinking that she may have seen her at the Hall of Justice, heading for the Vice Detail. "Was she, by any chance, undercover?" Kate asked.

Jack hesitated. "I don't know for sure. I haven't seen her around for a while. But she was a redhead. Was your homicide a redhead?"

"Her head was covered," Kate said with a sinking feeling.

"I'll talk to the Lieutenant," he said.

The minutes dragged by as she waited. She heard men's voices in the background. They were talking in low tones, and she couldn't make out their words. She thought she heard Lieutenant Donaldson's voice in the background. Maybe she was mistaken. Maybe the victim just reminded her of Sarah Spencer. She hadn't actually seen the red hair. Maybe Spencer was out sick or on vacation. Maybe the victim had found the gun and it was all a big coincidence. She crossed her fingers.

"Hi, hon." Jack paused.

Those two words were enough. His tone of voice told her the answer.

"She was," Gallagher said when she replaced the receiver. "I can tell by your face that she was."

Kate sank into the desk chair.

❧❧❧

Sister Mary Helen heard the office door open. *That was fast*, she thought, glancing up. Light from a small window in the office framed the two homicide inspectors in the doorway. In the glare she could not see their faces, yet she knew by the straight, tight way they both stood that the telephone call had not produced good news.

As the pair came into the room, their faces confirmed her suspicions. Gallagher, cheeks burning, yanked at his tie as though it were cutting off his windpipe. Kate's blue eyes, glistening with tears, were enormous in her bloodless face. Without so much as a nod good-bye, the two inspectors hurried through the gathering room and out into the street.

"Where they be going so fast?" Peanuts asked nobody in particular.

My question exactly, Mary Helen thought, *and why?*

"*Where are you going to my pretty maid? I'm going a-milking, sir, she said,*" Crazy Alice called out. She must have forgotten that Monday was her day to listen.

"It can't be nothing good, makes them move like that," Miss Bobbie said, ignoring Alice. She caught Mary Helen's eye. "What's really going on here, girlfriend?" she asked.

"I have no idea," Mary Helen said truthfully and started around the room refilling iced-tea glasses. *I'm sure we'll find out soon enough*, she thought, her mind jumping like a nervous flea from possibility to possibility. What had happened to upset the two inspectors in such a short space of time? Had there been another murder? Were they called to another crime scene?

Mary Helen was still stewing and pouring iced tea when Geraldine burst through the front door as if she were steam driven. The wind had played with her new hairdo until it stood out around her head like an aura. Her brown eyes were bright with excitement.

"Hi, Genie," Venus called out, using Geraldine's street name.

Mary Helen wasn't sure that even the gift of tongues would help her keep the women's real names and street names straight. Some, she had discovered, had aliases as well. None of them, however, seemed a bit confused about who was who.

"Hi, you all." Geraldine scanned the room looking for the best spot. "I can't stay long," she said, sitting down at Miss Bobbie's table. "I got some news you all gonna want to hear."

"Iced-tea?" Mary Helen offered. Geraldine shook her head. Whatever her news was, apparently it was too important to postpone even for a little conversation and a cold drink.

"Well, what is it, girl?" Miss Bobbie demanded impatiently. "We can't wait all day. We got business, too."

Frozen-faced, Geraldine stared at her. For a moment, Mary Helen thought she might not tell her news after all.

"Don't pay her no mind," Peanuts said.

That was all the encouragement Geraldine needed. She

wouldn't let indignation get in the way of sharing some juicy tidbits. In fact, she looked relieved that she could both save face and tell all.

"Well, ladies, I be talking to my nephew." She paused, surveying the group. "Junior Johnson . . ."

An awesome hush fell over the room. The silence could not have been more profound if she had said, "I be talking to my nephew, the Pope." Mary Helen was impressed. This Junior Johnson must be something, all right.

She heard Sister Anne moving in behind her. "What does he know?" Anne whispered, making sure she wasn't overheard. "He's nothing more than a thug."

A thug with a lot of clout, Mary Helen thought. She smiled encouragingly at Geraldine, hoping she'd get on with it.

Venus was smiling wide enough to show her missing front tooth. "What that home boy say?" she asked.

Geraldine seemed to know that she had the crowd in the palm of her hand. She could have held them there, too, except that she was as eager as they were to have her tell all.

"Well," she lowered her voice, "Junior, he say that the lady who got herself killed—that Sarah—she was a police."

"She didn't look like no polices," Venus protested.

"She a—how you say it, girl?—a decoy."

"An undercover police officer," Crazy Alice said in a rare moment of lucidity.

Suddenly the gathering room became even quieter. The tension was electric. Behind her, Mary Helen heard Anne suck in her breath. All at once everything jigsawed into place—the woman's sudden appearance on the streets; her obviously cared for skin and teeth; Geraldine's suspicion that she was not really homeless; and, finally, Kate and Gallagher's sudden exit from the Refuge. Kate's phone call had probably established the fact that Sarah, who looked as if she could be traveling with Saint Teresa, was in fact traveling with the SFPD.

Now her travels are over, Mary Helen thought, feeling hollow. Who could have done such a thing? She almost pitied the perpetrator. The police force would leave nothing and no one untouched to find the murderer of a fellow officer. Surely whoever did this was unaware that Sarah was a policewoman.

"What she be looking for?" Miss Bobbie's voice was hoarse.

"What you mean?" Geraldine asked.

"If she be undercover, she be undercover for something. What Junior say?" The scar along Miss Bobbie's right eye twitched as she stared at Geraldine.

The older woman ran her tongue along her bottom lip, considering her answer. "Junior, he didn't tell me that," she said, "and you know what? I didn't ask him."

Peanuts let out a snort. "You make a fine detective, Genie," she said sarcastically. "Not asking no questions!"

Geraldine straightened her heavy shoulders. Looking at her, Mary Helen thought the woman had hurt feelings, but she should have known better. "I may be a lousy detective, Little Peanuts, but I be a wonderful auntie."

The room exploded with nervous laughter. Crazy Alice, her face oyster white, closed her eyes and giggled wildly. The sharp, high tingle of it made the hair on Mary Helen's arms stand up.

"This is awful," Anne whispered, her color gone. "Nobody's safe."

Ruth, wearing a stunned expression, joined them.

"It could have been one of us," Anne shivered. Her fear was back in full force.

"Only if it was a random shooting," Mary Helen said practically.

"What else would it be?" Ruth asked.

"I tend to agree with Miss Bobbie. The woman wasn't undercover for nothing," Mary Helen answered.

"This is like a nightmare." Anne's voice cracked. She pushed a strand of dark hair off her cheek. "A regular nightmare!"

Unfortunately, Mary Helen thought sadly, *it will still be with us when we wake up.*

❧❧❧

Inspectors Dennis Gallagher and Kate Murphy drove the few blocks back to the Hall of Justice in silence. It was as if a pall had been placed over the car, allowing each to wrestle with his or her private thoughts.

Kate scarcely noticed the homeless man on the island under the stoplight with his "Work for Food" sign. And she was only partly aware of the graffiti covering the Muni bus, which was taking its half of the road out of the middle. She couldn't seem to stop brooding about the beautiful Sarah Spencer with her full mane of auburn hair. What were her dreams, her fears? What had she expected from life? Were her parents still living? Did she have a husband and children? Above all, why had she been murdered?

When Kate and Gallagher finally reached the fourth floor of the Hall of Justice, it was obvious that their bad news had preceded them. Small groups spoke in hushed tones. Some officers simply sat staring into space and it was obvious that Myrtle, the Detail's secretary, had been crying. Her mascara had begun to run, giving her a slight raccoon look.

"How awful," Myrtle said the moment she saw them. It was almost as if she held them responsible. "She was such a nice young woman. We always talked when we waited for the elevator. She told me she was going to be married in the fall. And both her parents are alive. How will they cope?" She pressed her wet handkerchief under her runny eyes. "Who is going to tell them?"

"Don Donaldson and I are going over now," Lieutenant Sweeney answered from his office. Donaldson, not the most popular guy at the Hall, headed the Vice Detail. "And we better get there before the press does."

34

Kate checked her wristwatch—nearly four. "Where do the Spencers live?" she asked.

"In Lafayette." Apparently Myrtle had looked up the information for whomever had the sad duty.

Kate sank down into her desk chair and stared out the window at the crowded James Lick Freeway. An angry horn blared. Tires squealed and more horns blasted their opinions. *In all this traffic, even with the siren on, I doubt if they'll make it across the Bay Bridge and into Contra Costa County before the media*, she thought, but hesitated to say. There was no sense making a bad situation worse. She closed her eyes. What shock and sadness awaited the Spencer family and Sarah's fiancé. *It is a blessing that we can't see the future*, she thought. *Who could bear it?*

"Do we know why she was undercover?" Gallagher asked no one in particular.

The room was so quiet that Kate could hear the hum of the electric wall clock. Finally O'Connor spoke up from his desk where he had been sitting silently, a feat for O'Connor. "No one seems to know except the Lieut and the big brass. It was evidently a hush-hush operation."

Kate turned from the window. "She was from Vice," she said.

"So it probably had something to do with prostitution," O'Connor observed. "That would be my guess."

"But she wasn't dressed like a prostitute. She looked more like an eccentric bag lady," Kate said.

"That's odd." Myrtle joined the conversation.

"I'm sure it was the hair," Kate mumbled.

"Hair?" Myrtle propped herself on the edge of Kate's desk.

"Sarah had that unforgettable auburn hair. She needed to cover it in order not to be recognized."

Myrtle looked impressed but the telephone rang before she had a chance to say anything.

"Why would they send a woman with such a distinctive feature undercover?" O'Connor asked.

Gallagher shrugged. "Beats me," he said. "Maybe it was because she was young, eager, able to pull it off. Whatever. That's not our department. Donaldson has to answer for that and he probably feels like hell already."

He turned toward Kate. "We need to get statements from any eyewitnesses. First thing tomorrow morning we'll start along Eighth Street—the New You Tattoo parlor, the American Asian Food Market, McCormick's Auto Parts and, of course, the Refuge. Why are you staring at me, Kate? Did I say something wrong?"

"Was I staring?" she asked. "I was just thinking, that's all. As O'Connor said, it is peculiar to send someone undercover whose appearance is so distinctive."

"I'm sure Donaldson has a perfectly logical explanation." Gallagher loosened his tie.

"Maybe," Kate conceded. "And there's another thing—"

"What's that, Katie-girl?" Gallagher had begun to fill out the report.

"Did you bag any empty shells at the scene? I didn't see any brass on the sidewalk."

Her partner looked up frowning. "No," he said.

"Makes you wonder," she said. "Was our perp so neat and tidy that he stopped and picked them up? Or does he know something about crime scenes?"

"I just assumed they were in the street and that the tech team collected them," Gallagher said.

"Could be." Kate stared thoughtfully into middle space.

"We'll get the perp, Katie-girl," Gallagher assured her. "Don't you worry. We'll get him if we have to turn over every rock in this city, we'll get him. Nobody gets away with killing a cop."

For the rest of the afternoon Sister Mary Helen could think of nothing but the shooting death of the young undercover policewoman. Her mind would not let go of the image—the lifeless body lying like a brown mound in the middle of the dirty sidewalk. No one should die like that. Nor could she shut off the memory of the dying woman's last word. "Pity," she had whispered. Surely God would show her pity. The poor soul was little more than a kid.

Neither Crazy Alice's maniacal giggle nor Miss Bobbie's gentle prattle was able to distract her. Her body seemed to be on automatic pilot. She was vaguely aware of handing out soaps and toothbrushes and hand lotions on request, although she'd be hard pressed to name any of the recipients.

She didn't really remember saying good-bye to Ruth, who was nowhere to be found. Obviously, the volunteer had gone home.

At closing time the Refuge was still crowded. It was as if the women were loath to leave. Were they afraid to go back to the streets where they might stumble upon the murderer, or were they just afraid of missing something?

All afternoon Junior Johnson's shocking revelation that the victim was a police officer went around and around the room, embellished with every circle until it played like a full-length movie. The last time Mary Helen had caught a snippet of the story, the officer had been undercover to capture a crazed killer of homeless women. He was a vicious man that several of the refugees were sure they'd seen.

"Bet he be that new guy hanging at the Go-Go Market on the corner," Peanuts said. "And now that I thinks about it, I seen him at the tattoo parlor, too." She pointed toward the storefront.

"I think you be right," Venus nodded solemnly.

Miss Bobbie sucked in her breath and Mary Helen felt a shiver of fear run up her own spine.

"You all crazy," Geraldine said. "Scaring your own selves to death. It was probably just some fool kid with a gun showing off."

"Well he sure did hit the wrong target," Peanuts said, obviously annoyed that her story had not received the consideration it deserved. "Tomorrow the whole neighborhood will be full of cops." Her remark silenced them all.

"We're going to close now, ladies." Anne sounded almost apologetic, although there was no doubt that she meant business.

After a few moments of fussing with their plastic bags just to remind her who was really in charge, the last of the group shuffled out into the street.

"We better get home before the five o'clock news," Anne said, quickly locking up.

Mary Helen checked the lights. "What's the hurry?" she asked.

"It's just that a little while ago I saw the Channel 5 TV van rolling down the street. Since you're the one who was with her when she died, they might want to talk—"

Mary Helen didn't let her finish the sentence. "Quick," she said. "We're out of here."

❧❧❧

Officer Mark Wong and his partner, Brian Dineen, usually began their shift at 4 P.M. Today both of them reported in early and they were not the only ones. News of Sarah Spencer's death had spread quickly. The room was crowded with those coming in early and those staying after shift. Under other circumstances, the Detail would be alive with banter and horseplay. Today voices were hushed and conversations somber.

"It's a goddamn shame," Brian said, running his fingers through his short red hair, still wet from the quick shower he'd taken before leaving home. "A goddamn shame!" He loomed in the doorway like a brooding bear.

"You can say that again." Mark sat on the edge of Jack Bassetti's desk. "Gallagher and Jack's wife caught the case," he said.

"Bummer," someone remarked.

"Right, but they'll get plenty of help." Mark cleared his throat. "Susie just called—Susie Chang from the Chief's office," he explained unnecessarily. Everyone knew that Susie Chang worked for the Chief and that she and Wong were an item.

"Susie who?" someone joked.

The flush on Wong's face was the only indication that he'd heard the question. "According to Susie, the Chief is giving this case top priority. Wants us to roust everybody."

"Damn right!" someone said.

Brian glanced toward the darkened corner office. "Where's the lieutenant?" he asked.

"Gone with Lieutenant Sweeney from Homicide to break the news to Sarah's parents." Jack gave a doleful smile. "What a helluva job," he muttered.

"Got any ideas who our perp could be?" "Who was she getting too close to?" "Anybody know what she was working on?" "Why wasn't somebody covering her?" Questions bounced around the room like ping-pong balls and no one seemed to have any answers.

"Let's roll," Brian Dineen said at last and Mark Wong was glad to oblige.

"I'll circle the neighborhood. You look," Brian said, settling behind the wheel.

The two had been partners for so long that Wong didn't need to ask, "For what?" Not only were they partners, but they were also good friends. "You got to be friendly," Mark always said, "when you trust a guy with your life."

Their difference in height—Brian was six foot three inches and Mark was five foot seven—caused the other guys in Vice to refer to them as "the long and short of it." Ironically, Brian was also the long of it on patience while Mark was, well, not. "What he lacks in height, he makes up for in fight," Brian often joked.

Mark Wong felt that his partner was onto something, although Brian's bulk usually kept him from being put to the test. Tonight, he hoped, would be no different.

Deliberately the police car crept down Jones Street toward Market. Dineen stopped for jay-walking pedestrians while Wong scanned the street, peering into darkened doorways, hoping to spot anyone who might prove helpful.

He ignored two drunks on the corner—one hollering and pushing, the other barely able to stand. The beat cop would pick them up. Several prostitutes strolling Ellis Street quickly began to window shop when they saw the familiar car. He ignored what he knew was the drug deal, memorizing the two guys' faces so he could go after them later. Right now top priority was what had happened to Sarah Spencer.

"Look. Is that Olivia?" Brian asked, "If it is, she's got to know something."

Peering into a darkened alley, Wong spotted a skinny white woman with platinum hair fixed in an Afro. It had to be Olivia. Her hairdo always reminded Wong of a dandelion gone to seed, much as poor Olivia had. In her heyday her street name had been Candy, presumably because she was so sweet and desirable. Time had not been kind to Olivia. Although her hair was still platinum, it was brittle from too many years of bleaching. She was thin—too thin—and her eyes were too hard to make her look either sweet or desirable.

"Want to see what she can tell us?" Brian asked, pulling over to the curb.

Wong rolled down his window and watched Olivia stiffen.

"What the hell do you guys want?" she hissed. "Don't you know you're bad for business? Leave me alone."

"Can't you give us a minute?" Wong asked.

"No!" Olivia's eyes blazed. "Can't you see I'm busy? A girl's got to work to eat."

"Just a minute?" Wong repeated.

Olivia shivered. The fog was beginning to shift into the downtown area, forming little haloes around the streetlights. Goose bumps ran up the woman's bare arms. Her toes crammed into high-heeled sandals were white with cold.

Wong felt a sudden pity for her. Not only must she be freezing, but she must also be hungry. What a helluva way to live! He made a great show of checking his wristwatch. "It's dinner time for us," he said. "How about we buy you some dinner while we talk? That way you won't run the risk of missing a meal ticket."

Olivia looked skeptical but she didn't say no.

"How often does anyone offer you a free meal?" Wong coaxed.

"There's no such a thing as a free meal, Wong. You know that. Especially dinner." Olivia sneered but Wong could tell she was already deciding what to order.

❧❧❧

Officer Brian Dineen drove to Sam's Café, a small coffee shop just off Market Street. Sam, the owner, led them to a booth in the back where they could have a little privacy and where they wouldn't frighten off any of his other customers.

"I really don't know nothing," Olivia said, studying the fly-specked menu.

Wong watched her lips move while she read the choices and waited until she'd finished before he spoke. "You must have heard that a police officer was killed today," he said quietly.

"You'd have to be deaf, dumb, and blind to have missed that," Olivia snapped. She poured a little mound of salt on the table and began to play with it.

"What did you hear? Brian asked.

"Let's order first," Olivia said coyly and Wong motioned for Sam.

"Burgers for you two guys and the turkey blue plate special for the lady," Sam repeated. "How do you stay so skinny?" he asked Olivia who shot him a seductive smile.

While they waited for the meal, Olivia excused herself. "Got to go to the little girl's room," she said. Brian watched her go.

"Do you think she knows anything," he asked, "or have we just been suckered into a free meal?"

Wong shrugged. "It's worth a try," he said.

Olivia and the meal arrived at the table together. Wong watched the woman eat everything, even the parsley, and then mop up the last remnants of the turkey gravy with a piece of Parker House roll. "Was it good?" he asked.

Mouth still full, Olivia nodded and gave him a half smile. "Delicious," she said.

Wong noticed his partner checking his watch. They needed to get back on the streets.

"Now then," Wong said, "what can you tell us about Sarah Spencer's murder?"

"Sarah Spencer? Was that the girl's name?" Olivia asked, moving her plate so that Sam could set down the glass dish with a scoop of vanilla ice cream in it. "Comes with the blue plate," he said.

"Sarah Spencer," Olivia repeated. "That's a nice name. Kinda old-fashioned, huh?"

Wong could feel impatience knotting his stomach. "Come on, Olivia," he said. "Tell us what you know."

"All I know is what I hear on the street."

Brian Dineen leaned forward in his chair. Olivia blanched. He didn't need to say anything. His size alone was intimidating.

"Honest, fellows, all I know is what I hear."

"And that is?" Brian's voice was low.

"Someone said that Junior Johnson said—"

"Now we're getting somewhere," Wong muttered.

Olivia took a spoonful of ice cream and savored it. "Junior

said that the guy who shot the girl was not from the neighborhood."

"What does that mean?" Wong asked.

"That it's not somebody we know." Olivia studied the two police officers as though she was deciding just how much more to tell them. "Junior thinks he's probably long gone back to where he came from. So there's no use hassling people around here."

Dineen brought his face close to hers. "How does Junior know that?" he asked.

Olivia's brown eyes blinked nervously. "Junior knows all kinda things," she said, "you know that. The best thing is to ask Junior, not a working girl like me."

"Where do you think we can find Junior tonight?" Dineen asked. Olivia frowned, her spoonful of ice cream in midair. "You know what, fellows? Now that I think of it, I ain't seen Junior around since about noon."

"Yeah," she said, scraping her ice-cream dish clean. "Junior real busy with something."

🙟🙜

When the convent car rolled into the garage, old Donata was there to greet Mary Helen and Anne. "Therese has got herself into a real tizzy," Donata said without introduction. "Is it true that there was another murder at the Refuge?"

Mary Helen felt as though someone had punched her. "Why don't you just come right out and say what's on your mind," she asked, hoping it sounded light.

"At my age who has time for games?" Donata snapped. "Are you two involved in another murder?"

"Certainly not!" Anne sounded indignant.

"Then why did Therese's niece tell her you were?"

"I have no idea," Anne said stiffly. "A woman was shot down

the street," she conceded. "But how can we be held responsible? It's a rough neighborhood."

"Down the street?" Donata pondered that news. "You must have had something to do with it to get Therese so upset."

"As we both know, it doesn't take much to upset Therese." Mary Helen slammed the car door. "Where is she now? I'll talk to her."

"At the television—where else? It's time for the five o'clock news."

By the time Mary Helen and Anne arrived in the community room, every seat was taken. No one seemed to notice them standing just inside the door since every eye was focused on the television set. Anchorman Dave Chavez solemnly reported the shooting death of Sarah Spencer, a young police officer, on her first undercover assignment.

There was footage of the sidewalk where her body had fallen, bare now except for the brown stains of her blood and a chalked outline. Her fiancé, looking distraught, had mumbled a few words into the outstretched microphone. Her parents, pale and teary-eyed, asked to be left alone. Finally, the Chief of Police assured the viewers that whoever did this would be found and prosecuted. "I'll do everything in my power," he promised.

"What did he say about the hour?" Donata asked. She must have turned down her hearing aid.

"In his power," Ursula repeated patiently.

"I don't know why they have to mumble," Donata complained.

Mary Helen was sure that the segment was over and that no mention would be made of the Refuge, when the anchorman lowered his voice. It was as if he were about to share a dark secret. "A reliable source," he said, giving the camera his sincerest expression, "informs this reporter that an elderly nun from the Refuge happened to be with the policewoman when she died."

"Why couldn't he have just said 'nun'? Mary Helen fumed as all eyes suddenly shifted toward her.

"I knew it!" Sister Therese's reedy voice pierced the silence. "And, if you ask me, it's a disgrace. We have no business dabbling in this sort of business."

"If you ask me," old Donata piped up, her hearing obviously improved, "it's one of the corporal works of mercy—*Comfort the dying*."

"I think you've got it confused with *bury the dead*," Ursula, ever exact, corrected.

"Whatever!" Donata said impatiently. "You know exactly what I mean."

Ursula's face flushed. "I suppose it could be compared to visiting the sick . . ."

"Stop!" Mary Helen tried to keep her voice even. "I didn't want to be there. It just happened. Do you think I enjoyed watching the beautiful young woman's life fading away?" Without a word she left the now silent room. She was exhausted. It had been a long day. Although she wasn't hungry, she should get some supper and go to bed. But first she needed to unwind. Regardless of the time in Ireland, she decided to call Eileen.

To say Eileen was surprised to hear from her again so soon was an understatement. "Do you know what time it is, Mary Helen?" her friend asked, in a voice thick with sleep. "This better be good."

Quickly Mary Helen told her of meeting Sarah at the Refuge, being told that something bad was going on down the street, and getting to the woman to hear her dying word. Eileen listened without comment.

"What do you think I should do now?" Mary Helen asked finally.

"To be perfectly honest, I think you should leave it to the police. Whoever killed that woman has a gun and is not afraid to use it on anyone."

Mary Helen was taken aback. Eileen was usually so fearless. She had fully expected her old friend to say, "You surely should do whatever you can to help Kate and Inspector Gallagher find the killer." Then make up an old Irish proverb to prove it.

Maybe she hadn't heard correctly. Could they have a bad connection? It probably hadn't been such a good idea to wake up Eileen at two in the morning. Nobody is at their best when they're awakened from a sound sleep. "You mean not get involved?"

"That's exactly what I mean."

"What makes you say that?" Mary Helen asked in disbelief.

"Well," Eileen chose her words carefully, "for one thing, the last time I saw you, you were not yet bulletproof."

"So?" Mary Helen pressed.

"So, when I finally do get home, old dear, I'd like you to be there."

"Don't be silly," Mary Helen said, but not before she felt a chill run up her spine.

❧❧❧

As Kate Murphy drove out Geary Boulevard toward home, she was scarcely aware of the evening traffic. In all the congestion, her car seemed to operate on automatic pilot, stopping at stoplights, waiting for pedestrians to cross, and avoiding buses and aggressive bikers alike. It wasn't until she pulled up in front of her yellow peaked-roof house on Thirty-fourth and Geary that she noticed that great waves of fog had rolled in from the beach, covering the Avenues. She slammed her car door and felt the moisture in her hair. Soon the fog would be as thick and dense as her mind trying to make some sense out of the death of the policewoman, Sarah Spencer.

Kate was glad to see her husband's car. Jack was home. It was his turn to pick up their son from Sheila, the babysitter, and to make dinner. She was starving. No wonder. The last thing she remembered eating was a cookie at the Refuge. Then all hell had broken loose.

Beside her front stairs the wide leaves of the iron blue hydrangea bushes glistened in the dampness. Carefully she mounted the steps. The fog made them slippery, and she had no time for a broken bone.

"Hi," she called, pushing open the front door, fully expecting her son John to squeal and run to hug her. But the house was silent.

"Jack. Pal. John, it's Mom," her voice ricocheted through the empty hallway. "Jack, are you there?" she called toward the kitchen. The light was on, but there was no hint that a meal was cooking—no aroma of onions or garlic. Fear prickled her scalp. No matter what Jack was preparing, he always sautéed a few onions or a clove of garlic first, claiming that the smell alone relieved everyone's anxiety about dinner being served.

"Jack?" she called, controlling her urge to scream, and listened. Was water running in the upstairs bathroom? The shower? Yes. Someone was in the shower. It must be her husband. But where was her son? If he were in the shower with his father wouldn't she hear some noise?

Struggling to calm the whirlpool of dread, she started up the stairs. *Why must I always imagine the worst?* Kate wondered, gripping the banister. Was it an occupational hazard?

The jangle of the telephone pierced the house like a scream. Taking the stairs two at a time, she snatched up the receiver from their bedside phone. "Hello," she said, trying to keep the panic out of her voice.

"Hello, Kate," her mother-in-law chirped. "This is Loretta."

As though I wouldn't recognize your voice, Kate thought. "Hello, Loretta," she said, hoping she didn't sound impatient. Mama Bassetti had the unfailing knack of calling at the absolute wrong time. Tonight was no exception.

47

The shower stopped. She heard the curtain being pulled back. She desperately needed to talk to her husband. Where was their son? Had Jack done the unthinkable and forgotten to pick him up?

"Did Jack tell you?" Mama Bassetti asked.

"Tell me what? Kate was distracted.

"Then, I guess he didn't. That boy!" Kate visualized her mother-in-law, one hand on her ample hip, lips pursed, shaking her head. "I don't know what's wrong with my Jackie," she said. "I raised him better than that, Kate. I swear I did. His papa and I did our very best." She sighed. "What kind of a husband is too busy to call his working wife and tell her that they are going out for dinner? I ask you?"

When her mother-in-law paused for breath, Kate heard a familiar giggle in the background. It was John! He was with his grandmother. Quick tears burned her eyes. What in the world was he doing there?

The bathroom door swung open and Jack appeared in a cloud of steam smelling clean and fresh. "Hi, hon," he said, kissing the back of her neck. His wet hair dripped on her shoulder.

Suddenly angry, Kate handed him the receiver. "Your mother," she said. "Was there something you forgot to tell me?"

"What's up, Ma?" Jack asked. Except for an occasional grunt and a few "but, Ma's," he listened until Kate felt sorry for him.

"That was some wild Italian," he said when he finally hung up. "She didn't even give me a chance to explain that your car phone wasn't on."

"Oh, right," Kate said, realizing that she'd been too distracted to notice. She sat down on the edge of their bed, pulled off her shoes, and wiggled her toes. "What's going on?" she asked, suddenly exhausted.

Toweling his hair, Jack shrugged. "It seems that my mother heard from a neighbor whose friend's son is on the force that a policewoman was killed today. Of course, the neighbor has no name or other information to identify the victim, so my mother immediately jumps to the conclusion that it could be you."

"Oh, dear." Kate leaned back against the pillow. She knew all about jumping to conclusions.

"I just beat you home," Jack said. "It was hard to leave the Detail. We kept hashing and rehashing Sarah's murder. Although none of us knew her very well, we all liked her. It's a helluva thing to happen to a young kid. We should have protected her better."

Kate noticed the sadness in Jack's eyes and was ashamed of her own outburst. It was tough to lose a fellow officer, but especially someone in your own Detail. "I'm sorry, pal," she said, but Jack didn't seem to want to go there.

"Anything new come up in the case?" he asked.

"No. Like you, we were just hanging around trying to figure out what we know. Or more like it, what we don't know about her assignment."

"What do you mean?"

"Well, she was dressed like a bag lady—a crazy one at that. Wouldn't an undercover Vice cop be more likely to pose as a prostitute?"

Jack shrugged. "If you know that and I know that, pimps and madams sure as hell know it, too. Maybe that's the point—to throw them a curve."

"Maybe," Kate admitted. "But the thing just doesn't smell right."

"In what way?"

"Undercover cops usually blend in or, at least, they don't stand out. A woman with flaming hair? Like I say, it just doesn't smell right." She twisted a strand of her own auburn hair around her finger. "And we didn't find any brass near the scene. Unless the tech team picked it up without Denny or me being aware of it, it wasn't there. You have to admit that's pretty slick for your average perp."

"What's your point, hon?"

"I'm not sure. Something just doesn't smell right."

"You're a woman of few words," Jack said. "You just keep repeating them."

"Very funny!" Kate couldn't suppress a yawn.

"Tomorrow, talk to Donaldson," Jack suggested. "He'll probably be able to answer all your questions—at least about Sarah's undercover assignment. You're the homicide detective, but remember you have the whole department behind you. We'll figure it out."

Kate closed her eyes. Let's hope so, she thought. She felt the mattress move and the warmth of Jack's body beside her. It was good to be home. "How did John get to your mother's and how did we get invited to dinner?" she asked.

"Poor Ma has been bombarding Saint Michael with prayers for you all day."

"Saint Michael?"

"Patron saint of policemen."

Although Kate did not open her eyes, she raised her eyebrows.

"Sorry, police persons. Anyway, when she finally got me on the phone and found out that you were alive and well—I think it might be wise not to tell her that you caught the call—she offered to pick up John from Sheila's and make us a special dinner."

Kate's stomach rumbled. "Do you know what we're having?

"Ravioli, I think. She was going to North Beach to get them."

"I didn't realize I meant that much to her," Kate quipped, feeling Jack's arm around her. "I nearly panicked when I came home and didn't find you or John downstairs. I thought something happened."

"You're getting as bad as my mother," he said, gently kissing her temple. "I'm sure John is having a great time eating all the cookies his heart desires. And I'm right here beside you."

"What time do we have to be there? Kate asked.

"In about an hour."

She felt Jack's breath brush her ear. "That's plenty of time," she said as his hand tenderly touched her waist and ran down over her hip.

"It doesn't really matter if we're a few minutes late," Jack said, his lips reaching for hers. "There's no way you can really spoil ravioli."

❧❧❧

Kate and Jack had just started up the terrazzo steps of Loretta Bassetti's home in the Sunset District when the front door swung open. Mama Bassetti, wearing her company apron, loomed in the doorway. Little John's smiling face peeked out from behind her.

"I was just starting to worry about you," Mama Bassetti said, lifting her cheek to her son for their ritual kiss. "Was there traffic in the park or did you two get lost?"

As if he hadn't heard, Jack pecked at his mother, then swooped up his son in an enormous bear hug. Mama Bassetti's sharp brown eyes pinned Kate.

"I'm sorry we're late," Kate said, wishing they had remembered to bring fresh flowers or at least a bottle of wine. What had they been thinking? Her face flushed when she remembered.

"I hope we didn't spoil anything," Kate said sheepishly.

"Come in, come in out of the cold." Her mother-in-law seemed satisfied with the apology. "Here, let me take your coat. No, on second thought, Jackie," she called toward her son who was already horseplaying on the living room rug with John, "you take the coats, like a gentleman should. It's a good example for your son." She wagged her head. "Although God knows your papa, may he rest in peace, and I tried our best to give you a good example, for all it got us."

"I am a perfect gentleman, Ma. In fact, I am a gentleman for all occasions," Jack joked, winking at Kate. It continually astounded her that his mother's nagging never seemed to faze him.

He gave a waist-deep bow and put on his best Jeeves accent. "As a matter of fact, Madame, not only will I take Kate's coat and hang it up, but I will make you, beloved mother, and you, adored wife, both an old-fashioned. Will you assist me, John, old fellow?"

"Not too many bitters," his mother called, watching the two disappear into the kitchen. She didn't speak until she heard the clink of glasses and ice.

"Kate." She put her thick hand on her daughter-in-law's arm. "Sit down, I want to talk to you while we're alone."

Kate stiffened. What was wrong?

Loretta's eyes widened and for moment she looked apprehensive, a look Kate scarcely recognized on her. Something was definitely wrong.

"All day long, after my neighbor told me a policewoman was killed, I was worried to death about you."

"If I had known . . ." Kate started, but her mother-in-law cut her off.

"I was afraid that you were the policewoman, God rest her. Silly, I guess, but it could have been you, you know." She patted Kate's hand. "Thanks be to God, it wasn't. Anyhow, after I talked to Jackie and found out that you were all right, my neighbor called again."

You and your neighbor have little to do, Kate thought, but knew better than to say so.

"Her son who's on the force, too . . . that's why we talk a lot . . . he said that the woman who was killed was young and inexperienced. Then she dropped her bomb. Do you know what she told me?"

Kate shook her head.

"That she was in Jackie's Detail."

Where is this going? Kate wondered.

"Jackie doesn't know this, but after I talked to my neighbor, I began to think about it. Stew, I guess. And before I knew what happened, I was hot."

"Hot?" Kate couldn't remember ever hearing her use that word before.

"You know, mad," Loretta said. "And with good reason, too. Why would any man, especially the man in charge, send a young, inexperienced girl undercover? Bad enough for an experienced man, but for a young girl?"

"Isn't that a little sexist, Loretta?" Kate said.

"Sexist, mexist!" Her red cheeks flushed. "It's poor judgment and poor leadership, if you ask me." She paused. "I never did like that Donaldson kid very much. He was a little bit of a bully in the neighborhood. Although, I never could figure out why his mother named him Don . . . Don Donaldson? Poor woman, she did her best to keep him in line. I remember her well from the PTA. The father, God rest him, was no help. So, I did what any good citizen would do."

Kate waited, hoping she hadn't guessed what her mother-in-law had done.

"I called Lieutenant Donaldson. Even if he is Jackie's boss. I was acting as a private citizen and a taxpayer."

"Does Jack know?"

"This is not Jackie's business. Anyway, I told that Donaldson boy exactly what I thought about his sending a young girl on such a dangerous assignment. What was he thinking of, anyway?"

"What did Donaldson say?

Loretta Bassetti pushed a strand of gray hair off her forehead. "He wasn't exactly insulting, but I certainly did not like his attitude. His mother, and I just might tell her if I get the chance, would not have been proud of the way he talked to an older woman."

Kate decided to let that lie. "Did you tell him that you were Jack's mother?"

"I didn't intend to when I called. In fact, at first I didn't give him my name, but he got so sassy that it just slipped out."

"Did anything else slip out?"

"No. Only that my Jackie would not approve of anyone speaking to his mother in that tone. And that my good friend, the police commissioner, wouldn't either."

"Do you know the police commissioner?"

"One of my neighbor's sisters used to live next door to the commissioner's cousin, and they were very close."

"Hello, again, ladies." Jack came in balancing a tray of drinks. Little John followed with crackers and Brie cheese on a glass plate. Mama Bassetti rose quickly to grab the knife that wobbled on its edge.

"What are you lovely ladies so deep in conversation about?" Jack's eyes twinkled.

He hasn't a clue, Kate thought.

"Kate will tell you," Mama Bassetti said, straightening her apron. "John, after you take a few crackers, put them down and come help Nonie with the ravioli."

John didn't need to be invited twice. "Can I drop them in the boiling water?" he asked. Although to her knowledge none of the Bassetti children had ever been scalded, Kate was just as glad she didn't hear the answer.

"Tell me what, pal?" Jack was still smiling. "What's going on?"

Without meeting his eyes, Kate told him as quickly and as painlessly as possible.

"Stop that shouting, Jackie," Mama Bassetti called from the kitchen, "right this minute. Do you want all the neighbors to hear you talking that way about your mother?"

❧❧❧

With a sense of relief, Sister Mary Helen shut her bedroom door and listened to its solid click. *Please God*, she prayed earnestly, *don't let anyone knock to see how I'm doing or if I need anything.*

Dinner had been a nightmare. By the time she had finished talking to Eileen and made her way to the dining room, most of the nuns were already there. When she walked in, the silence hit her like a hot wind. Apparently her outburst in the Sisters' Room had upset them all. For several anxious seconds, no one spoke.

"Are you still mad?" It was old Donata.

Someone groaned. "Really!" Therese sniffed, clearly incensed. "Have you no finesse?" she hissed.

Mary Helen smiled. She rather enjoyed Donata's flat-footed approach. At least you never had to guess what she was thinking. "I wasn't angry, Donata," Mary Helen said, her voice filling the still room. "I was just frustrated. I'm sorry if my reaction upset everyone."

Ursula rose from her chair. "We are the ones who should be sorry," she said piously and glanced around, waiting while the low murmur of agreement spread through the group. Satisfied, she sat down, and quiet conversation gradually began to melt the tension.

Relieved, Mary Helen picked up her dinner tray. All at once her appetite returned. The spicy aroma of tonight's stew made her realize that she hadn't eaten much solid food all day. In fact, she felt hollow. Balancing a tray with a large helping of stew over rice, crisp sourdough bread and butter, and a tall glass of iced tea, she decided to come back later for dessert. The chocolate éclairs looked especially inviting.

Slowly Mary Helen made her way toward a vacant place at the end of a half-filled table where she could eat in peace. Crossing the room, she smiled benignly at a Sister who smiled at her. "How do?" she said to another. What was it Eileen always said? "A kind word never broke anyone's jaw."

"Mary Helen, I saved you a place." It was Sister Patricia, a college president.

"Thank you," Mary Helen said, although tonight she'd much rather have sat alone. She was just placing her napkin in her lap when a familiar voice rose above the others.

"I'd like to say something." It was Anne. She must have just come in. Had she been crying? Red-faced, her hazel eyes blazing, she stood tall and stiff, like Saint Joan of Arc at the stake. *All she needs is the fire*, Mary Helen thought.

"Now what?" Patricia muttered. Mary Helen wondered the same thing. Neither had long to wait.

"Although I'm sure none of you means it," Anne began in a strong voice, "I just want to tell you how difficult it is for Mary Helen and me to come home after working all day with homeless women and their desperate needs and tragic lives and have some of you"—her eyes narrowed and swept the room—"some of you," she repeated, "make our work more difficult by blaming us for the tragedies we stumble upon." Her voice choked.

All eyes shifted like searchlights toward Sister Mary Helen, no doubt expecting her to say something, anything to save the day. She pushed her bifocals up the bridge of her nose and cleared her throat. Without warning her mouth felt furry and her mind went blank.

"What in the world is she thinking?" Patricia whispered. "Wasn't one scene at dinner enough?"

Apparently not. Anne went on. "As I said, I'm sure no one means it and Mary Helen would never complain, but it hurts."

"What is Anne saying about Mary Helen?" Donata's voice pierced the frozen silence. "Did she complain about the desserts?"

Following a moment of shock, the room burst into laughter. Mary Helen was never quite sure whether or not Donata had made an honest mistake, not that it mattered. The spell was broken. As someone once said, the next best thing to solving a problem is finding humor in it.

Mary Helen fully expected that the situation was on the mend. It never occurred to her that she'd spend the next two hours accepting apologies, explanations, and fending off offers to help, etc. By the time she had shut her bedroom door she could have happily strangled Anne.

After a relaxing bath she settled into bed with the latest Gloria White mystery, hoping that Ronnie Ventana, private investigator, would take her mind off the events of the day. But even Ronnie wasn't tough enough for that assignment. Giving up, she turned off the light and lay in the darkness waiting for sleep to come. Heaven knows, she was tired enough. She turned on her side toward her bedroom clock where the glow-in-the-dark numbers read 10:15.

Had it only been sixteen hours since her day had begun? It seemed like a lifetime ago that Father Adams had spoken of the corporal works of mercy in his homily. She had bargained for feeding the hungry and sheltering the homeless, but never had she anticipated dealing with another death.

Even with her eyes closed she could still see Sarah Spencer crumpled on the sidewalk. She watched the young woman's face grow pale as her blood slowly ran toward the curb. She felt Sarah's breath on her ear as she strained to hear her dying words.

Didn't that make her somehow responsible for trying to find the woman's killer? *The police will take care of that*, a still, small voice warned her. Her dear friend Eileen had cautioned her against getting involved, too, but she was already involved.

Lord, she prayed in the quiet of her heart, remembering the shadow she thought she'd glimpsed in the doorway, *what harm would it do to try to find out if anyone was there? And if so, what had he or she seen? Then I can pass the information on to Kate Murphy. She and Inspector Gallagher must be swamped. It would be a real act of charity. You know, Lord, what Scripture says about charity—that charity never fails.*

"I see. I thought you might have another passage in mind," the Lord said.

And what passage is that? Mary Helen asked, sensing that she was walking into a Divine trap.

For an instant she thought she heard a deep, hearty chuckle. "That charity covers a multitude of sins, old friend," the Lord said.

That, too, Mary Helen answered and fell into a peaceful sleep before the Lord had a chance to go into detail.

Tuesday, June 5

❧❦❧

Feast of Saint Boniface, Bishop and Martyr

The first thing Sister Mary Helen heard when she awoke was the hum of the garbage truck coming up the college hill. *It must be Tuesday*, she thought, her eyes still closed, *and nearly seven o'clock!* Abruptly she sat up. Had she overslept or was the Sunset Scavenger early? One glance at her bedside clock told her that as usual, the truck was on time.

This is getting to be a bad habit, she thought, turning back the corner of her window shade to check the weather. A screen of thick fog shrouded the college. In the dampness the lawn glistened and dew on the startlingly orange and red Tropicana roses shimmered like tiny sequins.

Quickly Mary Helen slipped into her navy blue skirt and a white cotton blouse, and then took her Aran sweater from the closet. Layers was the only way to dress for a San Francisco summer day.

Father Adams and she arrived in the chapel at exactly the

same time. "Today is the Feast of Saint Boniface," he began from the altar, "the patron saint of Germany."

At the mention of the Saint's name, Mary Helen's mind leap-frogged from the man to the church of Saint Boniface in the heart of San Francisco's Tenderloin. For years the Franciscan Fathers had fed hundreds of homeless men, women, and children each day. Most of the women from the Refuge had their main meal at St. Anthony's, the church's free dining room. *How*, she wondered, *had the women fared last night?* She hoped that they hadn't been as haunted by Sarah's murder as she had been.

It wasn't until Sister Anne and she had picked up the day-old doughnuts and were nearly at the center that she realized just how drastically the women's lives actually were being affected by the murder of this young officer.

"Look at the police." Anne pointed out the car window. They had turned off Geary Boulevard and were making their way down Jones Street. Police officers were everywhere.

"It's must be some kind of sweep," Mary Helen said, watching pairs of uniformed patrolmen circuiting the streets, stopping people. A number of cars that obviously did not belong in the neighborhood were parked along the curb.

"It looks like a scene right out of a police drama," Mary Helen said. "If I didn't know better, I'd think they were filming."

"*Nash Bridges* maybe," Anne said.

More like NYPD Blue, Mary Helen thought, but let it go.

A knot of women stood in the front doorway of the Refuge when the two nuns arrived. "You late, girlfriend," Miss Bobbie called, "and we needs our coffee this morning." The scar around her right eye twitched.

Venus smiled her one-tooth-missing smile. "We sure do," she said with a shiver.

"What's going on around here?" Anne asked, unlocking the front door.

Tiny Peanuts held the door back so that the two nuns could

60

go in and start the coffee. "You don't want to know," she said, but that didn't seem to stop her from telling them. "Them polices are all over asking questions, picking up peoples with warrants, hassling you for jay-walking, asking if you seen any thing—"

"Did you?" Mary Helen asked.

"If I did, I ain't telling," Peanuts said.

Miss Bobbie sat down at her usual place at her usual table with a cup of coffee and two sugar doughnuts. "It's that policewoman got herself shot," she said. "It wouldn't make no matter if one of us be shot. They'd just go on, business as usual."

"I don't think that's true," Mary Helen said. "I'm sure the police are very concerned no matter who is killed. Look how quickly they solved Melanie's murder."

For a moment Miss Bobbie looked as if she might argue. Instead she shrugged. "That's 'cause you got into it," she said. "You going to get into this one, too?"

Mary Helen stopped short. She couldn't believe Miss Bobbie had asked that question. Was it just a coincidence or was her question somehow providential? Was it some sort of sign? One look at Anne's face and Mary Helen knew that she'd better not go there—at least, not out loud.

"Morning, you all." It was Geraldine. Mary Helen was glad to see her. Something Geraldine had said yesterday was bothering her.

"I can't stay long," Geraldine said, pouring herself a cup of coffee and dumping in four teaspoons of sugar. "I can't stay long," she repeated, sitting down at the table with Miss Bobbie.

Almost at once several groups of women came through the door. Soon the Refuge was crowded and Mary Helen was busy giving out shower rolls, replenishing the donuts, making more pots of coffee, and answering the telephone. Unfortunately, one of the calls was from the morning volunteer saying that after yesterday's murder, her husband was too afraid to let her come down. Men, Mary Helen thought, hurrying to call a substitute. Judy, who happily was not busy, promised to be there in twenty minutes and she was.

At the first break in the action, Mary Helen found an empty chair beside Geraldine.

"What's happening, Sister?" the woman's dark eyes looked wary. "You all right?"

"I was just wondering—"

" 'Bout what?"

"About something you said yesterday, Geraldine."

"Yesterday? What I say yesterday?" The eyes shot open and her heavy shoulders stiffened defensively.

"You mentioned that your nephew, Junior Johnson, knew that the woman who was killed was a policewoman."

"That part right." Her words were clipped.

"My question is," Mary Helen tried to keep from sounding threatening, "how did he know so quickly?"

For several seconds Geraldine studied her. *She is wondering, no doubt, just how much to tell me,* Mary Helen thought. *I can't blame her.* Geraldine leaned forward. She must have made a decision.

"We need to talk private," Geraldine said and looked toward Miss Bobbie. One glance told them both that Miss Bobbie was not moving tables, no matter how much they needed to be alone.

"What about the office?" Mary Helen offered, but Geraldine had already decided that another table at the far corner was private enough.

When they were settled again, Geraldine bent forward and whispered, "My nephew Junior is an important man around here. People tells him things."

"Like what?" Mary Helen asked.

"Like things. Take, for instance, that pink stucco house on Brannon—you'll see it if you drive by—it's a house for working girls. Everyone in the neighborhood knows that, not just Junior. Anytime some new face around lookin', Junior's friends tell him and he checks them out."

"If everyone in the neighborhood knows it is a house for working girls," Mary Helen said, presuming that working girls meant prostitutes, "why don't the police know?" It didn't make any sense.

"You is simple, girl, ain't you?" Geraldine asked in amazement and Mary Helen didn't know whether to be flattered or insulted. What in heaven's name was the woman implying?

"Are you saying the police do know?" she asked, fear creeping into her chest.

Geraldine narrowed her eyes until all Mary Helen saw were slits. "I'm not saying nothing, for sure. I just be minding my business." Her tone was cold. "But don't it stand to reason? There must be something more if they sends that pale face woman as a decoy. They knows what it is. Why not just move on it? Got to be something more."

"What more has there got to be?" Mary Helen asked, a little short of breath. This was getting very complicated. "What does Junior say?"

"I don't ask him, he don't tell." Geraldine let out an unexpected guffaw. "Like them gays in the military."

"Do you think I can speak to Junior?" Mary Helen asked.

Geraldine shrugged. "It ain't up to me. It be up to Junior."

"How can I get in touch with him? Is he around somewhere?"

Geraldine stared into her coffee cup as though the answer might be written on the bottom of the mug. "You know, Sister, now that I thinks about it, I ain't seen Junior yet this morning. Not since yesterday. He may be doing business somewhere."

"Could his business have anything to do with the house on Brannon?"

Geraldine gave a hollow laugh. "Not that house," she said. "Like I says, that ain't no ordinary whorehouse."

"I don't understand," Mary Helen said. "What do you mean no ordinary house?"

"For a smart woman, you be awful dumb sometimes." Geraldine shook her head. "You thinks about it. You can figure it out." All at once, her dark eyes hit Mary Helen like a shot. "What you think about the police knowing and nobody doing nothing until Miss Sarah come along and then somebody kill her? Huh? What you think about that? I ain't saying nothing more."

"If you are asking if I think the police are responsible for Sarah's death, I certainly do not!" Mary Helen said emphatically. "Do you?" she asked and watched Geraldine's face become impenetrable.

"Like I told you, I ain't saying nothing more," Geraldine said, "except watch your back, old lady. Watch your back."

You can bet on that, Mary Helen thought, her heart plummeting. Although she did not believe what Geraldine had said for one minute she was glad when the telephone rang. She needed a little distraction.

Sister Anne, however, picked up the receiver before Mary Helen reached it. She could tell by the tightness around the young nun's mouth that the call was not a pleasant one.

Without a word, Anne pushed the hold button. "It's for you," she said, thrusting the receiver toward Mary Helen. "It's somebody from Channel 5. They want to set up an appointment to interview you about Sarah Spencer's murder."

Mary Helen stepped back, shaking her head.

"What shall I tell them?" Anne asked, staring at the receiver as if the thing might bite her.

"Tell them that I've stepped out for a few minutes, which I'm just about to do. And tell them that you don't know when I'll be back, which, of course, you don't."

Before Anne could comment, Mary Helen was out the front door of the Refuge. Outside the morning was beginning to warm up. The leaves of the straggly maple trees along the sidewalk gleamed in the weak sun. Up the block the tower of the Holiday Inn loomed above the storefronts. Cars flowed down the street on their way to the Bay Bridge. Pedestrians, alone and in groups, filled the sidewalk. For all appearances, it was just another summer day in San Francisco. No one seemed to remember that just yesterday, Sarah Spencer had been killed on this very street. All that remained of her murder was an ugly stain, yellow plastic tape, and a blurred chalk outline.

Death is often like that, Mary Helen mused. *Those who are touched by it are always astonished that nothing stops, that despite their heartbreak the world continues to go on as if nothing extraordinary had happened.*

All at once, she was aware of Venus, Sonia, and Crazy Alice. The three women stood in a knot beside the chain-link fence of the parking lot smoking cigarettes.

"Hi, Sister." It was Crazy Alice sounding unusually sane.

"Good morning, Alice," Mary Helen stopped, and then turned to include the others. "How are you all doing this morning?" she asked.

Alice thought for moment as if she were not quite sure. A dangerous sign, Mary Helen feared. Venus, her hair standing up on her head like black broccoli, rolled her large brown eyes. "We be fine. We just be smoking us a cigarette," she said pleasantly enough.

"What you be doing out here?" Sonia asked, cocking her head. The woman's dark skin had a sickly gray cast to it. Mary Helen wondered if her sickle cell anemia might be acting up.

"Me?" the old nun asked. "What am I doing out here? I just stepped out for minute."

"You needs some fresh air. Right?" Venus nodded. "I know what you means. All that talk about that decoy's murder. It be getting on my nerves, too."

Mary Helen was just about to protest when Crazy Alice began

to giggle. "How am I?" she mumbled as though she had decided at last. *"Sugar in the gourd and honey in the horn, I never was so happy since the hour that I was born."* Tumultuous giggling filled the air. Crazy Alice was totally unaware of the three women staring at her.

"Lord, help us. It ain't much better out here," Venus said, flicking her cigarette butt over the edge of the curb.

Sonia turned away from Alice in disgust. "You ain't nothing normal," she snapped and followed Venus into the Refuge.

Crazy Alice didn't seem to hear or see either one of them. Still tittering and looking neither right nor left, she stepped into the busy street.

"Stop!" Mary Helen shouted, but Alice kept on walking. Instinctively Mary Helen squeezed her eyes shut and waited for the thud. Instead she heard the screeching of multiple car brakes, the blare of a dozen horns, loud curses, and, above it all, the high-pitched giggle.

When the traffic finally began to flow again, Mary Helen opened her eyes. Crazy Alice was on the opposite side of the street safely strolling along the sidewalk. Unaware of anyone around her, she waved her arms as though she were directing the San Francisco Symphony Orchestra in full practice.

All the commotion had brought several shopkeepers out onto the sidewalk. Mary Helen waved to the mechanic from McCormick's Auto Parts who was talking to the owner of the American Asian Food Mart. Down the street, like an answer to prayer, was the tattooed man from the New You Tattoo Parlor. He stood in front of his shop staring after Crazy Alice.

"How do," Mary Helen said, approaching him quickly. "I'm Sister Mary Helen from the Refuge. I don't believe we've met."

The tattoo man, whom she judged to be somewhere in his mid-forties, was a tall man and had a beard that reminded her of Abraham Lincoln on a five-dollar bill. He looked down at her with clear blue eyes, which were neither warm nor friendly.

After coolly appraising her, he said in a deep voice, "I'm Tim."

Tim, the tattoo man, Mary Helen thought. Catchy! "How do, Tim," she said. Smiling up at him, she tried not to stare at his bulging arm muscles, covered with intricate tattoos. With effort she managed for the most part to concentrate on the man's face, which was pleasant enough, although her eyes kept shifting down to the ornate blue dragon curling around the back of his neck.

"Looks as if we almost had another fatality," Mary Helen commented, hoping her remark would lead naturally into the subject to Sarah Spencer's murder.

Tim didn't bite. Instead, he shoved his hands into the pockets of his Levis. Only his fingertips fit, really, and Mary Helen noticed that one set of knuckles had the word MOTHER tattooed across them. She couldn't imagine any mother being pleased about that.

All the while, Tim continued to stare straight ahead. *This is going to be a tough one*, she thought, studying the array of tattoo samples displayed in the New You window. There were delicate butterflies and long-stemmed roses, skulls and swastikas, an elephant's head with a shortened trunk, swords and sunsets all in color. Something for everyone, she reckoned.

Turning back, she found that Tim was staring at her. "Is there something I can do for you?" he asked, following her gaze to the tattoo display.

Mary Helen felt the color rush to her cheeks. "Oh, no!" she said, then hoped she hadn't sounded too horrified. Obviously the man took pride in his work. It would never do to insult him.

"Just wondering," he said with a smirk. "You seemed awfully interested." He turned to go back into the parlor.

It is now or never, Mary Helen thought. "Mr. Tim," she called above the din of the traffic, "did you by any chance see anything when that young woman was shot yesterday morning?"

The man stopped dead, then spun around to face her. "What

did you say?" His voice was low and threatening.

Sister Mary Helen pulled herself up to her full five foot three inches, pushed her bifocals up the bridge of her nose, put on her "schoolteacher" face, and repeated her question. If there was anything she hated, it was being bullied.

Although Tim's face assumed a placid mask, his blue eyes burned. "That's what I thought you said. Come inside, Sister," he ordered. When she didn't budge, he added, "Please."

To her surprise, the shop was light and immaculately clean, like a doctor's office really. Sample tattoos were artistically arranged on the walls and a thick photo album lay on the counter, filled, no doubt, with pictures of more choices.

The price list was placed unobtrusively on the wall behind the cash register and Mary Helen was shocked to see that the price of tattoos began at fifty dollars and went up as high as five thousand dollars.

On her left was a doorway, which led to a second room with a lounge chair and table, undoubtedly for the comfort of the "tattooee." She would have liked to look around more, but this was not the time.

Tim shut the front door. Mary Helen's stomach jumped with the click of the key in the lock. "Sister," the man said evenly, "have you any idea how dangerous that question could be?"

The hum of the traffic from the street outside filled the silent shop. To be honest, up to this point she hadn't considered the danger of her question. Let alone the danger of coming into a locked shop with a man she had just met. Slowly fear crept through her body like a chill. She felt a little lightheaded.

"It is very dangerous!" Tim answered his own question.

"I suppose you're right," Mary Helen said, struggling to keep her voice steady.

"Damn right, I'm right!" Tim strained his words through clenched teeth.

"I was just trying to help the police," she explained reasonably.

"Well, don't!" Tim, the tattoo man, leaned forward. She felt his warm breath on her cheek.

"And for your information, Sister, I want you to know I am the police."

Mary Helen was astonished. She couldn't believe her ears. "You don't own this shop?"

Tim shook his head. "It's just a front. The guy who owns the shop is an ex-cop who agreed to let me use it. I wouldn't know one end of a tattoo needle from the other."

Mary Helen was astonished. "What do you do if someone comes in who really wants a tattoo?"

Tim shrugged. "I set up an appointment and my friend comes in. I'm here because I'm undercover."

"Like Sarah?"

"Yeah, like Sarah."

"And you didn't see anything?" Mary Helen couldn't resist.

Suddenly the man's eyes were wet and he swallowed hard. "The less you know about what anybody saw, the better off we all will be, Sister," he said finally. "Nobody wants you to be the next one with a chest full of lead. Now, please go back to the Refuge."

"One more question," Mary Helen couldn't seem to help herself.

Tim's eyes narrowed dangerously.

"Not about the case," she added quickly. "I'm just curious about the tattoos. Are all of yours real?"

With a crooked smile, Tim wagged his head. "No, thank God," he said. "They're those paste-on things. The only real one is this one." He pointed to the word MOTHER.

❧❧❧

"At last, you're back," Sister Anne said, trying not to sound as peeved as she felt. "What in the world have you been doing? Judy and I were starting to worry."

Mary Helen looked at her blankly, her cheeks flushed and her eyes a little glazed.

"Sister Mary Helen?" Anne felt the muscles in her neck tightening. "Are you all right?"

"Of course I'm all right." Mary Helen blinked as though she were coming out of a dream. "Why wouldn't I be all right?"

Taking a deep breath, Anne struggled to keep her composure. *Now I know for sure where the expression "pain in the neck" comes from*, she thought, slowly circling her head. "Well, for one thing," she said crisply, "you've been gone for quite a while to who-knows-where to do who-knows-what. Anything could have happened to you and we'd never have known."

From the expression on Mary Helen's face, Anne could tell that she was being totally ignored. "Actually, Judy was more concerned than I was," she said, crossing her fingers.

Mary Helen frowned. "Judy? Judy who?"

"The volunteer you called to come in as an emergency substitute." Anne pointed toward a small, pudgy woman with neatly cut, frosted hair wiping off tablecloths and collecting abandoned cups from around the room.

"Of course," Mary Helen said. "Judy." She still seemed a little foggy to Anne. "She was concerned?"

"Very," Anne said, hoping that Judy wouldn't come over and make a liar out of her. Actually, the volunteer had been so busy that she'd hardly noticed Mary Helen was gone until Anne mentioned it.

"Where were you?" Anne pressed.

"You won't believe where I was," Mary Helen said.

Which doesn't answer the question, Anne thought, wondering if she'd be better off not knowing.

"I was with Tim, the tattoo man."

Mary Helen had been right. Anne could scarcely believe it. "Why?"

"Because I thought he might have seen something or someone when Sarah Spencer was shot that could prove helpful to the police."

Anne was about to protest, but Mary Helen raised her hand like a school crossing guard. "And you'll never guess what I found out."

I'll bet I won't, Anne thought.

"That he's a police officer, too. Undercover."

Right again, Anne thought, *I would never have guessed.* "How do you know that?"

As quickly as possible, Mary Helen told her. She began with Crazy Alice walking into the street and ended with Tim taking her into the New You Tattoo Parlor.

"No wonder Kate Murphy called," Anne said. She watched Sister Mary Helen's jaw tighten.

"What do you mean, Kate called? What did she want?"

"She wants you to telephone her at the Hall of Justice, ASAP." Anne said.

Purposefully Sister Mary Helen surveyed the gathering room. "Honestly, Anne," she said, "look at this place. We have more to do around here than to spend our time trying to contact the police. Besides, Kate and Inspector Gallagher probably have left the Hall of Justice by now. And I'd just be wasting my time. I see no point . . ."

"As Soon As Possible," Anne repeated, taking perverse pleasure in watching Mary Helen squirm.

"A perfect waste of time," Mary Helen repeated. "Kate's time as well as my time. And I'll bet you anything that it was that Tim fellow who called her. The insufferable old tattletale!"

"Sister Mary Helen, telephone for you," Judy the volunteer's voice startled Anne. She hadn't heard the woman approaching nor had she even heard the telephone ring. "It's that policewoman again," Judy said. "It must be important."

Rolling her eyes, Mary Helen set her chin and walked toward the office like a soldier marching into a decisive and dangerous battle.

Curious, Anne followed. After Mary Helen's initial "Hello," Kate seemed to be doing all the talking. It was difficult to tell from Mary Helen's monosyllabic answers what Kate's point was exactly. Although the "buts" coming from the old nun would indicate that Kate had the upper hand.

"Nice to talk to you, too," Mary Helen said at last and replaced the receiver.

From the expression on Mary Helen's face, Anne knew that she was not happy about whatever it was Kate had told her. Anne contained herself for as long she could—which was about thirty seconds. "What did she want?" she asked.

"What she wants, if you ask me," Mary Helen said, her words clipped with anger, "is to scare me to death."

Fat chance, Anne thought.

"All that talk about the brazen gunman, and the underbelly of society, and the complicated police plans, and the unknown danger I might be in." Mary Helen's eyes flashed.

"And did she succeed at scaring you?" Anne said as the telephone rang again. She picked at the receiver but covered the mouthpiece with her hand, waiting for Mary Helen's answer. It was quick in coming.

"What is it Eileen always says? 'Fear is a fine spur.'" Mary Helen grinned. "If anything, Anne, I must admit I feel spurred on."

Anne's stomach fell. Exactly what she was afraid of.

❧❦❧

Inspector Kate Murphy, her face burning, slammed down the telephone receiver much harder than she had intended. *That has got to be the most infuriating woman on God's green earth*, she thought, slowly releasing her breath.

"So she finally got to you, too, huh?" her partner taunted, pointing to the telephone.

"What are you talking about, Denny?" Kate forced a smile. She had figured that Dennis Gallagher would be in the coffee room for at least another ten minutes chewing the fat with the other guys, but she had figured wrong. Here he was, standing in front of her with two steaming coffee mugs and a silly grin on his face. Kate would rather burst than give him the satisfaction.

"The receiver simply slipped. I just put on some hand lotion and it's greasy," she said, which was partially true. The juniper lotion was new. She stuck the palm of her hand under Gallagher's nose.

"Get that away from me." Gallagher pushed her hand away. "You smell like a goddamn rain forest."

Sniffing her own hand, Kate didn't know whether or not to be affronted. She rather liked the woodsy, breezy aroma. Best of all, it had taken Gallagher's mind off Sister Mary Helen. At least she hoped it had. She dreaded telling him about Tim Moran's call. Thank goodness she'd been the one who'd received it.

"What's happened?" Gallagher asked, setting Kate's mug down in front of her. Easing into his desk chair, he leaned forward. "You ought to know by now," he began, then stopped to blow on his hot coffee, "that changing the subject or even throwing in a diversion like that stinky hand cream isn't going to work." He leaned back in his chair and stared out the window at the James Lick Freeway, continually crowded with commuters. "Will you never learn, Katie-girl?" He sighed.

Ignoring him, Kate smelled her fingers. "What's stinky about the stuff?" she asked. "It's juniper. Who doesn't like the clean, pungent aroma of juniper? Only some kind of nature hater."

Gallagher swiveled to face her. "Enough already about the

plants and bushes, Kate," he said. "Let's get to the point. What were you talking to Sister Mary Helen about?"

Kate could tell by the set of his mouth that he was getting angry even before he heard the story. "You are clearly prejudiced, Denny," she said. "You know as well as I do that the woman has our best interests at heart."

"That bad, huh?" Gallagher groused. "Spare me the beating around the bush, will you, Katie-girl? What did she put her foot into this time?"

"Nothing," Kate snapped. She felt Gallagher's eyes on her. "Actually, I called her after Tim Moran called me," she said.

"Moran?" Gallagher drummed his fingers on his desk. "Moran from Vice?"

Kate nodded. "That's the one."

"Has he got something that will help us?"

"Maybe."

"What do you mean maybe? If he hasn't got anything to help us why did he call? Wait a minute . . ."

Kate could almost hear Gallagher's detective mind snapping facts into place like couplings on a train. He gave a sarcastic chuckle. "Let's see—this Moran called us because the old nun called him. Right?"

"She went over to the place where he's working undercover." Kate clenched her teeth and waited for the explosion. Surprisingly, there wasn't one. She checked her partner's face. Had he heard her?

Gallagher looked puzzled. "Which is?" he asked.

"Which is what?"

"The place where he is working undercover?"

"The New You Tattoo Parlor, a few doors down from where Sarah Spencer was murdered. Seems Sister Mary Helen wanted to ask Moran if he saw anything the day Sarah was shot. He tried as persuasively as he could to explain to her that Sarah's killers weren't fooling and that it could be very dangerous to go around asking those kinds of questions."

"Did he get anywhere?" Gallagher asked, loosening his tie.

"As far as anyone could get with Sister Mary Helen, I suspect."

Gallagher pointed at the phone. "Did you make it clear that she was to stay away from questioning anyone for fear that she might just land on the wrong person and end up as dead as Spencer?"

Kate glared at him. She did not like his tone. He made it sound as if she had encouraged the old nun to get involved. "I gave it my best shot," she said. "Although I wouldn't swear that it will do any good. Not that your berating her achieves any better results. If you ask me, I think you just make her more determined."

Gallagher stood abruptly and pulled up the waistband of his trousers to cover his paunch. He glared at her over his horn-rimmed glasses. "I'll tell you what's going to achieve some results," he growled. "One of these days I'm going to arrest her. Swear to God, I will—"

Kate couldn't help laughing. "That would make a great police brutality story. I can see it now on page one of the *Chron.*"

Gallagher tried not to grin. "What's going to be on tomorrow's front page," he said, "is a story about all of San Francisco's finest not being able to locate one cop killer.

"Seems to me that we ought to get over to that tattoo parlor and talk to Moran," he went on. "Hell! The old nun knows more than we do."

Kate watched her partner pile all his papers into one stack. Then he put his half-filled coffee mug on top of them like a paperweight.

"What if someone bumps into that and it spills?" she asked.

Gallagher shrugged. "What are the chances of that happening?" He studied her for a minute. "You know, Kate, you worry about the damnedest things."

True, she thought, following him out of the Detail. They stood side by side waiting for the elevator.

"Why do you think no one told us about Moran being at that tattoo parlor only yards from where Spencer was murdered?" Gallagher asked. "And I don't mean the nun—I mean Sweeney."

Kate studied the numbers in a half circle over the elevator. The light didn't seem to be moving either up or down. She twisted a small piece of hair around her index finger, then pushed it against her scalp into a curl.

"What are you thinking?" Gallagher asked, recognizing the sign.

Kate shrugged. "Maybe the Lieut didn't know. Maybe Donaldson didn't tell him."

"Where the hell is this thing?" Gallagher hit the elevator button again. "Funny thing to withhold," he said.

"I agree." Kate offered her partner a butterscotch LifeSaver, which he took. "Makes you wonder why."

"Maybe if this elevator ever gets here," Gallagher said, without meeting her eye, "we can ask."

❧❧❧❧

All morning long, even while Sister Mary Helen went about the business of running the drop-in center, she thought about Kate Murphy's phone call. She could not believe that the policewoman had been so testy. It wasn't like Kate—not at all. She had acted as though Mary Helen wasn't going to return her call. Of course she was. Just as soon as she could.

At the first lull, when the majority of the women had gone to Saint Anthony's dining room for their main meal, Mary Helen escaped to the quiet office. Sitting in the dark, she closed

76

her eyes and forced herself to relax. Everyone's emotions were running high. In fact, this whole thing was getting way out of hand. They were starting to hiss at one another like so many Halloween cats with hunched backs. Fighting among themselves would never get the "good guys" anywhere. And she considered both the police, and Anne and herself, the "good guys."

It took the old nun several minutes of deep breathing to actually calm herself and begin to think sensibly. Junior Johnson—yes, she needed to talk to him. His Auntie Geraldine could arrange it if she wanted to. She'd talk to Geraldine.

After that, she probably should talk to Tim, the tattoo man, again. She ought to find out the man's last name. "Tim the tattoo man" was a little too cutesy to be taken seriously. Some of the things that he'd said were gnawing at her. He had hinted that he'd seen something when Sarah Spencer was shot. What exactly was it and why would she be better off if she didn't know?

Mary Helen took another deep breath and tried to sort out the uneasiness that was wrapping around her like a web. She knew that it had something to do with Geraldine warning her to watch her back coupled with Tim's reference to having her chest full of lead. Most especially it had to do with her friend Sister Eileen's reluctance to encourage her to get involved.

Was she in over her head? Had she lost her touch? Yes, she needed time to sort things out, time to think.

The office door swung open, startling her. "Oh, here you are." Anne sounded relieved. "I wondered where you had run off to—again."

Again? Mary Helen felt her hackles rise. Had she detected a slight tone? She glared at Anne, who blinked back innocently.

Calm down, she warned herself. *Anne didn't mean anything.* "What's up?" she asked, sounding as cheerful as she could.

Without answering her question, Anne sat in the chair across from her. "The crowd is thinning out and Judy, the volunteer, can cover for a few minutes," she said. "We need to talk."

Now what? Mary Helen thought, studying Anne's face. The young nun's cheeks burned in two red splotches, as though someone had slapped her. Her mouth was drawn up in a tight nervous smile. Her hazel eyes were solemn and Mary Helen was afraid that she might start to cry. What in heaven's name was wrong?

"I've been thinking about what you said," Anne began in a quivering voice.

Which thing that I said? Mary Helen wondered, determined not to interrupt. She nodded encouragingly, knowing from Anne's demeanor that it was important to let her have her say.

"About being spurred on by fear," Anne continued. "And . . ."

Mary Helen waited. It took all the patience she had left not to say, "Get to the point, will you?"

"And," Anne swallowed hard, controlling her voice, "it scares me to death." She reached out for Mary Helen's hand and squeezed the bottom of it. "I don't want anything to happen to you."

Sister Mary Helen's heart sank. She had never intended to upset Anne. "Do you want me to let it go?" she asked, hoping that she didn't sound too much like a martyr. The thing she had always noticed about martyrs was that they died very lonely deaths.

"No, that's not it. What I want is for you to be careful."

"Not to worry," Mary Helen said reassuringly. "Nobody wants me not to get hurt more than I do."

Anne frowned, looking as if she were trying to translate. "Right!" she said finally.

"Is that all?" Mary Helen asked, sure that it wasn't. One can always hope.

"No." Anne took another deep breath. "I think we need to solve this thing," she paused.

Mary Helen waited for the "but." She was pleasantly surprised when the word that came from Anne's mouth in a throaty whisper was not "but." It was "together."

⊱⊰⊱⊰

When Officer Mark Wong fell into bed in his flat off Judah Street he was dog-tired. And he had every right to be. With his partner, Brian Dineen, he had spent the entire night combing the Tenderloin, then spreading out to the area around it. Methodically they had stopped pimps and prostitutes and drug dealers. Some they knew by name, some only by face.

"What can you tell us about the murder of the young bag lady?" they had asked over and over. And over and over they had received only blank stares with muttered pleas of ignorance.

Most admitted that they had heard about the murder and that they had heard that she was an undercover cop. All denied that they had known it before she was killed.

Pulling the bed covers up around his shoulders, Wong lay in the cool, dark bedroom. His eyes closed, he tried to blot everything out of his mind, not that there was much to blot. The entire shift had been more or less a bust. They had come up with nada—nothing—zilch—that would lead them anywhere.

Street noises floated in from Judah—the rattle of the N street car rocking along the tracks; the shrill conversation of two Asian women lugging home their shopping bags from the Twenty-second and Irving Street market; the inevitable impatient blare of a car horn. Overall, his flat was quiet during the day. He was lucky to have rented it when he did, before prices in the city skyrocketed. With rent control he was paying only a fraction of what it would cost him now.

His landlords, an elderly couple, lived upstairs and seemed to like him. If his luck held, he wouldn't have to move until he had saved enough money for the down payment on a house. Maybe if he and Susie Chang ever really had time to get to know one another—but with him on nights and her on days, what were the odds?

In the distance Wong heard the scream of a police siren. Some hotshot on the day shift probably doing the same thing that Dineen and he had been doing all night—rousting everybody they could, hoping to apprehend Sarah Spencer's killer as soon as possible.

A brisk ocean breeze riffled the bedroom curtains and sent the Venetian blinds tapping against the window frame. Wong took a deep breath and let it out slowly. Relaxed after his hot shower, his limbs felt numb and heavy, yet tired as he was he could not seem to fall asleep.

For some reason he could not put his shift to rest. Something was wrong. He had sensed it, but he and Dineen had been so busy that they had not had the time to put a finger on it. Reluctantly Wong pulled himself out of bed and padded barefoot into the kitchen. Maybe he was just hungry.

Opening the refrigerator he was surprised to discover, buried deep in the back of the bottom shelf, a leftover piece of cherry pie, still in its pie tin. He tried not to figure out how long it had been there. He poured himself a glass of milk, then perched on a kitchen chair. A little soggy but not bad, he thought, swallowing the pie in four bites. Not bad at all. He scraped the tin. Just like Olivia scraping her ice-cream dish, he thought, putting it into the sink and adding a little water, in case of ants.

Olivia! That was what was bothering him. She had said that she hadn't seen Junior Johnson around, that he must be busy with something. They hadn't spotted him all night either, which was unusual. Junior was "the man" around the neighborhood. He had a finger in almost everything illegal that was going on.

On any given night, Dineen and he would usually run into Junior more than once. Not that he'd give them cause to arrest him. Junior was too slick for that. But he was around, strutting like a rooster among his hens—bold as a cock with the lowlifes in the neighborhood. If Junior was missing, he was up to something.

Had he been the one who had killed Sarah Spencer? Now that the Department was putting on the heat, had he been forced to skip town? Maybe. Or had some beat cop picked him up? Dineen and he weren't the only ones aware of Junior's activities. Could Junior be missing because he had been collared and was in jail? That would be easy enough to find out.

Wong checked the clock over the stove. It was almost noon. If he didn't get some sleep soon, he'd be good for nothing tonight. Picking up the telephone, he dialed the jail and identified himself. Within minutes he had his answer. Junior Johnson had not been booked. He was not a guest of the City and County.

Well, where the hell is he? Wong wondered, replacing the receiver. Running his fingers through his short, dark hair, he made his way back to his bedroom. First thing tonight, Dineen and he would have to figure that out, but for now he had to get some sleep.

❦❦❦

After lunch women slowly began to trickle back into the Refuge. Sister Mary Helen made several pots of coffee to keep up with the swell while Sister Anne and Judy, the volunteer, replenished the supply of sweets. Fortunately, that very morning Kevin, a Nabisco driver, had donated a dozen cartons of Fig Newtons. The cookies were disappearing almost as quickly as they appeared on the snack table.

"You be fattening us up, girlfriend," Miss Bobbie said. Smiling at Mary Helen, she popped a fourth cookie into her mouth and chewed it slowly, savoring the taste.

She made it seem so delicious that Mary Helen was tempted to have one, too. Fortunately the snug feeling in the waistband of her skirt brought her to her senses.

"Anybody sitting here?" Peanuts asked, pointing to a vacant chair at Miss Bobbie's table.

Still chewing, Miss Bobbie shook her head.

The tiny woman, her short hair slicked back, revealing a few strands of gray, sat down. Methodically she stacked her cookies on the table in front of her, much as a miser might stack his gold. The two women munched in contented silence.

"We needs more sugar," someone called from the snack table. Mary Helen picked up the empty container and hurried to the kitchen to refill it. Watching the white stream flow into the large bowl, she wondered how best to approach the subject of the whereabouts of Junior Johnson without her questions sounding like she was conducting an interrogation. Although his aunt Geraldine was her best bet, Mary Helen was positive that someone else in the room knew—someone she could ask in case Geraldine did not show up.

Still puzzling over the best approach, Mary Helen walked back into the gathering room and started toward the table.

"You hear about Junior Johnson?" Venus's voice greeted her. It was as if the woman were reading her mind.

Looking up, all ready to jump in, Mary Helen realized that Venus wasn't talking to her at all. Settled at Miss Bobbie's table, Venus was, in fact, talking to anyone who would listen.

Miss Bobbie nodded, ever so slightly, and tucked a stray piece of hair into one of her braids. "If I was you, girl, I'd watch my mouth," she said.

"What I say wrong?" Venus's dark eyes narrowed into surly slits. "Ain't nothing wrong with asking a question."

Peanuts leaned forward. "What you hear about Junior Johnson, makes you ask that question?" Her words dripped with menace.

Venus pretended not to notice. "I hear something," she said coyly.

Sonia, sitting several tables away, perked up. "Tell us, girl," she said, taking a small dented compact from her shoulder bag. Carefully she examined her lipstick, then added more to her already very red bottom lip.

Venus smiled, showing her missing front tooth. "What you getting all fixed up for, Sonia, girl, if Junior not around?"

Sonia snapped the compact shut and glared at Venus. "Who say Junior not around?" she asked.

Mary Helen couldn't tell from her tone whether she was pleased or displeased at the prospect.

"I just hears it," Venus said, then took a sip of her coffee. "I hear that Junior Johnson not such a big man no more. It got hot and he gone missing."

"What you saying, Ho, about my nephew Junior Johnson?" Geraldine's angry voice shot through the room.

Mary Helen hadn't noticed the older woman come in. Neither, apparently, had Venus. Her face paled. The room took on an unnatural silence. The only sound was water filtering into the coffee pot.

"You, Venus," Geraldine's eyes blazed and her body seemed to fill the doorway. She pointed toward Venus. "I be asking you a question, girl," she said, the veins in her neck protruding.

Mary Helen held her breath and watched Venus. *Uh-oh*, she thought. From the way the young woman hesitated, it was apparent that she was struggling with how to react. Should she save face and strike out or should she play it safe and fold?

With a belligerent stare, she slowly hauled herself up from the table. Mary Helen feared that saving face had won. Still holding the sugar bowl, like a frozen photograph, she wondered how best to defuse this situation. They had enough trouble already. They didn't need any more violence.

"You hear me, girl?" Geraldine's words sounded as if they had slipped off the end of a knife. "I be talking to you!"

Sneering, Venus squared her shoulders, her hands hanging loosely at her sides. She glowered at Geraldine.

Geraldine's mouth twisted. Raising her chin, she slipped her hand into her jacket pocket. "You hear me?" she taunted, daring Venus not to answer.

In the flat silence Mary Helen heard her heart thudding. She sensed that Venus was about to lunge forward. Did Geraldine have a knife in that pocket? "Stop!" she tried to shout, but the word stuck in her throat. *Lord, help us*, she prayed, glancing around for Anne. Now would be the time to call Kate Murphy. She was afraid to take her eyes off the two women who had begun to move closer to one another. Each seemed to be waiting for the other to act. It was only a matter of seconds, she feared, until one of them would.

With a startling strong bang, the front door flew open. Its force knocked Geraldine aside. Venus grunted in surprise.

Framed in the back glow of the doorway was Crazy Alice. Her eyes, shining manically, swept the room. Her head jerked. Carefully she folded her hands in front of her and took a breath, like a prima donna about to begin an aria. *"There was a little man, and he had a little gun,"* she chanted grimly, *"And his bullets were made of lead, lead, lead. He went to the brook, and saw a little duck, and shot it through the head, head, head."* She ended with a radiant smile.

Shock covered the room like frost. The other women stared in disbelief. "She ain't nothing normal," Sonia said in a whisper.

Without warning Crazy Alice began to titter. She covered her mouth, trying to stop it. Still it grew into a giggle and grew and grew until the shrill, wildly insane sound filled the entire room like a scream.

It took several minutes for the women at the Refuge to settle down. Sister Mary Helen was continually amazed at how quickly they were able to assimilate the most bizarre events and go on as if nothing out of the ordinary had happened. Or perhaps what, to her, seemed very unusual was to them simply ho-hum.

Glancing around, she noticed that Venus was gone. It was

just as well. That way neither she nor Geraldine felt obliged to prove anything.

"What happened?" Anne whispered. Although she had missed all but Crazy Alice's shrill laughter, she knew by the tension still hanging like cobwebs in the corners of the gathering room that something had happened.

Quickly Mary Helen filled her in. She was careful to omit her inability to get out the word, "Stop!" There was no sense upsetting Anne any more than she already was.

With the help of the volunteer, the two nuns brought out some sliced fruit that Anne had saved for an occasion such as this—one when no more sweets were needed to add to the hyperactivity.

A sense of peace began to descend on the Refuge. Several women spoke quietly to one another. A few even nodded off. Mary Helen seized the opportunity to single out Geraldine who, luckily, was alone at a table.

"How are you doing, Geraldine?" she asked, sitting down with a mug of coffee next to the older woman.

"Fine, Sister," Geraldine said, looking up.

Mary Helen was shocked to see how worn out the woman looked. Deep lines etched her dark face, leaving the flesh under her eyes puffy. Her hair, usually neatly done up, was uncombed. Her liquid brown eyes had the vacant stare of one whose mind is miles away. Even her voice, usually strong and clear, quavered like an old woman's.

"I be sorry about shouting in here," she said. "I didn't mean you no disrespect."

"I know you didn't, Geraldine," Mary Helen patted her hand.

"I just hates it when they be mocking my Junior." Her face tightened and Mary Helen feared that she was about to get angry all over again.

"I'm sure Venus didn't mean to mock him," Mary Helen was about to say, but thought better of it. As a rule nobody likes to be told that she is wrong, especially when she is still furious. Mary Helen sensed that Geraldine was no exception. With heroic control, she said nothing, simply sipped her coffee.

"My Junior be a good boy! He be a brave boy! If he be gone, something wrong! Lordy, I know something be wrong." Geraldine rocked back and forth in her chair as if she were in pain. "Help me, Jesus."

"Are you sure he's gone?" Mary Helen asked. "Maybe he's just not taking his calls."

Geraldine looked at her as if she had lost her mind. "I called. Yes, ma'am, I called every place I knows. Talked to his friends. Nobody seen him."

"For how long?" Mary Helen asked, trying not to sound worried.

Geraldine's eyelids fluttered as she paused to think. "Today be Tuesday. Yesterday—Monday. Nobody I talked to seen him since about noon Monday. So he be missing a whole day now." She wagged her head woefully. "I don't understand. That not like Junior. Not like him at all!"

Unless he was responsible for Sarah Spencer's death, Mary Helen thought. *Then it would be quite understandable.* With all the heat the police department was putting on, the most understandable thing for the killer to do was to get as far away from San Francisco as possible.

"I'm sure he'll show up soon," Mary Helen said, not really sure at all. In one sense, his disappearance was progress. If he had killed Sarah Spencer, then taken off because he had, the case would soon be closed.

Feeling somewhat light-hearted, Mary Helen sipped her coffee and wondered how to gracefully excuse herself. She was relieved to hear a refugee ask for a towel roll for the shower.

When she was sure that the woman had what she needed and was under the hot water, Mary Helen stood by the bathroom door thinking.

As soon as she saw Kate Murphy—and she wouldn't be surprised if the woman dropped in later today—she would tell her about Junior Johnson's disappearance and her suspicions that he might be the guilty one.

The other item on her agenda today—a minor one—was to find out Tim the tattoo man's last name, so that when she asked Kate about him, she'd sound, at least, informed. Walking toward the front door, Sister Mary Helen took a quick look around the gathering room. A number of the women had gone. Judy was sitting at a table chatting with a new refugee. Anne was in the laundry loading towels.

"I'm going down the street for a minute," Mary Helen shouted over the sound of running water. "I'll be right back."

Anne looked up and smiled.

That was easy, Sister Mary Helen thought, hurrying down the street. *Too easy*, a little voice said, which she summarily ignored.

Scarcely noticing the traffic speeding past her on Eighth Street, Sister Mary Helen mulled over her meeting that morning with Tim. What had he seen? Why would she be better off not knowing? Was he serious about her being in danger? She doubted that he would be willing to elaborate on any of her questions, save "What was his last name?" Then again, what was the harm in trying?

❧❧❧

"How do?" Sister Mary Helen called, opening the front door of the New You Tattoo Parlor. Aside from the tinkle of a small bell over the door jamb, the place was silent. "How do?" she called again, noisily shutting the front door. Surely he'd hear that.

"Tim?" Mary Helen hesitated at the counter. Except for a slit of light showing beneath a door in the back, the place was dark. Could Tim have stepped out and forgotten to lock the front entrance? Hardly. "How do?" she called again. "Tim? Are you there?"

She listened. Nothing. Anxious thoughts began a slow roll through her mind. Was the man all right? Where in the world was he? Had something happened to him, too?

Skirting the counter, Mary Helen stood for a moment. This really was none of her business, but if something had happened to him, she couldn't just leave him, could she? Of course not.

Cautiously she made her way toward the back room, pausing at the door. Her heart pounding, she pushed it. The door opened a few inches, then stopped. She pushed again but it was stuck. Warily she peeked around it. Fear slid down her spine.

The small back room looked as if a tornado had ripped through it. Papers were everywhere. The door itself was stuck on an overturned lamp. Someone had slashed the shades and torn the curtains from the windows. The dirt from one lone philodendron plant spread across the linoleum like a brown ribbon. Even the desk chair was overturned and pencils thrown everywhere as if someone had been unable to control his rage.

"What the hell—" An angry voice ricocheted off the wall.

With a startled gasp, Mary Helen spun around. Tim was behind her, his eyes a cold blue. Pushing past her, he stepped into the room. She watched his face grow burning red. His beard twitched. With a howl he kicked aside the lamp and stalked into the room.

Arms bulging, he righted the chair. The blue dragon curled around his neck seemed to take on a life of its own as he rescued the telephone from under a stack of scattered papers.

"What are you doing here?" he growled at Sister Mary Helen. His eyes shifted from her to the shredded window shade.

"I was simply looking for you," she said, scarcely able to catch her breath.

"What the hell for?" he asked, roughly dialing the telephone.

"To find out your last name."

He gave her a long, flat stare. "Moran," he said. "Tim Moran. Now get the hell out of here, will you?" He pointed.

Gladly, Sister Mary Helen thought, turning with as much poise as she could muster. "I'm relieved, Officer Moran, that you were not hurt," she said pleasantly.

His eyes shifted as if he hadn't seen her before. "Go!" he shouted.

And she did, but not until she heard him ask for Lieutenant Don Donaldson.

Struggling to salvage some of her dignity, she quietly let herself out of the tattoo parlor. Unfortunately, she walked right into Inspectors Dennis Gallagher and Kate Murphy, who were pulling up to the curb in front. From the scowl on Inspector Gallagher's face, she knew how he felt about seeing her there. Frankly, she was grateful that she could not hear what he was saying to Kate.

"Hi, Sister," Kate called, climbing out of the driver's seat of the car. Despite her effort to be pleasant, Mary Helen did not miss the edge in her voice when she asked, "What are you doing here?"

It's a free country, Mary Helen wanted to snap, but caught herself. "I might ask you the same question," she said with a smile that she was sure an alligator would envy.

Kate's blue eyes sparked. "I asked you first," she teased, in what Mary Helen knew was her final attempt at being amiable. To press it any further would be dangerous.

"I just dropped in on Tim, here," Mary Helen pointed toward the darkened storefront, "to find out what his last name was."

Kate frowned. "To find out his last name?" She looked over at her partner, who was coming around the car toward them, and shrugged. "I see," she said.

Sister Mary Helen turned to face Gallagher. "I didn't know the man's last name," she explained with a weak smile intended to appease him.

"His last name?" Behind his horn-rimmed glasses, Gallagher's eyes were smoldering. "Why would you need to know his last name, Sister?" His words were choppy with anger. "Didn't Kate

89

make it very clear that you were to stay out of this thing? As I understand it, even Moran here told you to butt out. What will it take? Someone to really hurt you?"

"I have no intention of being hurt," Mary Helen said with the last bit of moxie she could muster.

Exasperated, Gallagher rubbed the palm of his hand over his bald crown. "If I had a nickel for every corpse who thought that," he growled, "I'd be able to retire right now from this lousy job."

Mary Helen raised her chin and pushed her bifocals up the bridge of her nose. "I understand, Inspector, that you are concerned, but—"

"No buts about it." He seemed to chew each word. "Except you, Sister. You are to butt out!"

Their eyes clashed, Gallagher daring her to say another word. Mary Helen struggled to calm down.

"What in the hell are you still doing here?" Tim Moran's voice hit her like a shot.

"I'm on my way, Officer Moran. I was just talking to my friends here." She threw the words over her shoulder. *And good luck to you all*, she thought, *you—you ingrates!* Quickly she walked toward the Refuge, her feet slapping the cement. What was it Eileen always said? "When you are sitting on your heels, you will thank goodness for your old stool."

Taking deep breaths, she stole a glance at the three police officers standing in a worried knot. That is, if that bunch of know-it-alls will ever be able to admit that they—they are definitely sitting on their heels.

❧❧❧

With just a smidgen of sympathy, Kate Murphy watched Sister Mary Helen make her way back to the Refuge. Her short, round figure seemed smaller, more stooped than usual. *The poor thing was just trying to help*, Kate thought. The first chance she had she'd square it with Sister. Right now, Tim Moran needed her full attention.

It took her a minute to realize that Moran and the man she'd glimpsed talking to the uniform when Gallagher and had she responded to the murder scene were one and the same. Actually, his disguise was so good that she'd never have recognized him. In fact, she doubted if his own family would.

"Did Donaldson send you guys?" Moran asked.

"Donaldson? Why would Donaldson send us?" Gallagher frowned.

Moran held open the door of the tattoo parlor and Kate followed Gallagher in. "Because I just got off the phone with him. Somebody trashed the place," Moran said, scratching at his scrawny beard.

Kate and Gallagher trailed him down the hall to a small back room. "Whew!" Gallagher exclaimed, surveying the mess.

"Trashed" is an understatement, Kate thought, avoiding the broken glass from a light bulb. "Is anything missing?" she asked.

Moran shrugged. "I haven't had a chance to look yet."

"When did it happen?" she asked.

"It just happened." Tim Moran seemed dazed. "I was here all morning. I only stepped out for a few minutes. Hell, I couldn't have been gone for more than ten minutes—at the outside. When I came back the place was like this. And that nun was here"—his eyes grew cold—"snooping around."

"Why did you leave the shop?" Kate asked.

Her question seemed to take Moran by surprise. He eyed her suspiciously.

"Funny that you ask," he said. "I got a call from the American Asian Market up the street. At least, I thought it was. A woman called and told me the owner had fixed me something special to eat and asked if I could come over and get it. He does that every once in a while," Moran said. "Nice guy."

"Sounds like it," Gallagher agreed.

"Anyway, when I got there he was all shook up. He didn't want to offend me, but it seems he didn't know what I was talking about."

"Somebody's idea of a joke?" Gallagher asked.

"That's what I figured. Anyhow, when I went up there I thought the Chinese guy—"

"Does he have a name?" Kate asked.

"The Chinese guy? Yeah, of course he does. But somehow I don't think it's the one his mother gave him. It's Elvis. Elvis Lee."

Gallagher shot Kate a *stay-on-the-point* look. "You were saying?" he urged.

"Yeah, I thought Elvis had called so I switched off the lights in the front of the shop before I left so that it looked closed."

"Why didn't you just lock the front door?" Kate asked.

"I should have," Moran looked embarrassed. "Hell, I know better but I was just going to be gone a minute and"—he shrugged—"what's to steal?" His eyes shifted to the debris covering the floor.

"Let's find out," Kate suggested, starting to gather up the scattered pencils.

Within fifteen minutes, the room was back in some sort of order. "Nothing seems to be missing," Moran said. "At least nothing I can see right away."

With a grunt, Gallagher picked up the plant and made an attempt to scoop up some of the dirt still covering the linoleun. "There doesn't seem to be much reason to have knocked this over," he said, setting it on the edge of the desk.

"Maybe the perp was mad because he didn't find anything and he took it out on the philodendron," Kate suggested.

Moran studied the pot. "Unless someone thought there was a bug or something in it.

"Was there?" Kate asked in surprise.

Moran's laugh sounded a little like a bark. "No," he said, "although now I kinda wish there had been. I'd love to get my hands on the guy who did this."

I'll bet you would, Kate thought. There was something so infuriating about having your space violated.

"Could be somebody who found out you were undercover," Gallagher mumbled. "Might have put two and two together and come up with five."

"You mean somebody who has been in the shop thought that it could be bugged and came in looking for it?" Moran stared at the dirt on the floor.

"That makes as much sense as anything," Kate said.

"Mr. Tim?" A voice called from the front of the tattoo parlor, surprising them all.

"Back here," Moran answered.

A frail looking Asian man in a clean, white butcher apron large enough to cover two of him appeared in the doorway. He held a brown paper sack. "For you and your friends," he said smiling. "Lunch."

"Thank you, Elvis," Moran said, introducing Elvis Lee to Gallagher and Kate. "Will you join us?"

"Got to get back. Business, you know." Bowing, Elvis left the shop as quickly as he had come.

When Moran opened the bag, the delicious aroma of sweet fresh ginger, brown sugar, and warm pineapple mixed with tangy soy sauce and onion filled the small room. Steam rose from a carton of rice. "You guys hungry?" he asked.

"Starved." Kate pulled up three chairs around the desk. Tim Moran found paper plates and utensils and the three police officers settled at the makeshift table. Except for a few grunts of satisfaction, they ate in companionable silence. Moran managed to unearth a few tea bags and put a kettle of water on a hot plate.

"That was just what the doctor ordered," Gallagher said when they had emptied the last carton.

In fact, he does look better, Kate thought, *although it could have as much to do with his getting over seeing Sister Mary Helen as it does with the delicious lunch.*

When the kettle began to sing, Moran brewed the tea and passed around the fortune cookies that Elvis Lee had included in the bag.

Kate was the first to break hers open. " 'Nothing is impossible to the man who doesn't have to do it himself,' " she read. "I think this one's talking about you," she pointed to her partner.

"Never mind," Gallagher said, breaking open his cookie. He unwound his paper and groaned. " 'All you have is today. There's no such thing as tomorrow or yesterday.' Sounds a little fatalistic, if you ask me. Maybe I should get another one."

"Next," Kate said, ignoring him. "Your turn, Tim." Fascinated, she watched the letters of the word MOTHER, tattooed on the knuckles of his left hand, undulate as he cracked open his cookie. Slowly he unwound his paper, read it, and gave a humorless guffaw.

Is it my imagination, Kate wondered, *or did his face redden?*

"You think yours was bad," Tim said. "Listen to this. 'Keep your friends close and your enemies closer'—provided, of course, you know who they are," he ad-libbed, and Kate couldn't help feeling sorry for him.

Gallagher excused himself to wash some soy spots off his tie while she cleared the desktop. Since Moran and she were alone, Kate hoped to clear up some things that were bothering her.

"How long have you been undercover?" she asked, shoving the paper plates into a waste paper basket.

"A couple of weeks," Tim said, explaining that the real owner of the New You Tattoo Parlor, a retired cop, was taking some time off to renovate his kitchen. "But I guess I've blown my cover now," he said.

"You know, Tim," Kate said, her voice as nonchalant as she could make it, "my partner and I were wondering why nobody—and by nobody I mean none of the brass—told us that you were here, just yards from where Sarah Spencer was shot." Kate watched the color flood Moran's face.

He shrugged. "When you find that out, find out why nobody told me Sarah was digging around right under my nose. If I'd have known, I could have kept my eye out for her. Maybe this would never have happened. She was just a kid." His eyes filled. "Just a kid!"

"Thanks for the lunch." Gallagher's voice startled them both. "We'd better hit the street, Kate."

"Right," she said, noticing that enormous water spots had replaced the soy spots on her partner's tie.

"It'll dry," he said in response to her look of horror.

❧❧❧

After they left the New You, Inspectors Kate Murphy and Dennis Gallagher sat in the front seat of their unmarked car talking. Kate watched as several women leaving the Refuge spotted them. *Who do we think we're fooling?* she wondered, watching the women deliberately cross the street. One good thing about it was that everyone in the neighborhood knew a police car—marked or unmarked—when they saw one. So they were assured absolute privacy.

"What the hell do you make of it?" Gallagher asked.

"Make of what?" A number of things had Kate confused.

"Both of them undercover in the same area. Each one not knowing about the other." Gallagher sighed. "I'm assuming that if Moran didn't know about the girl, she didn't know about him. Makes you wonder why." Gallagher stared straight ahead. "Just like that old nun to stumble on it, isn't it?" he asked.

Kate laughed. "You're right," she said, twisting a piece of hair.

"It's almost as if Moran and Spencer were set up to spy on one another," she said, wishing she hadn't eaten so much.

"That's what I was thinking, too," her partner answered softly. "Do you suppose that Donaldson will tell us what this undercover operation was all about?"

Kate shook her head. "I doubt it. But it must be something big. Maybe Sweeney will find out for us," she said, confident that their own lieutenant would if he could.

Gallagher squirmed in his seat. "I feel a little hog-tied, not knowing exactly who is on whose team." He turned the key in the ignition. "Maybe we should head back to the Hall and find out."

"Before we talk to the ladies at the Refuge?" Kate asked.

Her partner nodded his head. "I've had enough of Sister Mary Helen for one day," he said. "Compared to her, even Pits Donaldson looks good."

❦❦❦

At the Refuge, Sister Mary Helen tried to keep her mind on the refugees and as far away from the goings-on up the street as possible. *After all, at my age who needs murder and intrigue*, she reminded herself several times. But as anyone who knew her— even slightly—could have predicted, it was a losing battle.

All afternoon her world had seemed topsy-turvy, as they used to say—*odd word*, she thought and wondered about its origin. Maybe she'd ask old Donata to research it on the Web. Donata was becoming computer friendly and might enjoy a project.

"What the matter with you, girlfriend?" Miss Bobbie asked. "You be so quiet."

"Sorry." Mary Helen managed a smile. "I'm just preoccupied."

"Say what?" Miss Bobbie wrinkled her brow.

"I'm busy thinking about things. My mind is a million miles away," Mary Helen said and sat down in an empty chair across from the older woman.

Miss Bobbie nodded to show that she understood. "You been mulling," she said. "And I bet you be mulling about that murder up the street."

"That and what I should do about it," Sister Mary Helen said honestly.

"Best thing you can do, girlfriend, is stay out of it." Miss Bobbie was solemn. "Ain't no good come from messing with the police, especially when one of them be killed." She took a deep breath. "No good at all."

You're telling me, Mary Helen thought.

Miss Bobbie leaned forward. Her false teeth clicked as she whispered, "Besides, the word on the street be Junior Johnson the one!"

Startled, Mary Helen studied Miss Bobbie's face, but it might as well have been carved from lava rock. "The one?" she frowned. "You mean the killer?"

Only the older woman's shifting black eyes showed any emotion. At first, Mary Helen wasn't sure if it was excitement or fear. A little bit of each, she concluded, watching Miss Bobbie scoot around in her chair until her back was toward Geraldine. Obviously Geraldine was to be one of the last to know.

Following Miss Bobbie's lead, Mary Helen moved, too. "What makes you think that Junior is responsible?" she whispered.

Miss Bobbie raised her eyebrows, her scar twitching. "I just knows. Trust me. Junior be the one."

"But I understood that he could not be found."

"You right. He gone missing! Which proves it for sure. Why else would the man go missing?" Miss Bobbie demanded. She waited, daring Sister Mary Helen to come up with a better explanation.

"I don't know," Mary Helen said, and indeed she didn't, but there could be other reasons. Under different circumstances she would have suggested some, but Miss Bobbie seemed to be running a little short on patience. "What does his Auntie Geraldine have to say about it?"

Miss Bobbie's lips curled into a tight smile. "If I be you, I not be asking." She rolled her eyes toward the older woman. "Not now anyway."

Sister Mary Helen saw that Geraldine was no longer alone. Olivia had joined her. Although it was next to impossible to tell what they were talking about, Mary Helen knew that whatever it was, it was serious. As Olivia spoke her platinum hair, standing out like a full-blown dandelion, bobbed nervously on her skinny neck. Her entire body was rigid and her gestures wooden.

Mary Helen felt a sudden pang of sympathy as she watched Geraldine. Although the older woman was listening to what Olivia was saying, her head was down and her heavy shoulders drooped as she played with a piece of doughnut on the table in front of her. She looked so sad, so alone, that Sister Mary Helen felt the tears burn in her own eyes.

Abruptly Olivia pushed back her chair and stood towering above Geraldine. Several of the women nearby quietly moved to other tables as if they feared getting caught in the crossfire. Mary Helen felt her own stomach knot. Olivia said something that Mary Helen was too far away to make out, but whatever it was seemed to add to Geraldine's anxiety.

When Olivia left, Geraldine continued to sit and stare, oblivious to the noise around her. As far as Mary Helen could tell Geraldine had been sitting at that same table for hours. Excusing herself on the pretext of refilling the sugar bowl, she went to the kitchen, determined to putter around for a few minutes, then, despite Miss Bobbie's warning, to talk to Geraldine.

"Oh, here you are." Anne's voice startled her.

"Were you looking for me?" Mary Helen dug a large scoop into an enormous barrel of sugar and filled the smaller bowl.

"Not really," Anne said, "but now that I've found you, would you mind helping Judy fix some shower rolls? Several women are waiting to take showers and it seems we've run out."

Sister Anne took the sugar bowl from her and Mary Helen went to the cupboard to help Judy. After she had put a hotel-sized soap, shampoo, and lotion into a washcloth, Mary Helen handed it to the volunteer who rolled it tightly in a bath towel. Soon they had taken care of all the women who were waiting, plus they had a small pyramid of bath rolls on the shelf for tomorrow.

"I think we've done it," Judy said with a pleased grin.

Sister Mary Helen must have looked at the volunteer strangely because Judy explained, "Caught up with the shower rolls." Mary Helen was glad that there had been two of them. She was so distracted with thoughts of Geraldine and Junior and murder rolling over and over in her mind that, left on her own, she couldn't be sure what she'd put in the washcloths.

Judy checked her wristwatch. "It's nearly three o'clock, Sister, and if you don't mind, I'd like to leave a little early. I'm going to get my hair cut."

"Fine," Mary Helen said, looking around the gathering room. Actually, there was no reason for Judy to stay. Many of the women had gone and most of those who did remain were starting to gather up their bags and sacks, ready to find shelter for the night. Only a few—the same few—made no effort to go. Mary Helen had noticed that every night these same women stayed until they were asked to leave and the doors locked. Their only reason seemed to be the hope that they would be overlooked, and able to spend the night at the Refuge. Some even hid in the bathroom or the sleep room. Despite their best efforts, Anne was always able to ferret them out.

Heartbreaking, Mary Helen thought, but Anne would need all sorts of permits and permissions to allow the women to spend the night. God willing, someday soon they might be able to expand into an overnight shelter.

Sister Anne had already begun to lock up when Mary Helen finally made her way to Geraldine's table. She was surprised that Geraldine was still there. "How are you doing?" she asked.

Geraldine looked up and without a word Mary Helen's question was answered. Dark half-moons had formed under her eyes and her cheeks were sunken. She gave a tight smile revealing that she had neglected to put in her upper plate. That wasn't like Geraldine at all. Was it a trick of the light, Mary Helen wondered, or did her hair have more strands of gray in it than it had just a few days ago?

Obviously the woman was distraught. Her liquid brown eyes jumped nervously. "Olivia bring me bad news," she whimpered, her mouth dry. "She say Junior be in trouble. He want me to come."

"Come where?" Mary Helen reached for Geraldine's hand, which was shaking. "Did Olivia tell you where?"

Geraldine's smile was pinched with pain. "She tell me the words, but she don't know what they mean."

"Oh?" Mary Helen waited for an explanation.

"It be like a code." Geraldine shut her eyes. Swallowing hard, she fought to gain control.

"But you know what he is telling you?"

Geraldine sighed. "Of course, I knows." She studied Mary Helen with a look of pity, then patted her hand. "You not be the sharpest knife in the drawer, girl," she said, "but you tries."

Remembering that a silent mouth never did much harm, Mary Helen decided to say nothing. She watched while Geraldine took another bite of her doughnut and a few sips of coffee. When she put down her cup, she seemed more like herself. A little of her old fire had returned to her eyes.

"He be waiting," Geraldine said. "I be going." She stood, her chair scratching against the rug.

"You can't go alone," Mary Helen blurted out. "It's getting

late and wherever you are going to meet him might be dangerous."

"And who is going with me?" Geraldine leveled her eyes. "You?" she asked with a sneer.

"Why not me?" Mary Helen said. Perhaps she'd have the opportunity to talk to Junior. Besides, she was a little weary of being deprecated. First the police, then Miss Bobbie, now Geraldine. "So, why not me?" she challenged.

"Why not you what?" Mary Helen had not heard Anne walk up behind her. She must have finished locking up quickly.

"Go with Geraldine to meet her nephew Junior Johnson," Mary Helen said without thinking.

Anne's face paled, making her hazel eyes seem enormous. "If you are going," she said stoutheartedly, "I'm going, too."

"All right," Mary Helen said after some hesitation. "That settles it. Let's go."

As the two nuns followed Geraldine out of the Refuge, Anne touched Mary Helen's arm. "Sister," she whispered as Mary Helen turned around. "Where is it exactly that we are going?"

❧❧❧

Geraldine insisted on sitting in the backseat of the convent car. Sister Anne would have preferred that she take the passenger seat next to her so that she could hear the directions more clearly. But the woman's mind was made up—backseat or no seat! After checking that Geraldine was locked in with her seat belt securely fastened, Mary Helen climbed in beside Anne.

"Where to?" Anne asked cheerfully, turning the key in the ignition.

Geraldine flinched. "Get out on the street first," she said. "Then I tells you."

Cautiously Anne pulled out of the parking lot and slipped into the traffic speeding along Eighth Street. Hearing Geraldine suck in air, Sister Mary Helen turned to look at their passenger. The woman's round face had lost some of its color, her eyes were squeezed shut, and her jaw was rigid. The knuckles on her left hand were white from clenching the door handle. *The poor woman is scared to death*, Mary Helen thought. "Are you all right?" she asked.

Geraldine did not speak, only nodded her head.

Anne must have seen the same thing in her rearview mirror. "Great," she said just loud enough for Mary Helen to hear, "not only are we driving Miss Daisy, but we are driving Miss Daisy with amaxophobia!"

It took Mary Helen a moment to remember that amaxophobia was what experts called a fear of driving.

"Now where?" Anne asked. They were streaming toward the Bay Bridge and she must be wondering, as was Mary Helen, if that was the direction Geraldine intended them to go. Once they'd hit the bridge there was no turning back until Treasure Island.

"Turn here!" Geraldine called out.

"Left or right?" Anne demanded.

"Left," Geraldine shouted, giving Anne just enough of an opening to do it.

This time it was Mary Helen who had her eyes shut. All she heard was the squealing of car tires and the blasting of several horns.

"Be careful," Geraldine hissed.

To Anne's credit, Mary Helen noted that she didn't say anything. She simply pressed her lips together in a straight line.

"You have to give her a little more warning, Geraldine," Mary Helen suggested. As soon as she did, she knew she'd made a mistake.

Geraldine pulled herself forward in the seat. "If you all are having problems with my directions, you can just pull right on over and I can take me the bus."

"Your directions are fine," Mary Helen said, trying to soothe feathers. "They just need to be given a little sooner."

Geraldine's eyes narrowed, but she said nothing.

"Where do you want us to turn next?" Anne asked. It was clear from the way Geraldine's eyes darted around that she did not know.

The reason for her confusion hit Mary Helen like a shot. Of course! She goes everywhere by bus! She simply gets on at a stop with which she is familiar and gets off at another that she knows. Riding in a car disorients her.

"Why don't you just tell us where you are supposed to meet Junior and let Anne figure out how to get there," Mary Helen suggested diplomatically. "She's a whiz at directions."

Geraldine made a "humphing" noise while she considered the idea. Mary Helen felt sure she'd give in eventually. What she needed was a little face-saving time.

Meanwhile poor Anne, her cheeks becoming more flushed every minute, wove in and out of traffic—up one-way streets and down crowded alleys. Obviously she didn't want to leave the area until she knew their destination for fear that she'd have to double back. The streets were already packed with commuters. In the next few hours it would only get worse.

Skillfully Anne maneuvered down a narrow alley which ran between newly converted work-live lofts, renovated Italian Gothics with stained glass windows and low pitched roofs, small factories, and parking lots. She slowed down to avoid a swarm of women exploding from one of the unmarked buildings. A sweatshop, Mary Helen thought, watching them stretch and blink in the light. It was after four o'clock. These women must have started sewing at seven this morning. Undoubtedly a night shift would replace them.

Already several people—Mary Helen couldn't tell if they were men or women—lay in the alley's sidewalk covered in dirty, drab blankets. They had wedged themselves like caterpillars against the sides of the buildings preparing to sleep through the night. Her heart ached to see them.

"Where to, Geraldine?" Anne asked, now a slight edge on her voice. Mary Helen wondered if Anne was regretting her offer to come along.

"You know the Dutch Windmill?" Geraldine asked.

Mary Helen thought for minute. "You mean the windmill in Golden Gate Park?"

Looking relieved Geraldine nodded. The Dutch Windmill, as Mary Helen remembered it, was an enormous windmill at the north end of the park. Surrounded by wind-bent trees, it towered above Queen Wilhelmina's Garden, an oasis of green lawn and brightly colored flowerbeds. It was only a few yards from the wide pavement of the Great Highway and the blowing sand of Ocean Beach. In mid-April, when the tulips bloomed, the sight was breathtaking.

"The Dutch Windmill it is," Anne said, leaving downtown San Francisco with the kind of skill and steady nerves that even Mario Andretti would admire.

When Sister Anne turned the convent car onto Fulton Street, Mary Helen noticed that Geraldine's face relaxed. Undoubtedly this was the way her bus went to the beach. She was on familiar ground.

Following the route of the Number 5 Muni bus, the convent Nova slipped along Fulton Street where the traffic was still flowing smoothly. To their left the broad avenue bordered Golden Gate Park. To their right it was a mixture of flats, apartment houses, and single-family dwellings.

Quickly the numbers of the Avenues mounted—Twelfth, Fifteenth, Thirty-second, Fortieth. Without speaking they passed several ornate park entrances and the Senior Citizen Center that once had served as the San Francisco Police Academy. Between the entrances great pools of flat, green nasturtium leaves filled with sharp orange and red blossoms covered the ground.

Nearing the end of Fulton, Mary Helen smelled salt in the air. On the horizon, the afternoon fog lay in a roll waiting to shift in from the Pacific. Before long it would cover the Avenues. The beach would be freezing. *With any luck we won't have to stay here that long*, Mary Helen thought. Simply find Junior and drop Geraldine. Surely she'd be in good hands with her nephew.

At Forty-seventh Avenue Sister Anne made a left turn into Golden Gate Park and wound her way past the Archery Field, deserted at this time of day, and a nine-hole golf course, which, if the number of cars in the parking lot could be believed, was crowded.

"There be Junior's car," Geraldine said as they pulled onto John F. Kennedy Drive. She pointed to a large pink Cadillac convertible with its top down. It was parked a few feet from the entrance to Queen Wilhelmina's Garden. Its angle and the fact that he had neglected to put up the top made Mary Helen think that Junior had parked in a hurry.

Sister Anne pulled in behind the Cadillac. She had scarcely turned off the ignition when Geraldine was out of the back seat. "He be waiting for me in our secret place," she said cheerfully. "I be right back." She turned toward the dirt road that ran behind the windmill.

"Would you like us to go with you?" Mary Helen asked, still hoping to talk to Junior. Besides, who knew what might be lurking in the bushes?

"I be fine," Geraldine said, her confidence apparently completely restored.

"Are you sure?" Anne asked.

In exasperation Geraldine raised her shoulders and her eyebrows. "I be sure, Sister Anne. Junior in our secret place. If you come, now how could it still be secret?" she asked logically.

"True," Anne conceded.

"I won't be long," Geraldine called, disappearing behind a clump of brush.

Mary Helen turned toward Anne. "I thought I might get a chance to talk to Junior," she said, feeling rather helpless.

"I imagine that when she finds him, they'll hook up and tell us to go. Maybe then you'd have a couple of minutes." Anne said. "In the meantime, let's sit. This is beautiful!"

"There's a comfortable looking bench," Mary Helen said, pointing to one close to them. In fact, the spot was full of comfortable wooden benches and vibrant flowers. Settled beside Anne facing the gigantic windmill, Mary Helen drank in the scene. Anne was right. It was beautiful. The tulips had been replaced with dahlias of bright orange, yellow, and red, with a few white blossoms scattered here and there. The geometric garden in the center of the green lawn was alive with red foxtails, orange, red, and pink impatiens, with a star-shaped bed of white petunias.

Above it all, like a giant salt shaker, towered the Dutch Windmill. A tour bus passed and slowed down for a quick look. Several bicyclists in helmets zipped along the road. A jogger pushing a jogger's baby stroller ran by. Overhead the four sails of the windmill moved slowly in the ocean breeze making a gentle *thunk* as they turned. An elderly couple sat silently on another bench. A young family speaking what sounded like French touched the fringed pinks to make sure that they were real.

What a peaceful place, Mary Helen thought, taking a deep breath. She felt her shoulders relaxing after a long day at the Refuge. She'd sleep tonight. And now that Geraldine had found her nephew, no doubt, so, too, would she. "Ah, peace," she said, closing her eyes. As the breeze brushed against her face she thought she heard the gentle hum of insects. Tension seemed to drain from her arms and legs and she felt as if she could drop off to sleep—and sleep—and sleep.

"I wonder what's taking her so long," Anne asked anxiously. Mary Helen blinked. Had she actually nodded off? Geraldine had only been gone a couple of minutes, hadn't she?

"She'll be here any second," Mary Helen assured Anne, watching a seagull swoop, then hover over the dome-shaped top of the windmill.

"We need to get going if we're going to take her back downtown and then get home for dinner," Anne let the thought dangle. "Maybe we could put her on the Muni."

"I'm sure Junior will drive her home," Mary Helen said, shivering a little. The fog, though not really cold, was damp. Soon it would blot out the vibrancy of the garden. She noticed that the older couple was leaving and the French family gathering up its toddlers. With them gone, the garden became so quiet that Mary Helen thought she heard the waves breaking against the shore.

"Do you think we should go looking for her?" Anne asked, a note of worry in her voice.

Before Mary Helen could answer, a horrifying, piercing shriek shattered the quiet. The old nun bolted upright.

"It's Geraldine!" Anne said, leaving the bench on a run. Puffing, Mary Helen followed. Without a word the two nuns hurried along the dirt path that they had seen Geraldine take. It was separated from Queen Wilhelmina's Garden by a chain-link fence.

"Careful," Anne whispered, pointing at the dry manure in the path. Mary Helen was more concerned about the fallen branches of the evergreens. About two hundred feet down the road after a blind bend, they came upon a green stucco shed, locked and hidden by heavy foliage.

"Geraldine! Where are you?" Anne shouted.

No one answered.

"I hear something," Anne called, darting toward the shed.

Out of breath, Sister Mary Helen caught up.

"Here she is!" Anne shouted to Mary Helen. The two nuns hurried to a sobbing Geraldine, crumpled on the ground.

"Are you all right?" Anne asked.

Mary Helen bit her tongue. *Of course she's not all right*, she wanted to shout. *Can't you see she's trembling like a person in shock? She doesn't even seem able to speak.*

"What is it? What happened?" Mary Helen asked gently. "Can you tell us?"

With one shaky finger, Geraldine pointed to a clump of bushes hidden behind the shed.

On her guard, Mary Helen crept toward the place and, separating the shiny leaves, cautiously peered in. Her stomach turned slowly as she saw what Geraldine had seen. Junior Johnson lay on his back. One side of his head was shattered and pieces of his brain clung to nearby branches.

"What is it?" Anne was behind her. "Junior? What—?" She heard the young nun gag. "I can't look," Anne said, moving quickly toward a cluster of calla lilies. "I just can't," she said before she was sick.

❧❧❧

Merging into the traffic on the Great Highway, he wondered how soon the body would be discovered. Although he had turned the car heater up as far as it would go, he was still shivering from the cold and dampness. Crunching in the bushes he had wondered how he'd ever gotten into this mess. It was as if he had stepped into quicksand and just kept sinking deeper and deeper. First Sarah Spencer, now he had to take care of Junior Johnson.

"Take care of the bastard." The familiar voice on the telephone had used those words, as though Junior were a small, solvable problem.

In a way, maybe he had been. Stupid bastard had tried to blackmail him. Big mistake! Then he'd used that hooker Olivia to tell his aunt where he'd meet her. A few bucks to a snitch and he'd known, too. Junior thought he was so clever telling

Olivia in a code so simple that even the snitch had figured it out.

He laughed to himself. He had paid the guy extra to trash Moran's office hoping that Moran would take the hint and back off. Nice touch, he congratulated himself, using a guy Moran had fingered. The guy had really put his heart into his work. And if Moran didn't back off? He didn't even want to go there. One problem at a time.

Despite the heat in the car, he shivered. Squatting in the dirt waiting for Junior, the dampness had crept up his legs. They had begun to cramp. He had been just about ready to stand up and stamp his feet for warmth when he had heard footsteps. Slipping his hand into his windbreaker pocket, he had felt for his gun with the silencer. He'd better have it out, he'd thought. Junior was a big boy and quick. The only way to take him would be by surprise.

He had listened as the crunch of footsteps moved closer and closer. Overhead seagulls had screeched. As he waited he felt the sweat begin on the palms of his hands. He clutched the gun tighter. One shot was all he'd have—like taking down a rhino. If he missed, the beast would attack.

He had risen slowly as Junior stepped into the clearing. The man's eyes had opened wide in surprise. For a puzzled moment, Junior had studied him. Then he knew.

Before Junior could react, he had put the gun to the man's temple and squeezed the trigger. Silently he watched the flesh being torn away. The big man had tottered a moment, then fallen backwards, leaving bits of tissue on the branches of nearby shrubs.

Junior's huge body lay on the ground, staring up at him unseeing. He had blinked, not sure at first whether or not those were Sarah's eyes he saw. Covering his face, he had tried to block them out, but they were there still. His throat had tightened and sweat had begun to soak his body. He had forced himself to take a deep breath. The pain in his chest had been so sharp that for a moment he was afraid he might be having a heart attack. Deliberately calming himself, he had stopped to rub out any of his shoe prints.

Checking the scene to make sure he'd overlooked nothing, he had tried to convince himself that he really had no choice. Junior could bring him down. There was no option. Besides the guy was a scumbag bastard. No loss to anyone. In fact, he was probably doing the world a favor taking him out. They should give him a medal.

Another seagull screeched at him as he had hurried down the path to his parked car. Eerie sound, he'd thought sitting in the driver's seat breathing heavily. Looking out the window, he'd met the bird's eye. His mouth went dry. It was Sarah's eye. Her eyes were everywhere. He couldn't seem to get away from them—from their sadness, their pity, their never-ending accusation.

When would they ever stop? he wondered, starting up the hill toward the Cliff House. And he knew, as well as he knew that the sun would soon set over the Pacific, that the answer was never.

❧❦❧

Holding the telephone receiver to her ear, Inspector Kate Murphy blinked in disbelief.

"What's happening?" her partner, Dennis Gallagher, asked without looking up from clearing off his desk. He was definitely ready to go home. "You look like somebody's reporting an invasion of aliens."

Don't I wish, Kate thought, replacing the receiver. "Even stranger than that," she said, checking her wristwatch. "And don't go anywhere yet, Denny."

"Why the hell not?" he asked, sweeping a stack of pink message slips off the corner of his desk.

"Let me call Jack," she said, watching most of them fall into the waste paper basket, "then I'll tell you."

Fortunately she caught her husband before he left the building and asked him to pick up their son at the babysitter's. "I'll be home as soon as I can," she promised, "and fill you in on what's happened."

"You better fill me in first and fast," Gallagher said once the receiver was back into its cradle. "Or else I'm out of here, Katie-girl. Oh, my aching back!" he complained, sinking into his desk chair. "So, quick, what's up? Even aliens can wait till tomorrow, can't they?"

Kate took a deep breath. She hated to break the bad news. He was exhausted. She would have known that even if he hadn't moaned about his back. The pasty color of his usually ruddy face and his watery blue eyes gave it away. And why wouldn't he be? She was. The two of them had spent a long and fruitless day tracking down every lead that came their way, only to run into one dead end after another. They hadn't even been able to locate Junior Johnson; that is—until now. A shiver skittered over Kate's skin.

"Aliens could wait, Denny, maybe," Kate said, "but not Junior Johnson."

Gallagher perked up. "Somebody found the guy? Great! Where is he?"

"At the Dutch Windmill in Golden Gate Park," Kate said.

"What the hell is he doing there?" Gallagher asked.

Kate shrugged. It was one place they never would have thought to look.

With a sudden surge of energy, Gallagher checked the large clock on the Detail wall. "How long do you think it will take them to bring him in?" He went on without waiting for an answer. "Makes no matter. I'll call Mrs. G. and tell her I'll be late. At last, maybe we can get some answers."

"Not from him," Kate said, hesitant to break the bad news.

Gallagher studied her, frowning now. "Who was that on the phone?"

"Sister Mary Helen," Kate muttered softly. "She's just found Junior Johnson."

"She found him?"

Looking at her partner, Kate swallowed hard. There was no way to avoid telling him the truth. She nodded. "She found him, all right," she said. "She found him dead."

Even with their siren on, it took Kate and Inspector Gallagher nearly thirty minutes to get through the dense traffic between the Hall of Justice and Ocean Beach. Gallagher's continued grousing about nuns in general and Sister Mary Helen in particular made it seem even longer.

Two black-and-whites, the paramedics, and the fire department beat them there. The patrolmen were trying to secure the crime scene with yellow plastic tape and to keep the curious moving. Soon the forensic team, the coroner, and all the other people who respond to a homicide would be tracking around.

After a cursory look at the body that still had Kate's stomach churning, she scoured the area for the nuns. She spotted them sitting on a wooden bench near a row of stiff snapdragons. Between them sat an older black woman whom she recognized. It was Junior Johnson's aunt, Geraldine. Hunched against the dampness, the three women looked so forlorn that Kate almost felt sorry for them. Almost—but not quite. What in the world where they doing here? She almost hated to find out.

While her partner was surveying the ground around the small stucco structure behind the windmill, looking for something—anything—that might provide them with a clue to Junior's killer, Kate walked toward the three women. At first Mary Helen avoided eye contact.

"Well, well, imagine finding you here," Kate said, hoping the sarcasm wasn't lost on the old nun. "Why am I not surprised?"

Sister Mary Helen opened her mouth to speak, but Kate shook her head. "No, Sister, before you get into the whys and wherefores of the *coincidence*"—she elongated her last word so that her meaning couldn't possibly be lost—Gallagher would be proud of her—"let me ask you some preliminary questions. First of all, did you hear anything?"

"Like a shot?" Anne asked.

"Like a shot," Kate said, turning toward her. Anne's face was the color of oatmeal with bright splotches of red at her cheeks. "Are you all right, Sister?" Kate asked. All she needed was for someone to get sick on the crime scene.

Mary Helen must have read her mind. "She is now, Kate," the old nun whispered softly.

A distant roar from Gallagher made her answer clear. "Who the hell upchucked?" he shouted.

Sheepishly Sister Anne raised one finger. "Sorry," she said, "I'm really not accustomed to—" Before she could finish, she gagged again.

Kate bit back the urge to ask, *Then why the devil are you messing with murder?* But the young nun looked sorry enough that she had become involved without her rubbing it in.

"To get back to my question. Did any of you hear a shot?"

The three women looked at one another then shook their heads. "And I think we would have heard a shot. It was quiet here," Mary Helen offered.

Kate focused on Geraldine. "I didn't hear nothing either." She dabbed her eyes. "I goes to the place where he say to meet him. And I wait and I wait, all cold. I be afraid I missed him. Then I look around, just in case and I found my baby . . ." She choked on the last words. Mary Helen put an arm around the woman's shoulders. Geraldine lowered her head and began to sob.

"Clearly Junior was shot before we ever got here," Mary Helen said.

"Unless one of you shot the man," Kate said coldly.

Anne looked as if she might collapse.

"Don't be ridiculous," Mary Helen snapped.

"In a homicide everyone is a suspect," Kate said ominously.

There was no harm in putting a little fear into them.

"Did any of you happen to notice anyone else hanging around?" Kate waited. "Or anyone or anything that might have struck you as suspicious?"

The three women seemed to be considering her question. "There was a tour bus," Mary Helen said, "but no one got off. And a jogger pushing a baby, and some bicyclists."

"And an elderly couple who left before Geraldine screamed and that French family," Anne offered. "Junior's car," she added, "It looked as if he'd parked in a real hurry. But nothing else."

Nodding her head, Geraldine remained silent.

"Are you sure?" Kate said. "Think now—anything." After a few minutes of silence she said, "I'll need to talk to each of you, but I don't want you to freeze to death." Shivering in the cold, she pulled up the collar of her jacket and pointed to the convent Nova. "Maybe two of you can sit in that car while I talked to the third one in there." She pointed to the unmarked police car.

They stared at her blankly. "You first, Sister Anne," she said. As Kate suspected, after a few minutes it was obvious that Sister Anne knew nothing, had seen nothing, and had no idea how she'd managed to get into such a mess.

Kate chose to speak to Geraldine next. It was clear from the woman's face, still wet from crying, that she was in shock and probably needed to get home.

"Are you all right?" Kate asked gently.

Geraldine nodded.

"Would you like me to have the paramedics give you something?"

Geraldine's eyebrows shot up. "No, ma'am," she said, shaking her head vehemently. "I don't want nobody messin' with my head."

"I just meant something to help you relax," Kate tried to

explain. "This must have been a terrible shock."

Geraldine would have none of it. "You just asks me what you need to asks me and let me tell you 'fore you start, I don't know nothing about Junior's business. Nothing."

"Can you tell me why you happened to come out to the windmill?" Kate asked. "It seems an odd place to come at this time of day."

Geraldine's expression froze as if a steel mask had suddenly slammed down over her face. "I come to see Junior," she said.

"How did you know he was here?" Kate asked.

"Someone tell me," Geraldine said, then pressed her lips together.

Clearly Geraldine wasn't going to give away any information that wasn't pried out of her. *This could go on all night*, Kate thought. "Who told you?" she asked patiently.

"I don't rightly remember."

"Have you any idea?"

"I thinks one of the womens at the Refuge."

Frustrated, Kate stared out at the Ocean Beach. The sky was leaden and a heavy bank of fog was already covering the Great Highway.

"You don't remember who told you Junior was here?" she asked.

"No, ma'am." Tears flashed in Geraldine's brown eyes. Kate watched one slip down her smooth cheek while she rummaged through her pockets, obviously looking for something to wipe it with.

"Can you think of anyone who might have wanted your nephew dead?"

Geraldine sucked in her breath. "No, ma'am," she said.

It is pointless to torture this woman, Kate thought, handing her a wadded tissue from her own pocket. At the sight of it Geraldine bent forward and began to rock and sob softly. Her short, gasping breaths slowly turned into a plaintive wail and she began to keen. The high mournful sound filled the police car. Kate's first impulse was to cover her ears.

A frowning patrolman tapped on the car window. "Is everything okay, Inspector?" He sounded worried.

"Fine, thanks, officer," Kate assured him. "I think this lady needs to get back downtown." She cocked her head toward Geraldine.

"Right," the patrolman straightened up and stepped away.

Kate turned back to the nearly hysterical woman. "I think you've had enough for today," she said. "What about the police officer taking you home and you trying to get some sleep. Tomorrow will be plenty soon enough for us to talk."

Raising her head, Geraldine nodded. Her face was soft and soggy from crying. "Thank you," she said hoarsely. "Tomorrow be a better day!"

Once Kate was sure that Geraldine was safely in the patrol car and on her way downtown she called Sister Mary Helen. Studying the old nun's face, Kate was shocked at how tired she looked. Fatigue had deepened the wrinkles around her mouth and behind her bifocals her hazel eyes were as glassy as marbles. Clenching her teeth to keep them from chattering, she climbed into the backseat of the car across from Kate.

She shivered and Kate felt the cold and damp radiating from her body. "I'll try to make this quick," she said. "First of all, how did you and Sister Anne and Geraldine happen to be out here and stumble upon Junior Johnson?" *Who, by the way, the SFPD has been looking for unsuccessfully all day*, she wanted to add, but thought better of it.

Adjusting her bifocals up the bridge of her nose, Mary Helen met Kate's gaze, paused for a few seconds as though trying to decide where to begin. "The ladies at the Refuge seem to know everything," she said at last.

Kate listened as Sister Mary Helen told her about Geraldine

hearing rumors that her nephew had killed Officer Sarah Spencer and that he had disappeared. She filled her in on the woman's reaction and her concern for her nephew, especially her distress over his disappearance. She told Kate about Geraldine's meeting with Olivia who had given her the code name indicating where she could find Junior. She admitted—a difficult admission for her—that she wanted to go with Geraldine in order to talk with Junior and that poor Sister Anne had really been suckered into it.

Kate held her peace, not sure just how long she could.

"I wanted to talk to Junior Johnson," Mary Helen confessed, "because there is a little undercurrent among some of the women that perhaps the police are looking the other way. I know that can't be true." Kate felt pinned by the sharp hazel eyes. "So I wanted to find out from Junior how the rumor got started."

At this the dam of Kate's patience finally broke. "Did it ever occur to you that you were playing a very dangerous game with a very dangerous man?" She leveled her eyes at Mary Helen. "This is the second homicide in two days. And I'm sure they are connected. What we don't need is a third. This is not a television program, Sister. You are not Miss Marple. This is real life and you have put yourself and your companions in extreme danger." Kate stopped for breath.

Mary Helen's eyebrows shot up like streaks of lightning and she pressed her thin lips into a tight line. "I am very aware of both the reality and the danger, Inspector," she said crisply. "I was simply trying to be of some assistance."

Kate thought she detected a little hurt as well as anger in Mary Helen's eyes and softened a bit. "I realize that you are trying to be helpful," she said, "and I appreciate that. I really do." She hoped her partner hadn't overheard her. "But what we don't need is a murdered nun or two in the mix. It's bad enough that we have one murdered undercover policewoman and one less suspect—also murdered. Do you understand?"

"Of course, I understand your concern but—"

"No buts!" Kate raised her hand and her voice. "I'm asking you, Sister—no—I'm demanding that you not involve yourself in this investigation in any way, at any time, with anybody, for any reason. Do you think you can do that?"

"Of course I can," Mary Helen said, rather too quickly.

"Ah! Will you please do that?" Kate asked. That was the crux of the matter. "I beg you," she added.

"There's no need to beg, Kate," Mary Helen said with an unexpected smile. " 'We, ignorant of ourselves, beg often our own harms, which the wise powers deny us for our good . . .' "

Kate must have looked puzzled.

"Shakespeare," Mary Helen explained.

"Whatever," Kate said, eager to get on with it. "Then we understand one another?"

"As always," Mary Helen said and reached for the door handle. "Have a nice evening, Kate," she said turning to face her, "and get some rest. You look exhausted."

Watching the old nun step out onto John F. Kennedy Drive, Kate felt oddly uncomfortable. Was she wrong or had her conversation with Sister Mary Helen gone far too smoothly?

❧❧❧

Officer Mark Wong walked into the Vice Crimes Section of the Hall of Justice well before his shift began. He wasn't surprised to find his partner Brian Dineen there ahead of him. "Howdy, big guy," he said, looking up at the tall redhead.

Brian yawned in response.

"Same to you," Mark said, noticing that if anything Brian looked as though he'd slept less than Mark himself had. "I see you've got your bags packed." Mark pointed to the charcoal puffs under each of Dineen's bloodshot eyes.

"Everybody's a comedian," Dineen grumbled.

"You guys are in early." It was Jack Bassetti.

"Yeah," Mark answered for the two of them.

Jack's shift was over and he was finishing up the last of his paperwork. He looked eager to get going. In fact, most of the day shift looked as if they could hardly wait to go home. And why not? It had been a long and frustrating couple of days for all of them.

The room rang with their banter and jokes. "How about a drink before we hit the road?" someone asked Jack.

Shaking his head, Jack declined. "Let me take a rain check on that," he said. "Tonight I have to pick up the heir apparent. The Queen Mum just called."

"A royal summons cannot be ignored," someone announced solemnly.

Mark knew that Jack's wife, Kate Murphy, was a homicide detective. He had wondered, when he thought about Susie Chang and himself, how that would work out. Two in the SFPD. It seemed to be panning out just fine for the Bassettis. Better than a lot of marriages on the force. Donaldson, for example, and Sweeney from Homicide—both divorced. And even his partner. Brian had hinted lately that he and his wife were having problems, although he didn't come right out and say so. It was not something you asked a guy, even if he was your partner.

"Anything new on Sarah's homicide?" Mark heard his partner ask.

"Not that I know of," Jack said, "although it's not for lack of trying. We've been beating the bushes all day long, weeding out every lowlife, needling every snitch in town. If anybody knows anything about the kid's death, sooner or later we're bound to uncover it."

"Did anyone locate Junior Johnson?" Mark asked.

Jack had already started to shake his head when Lieutenant Donaldson stepped out of his office. "Did I hear someone ask about Junior Johnson?" He leaned against the door jamb. Donaldson was a big man with a full head of steel gray hair whose mother, for some reason, had named him Don. Wong assumed it was her overactive sense of whimsy and not sheer meanness which had caused her to light upon the name. Whichever it was, the poor guy had put up with years of the other kids stuttering, "Don, Don, Don, Don Donaldson," as if it were a great joke.

In college he had played football for a small local school. Unfortunately, some of his muscle had turned to fat, especially around his gut.

"Yeah, Lieutenant, I asked about Junior," Mark spoke up.

Donaldson turned toward him. He looked worn out. His squared jaw seemed even more angular than usual and the lines that bad temper had etched at the corners of his mouth were even deeper.

"I just got a call from Sweeney in Homicide," he said, his voice flat. "They found him at the Dutch Windmill in Golden Gate Park."

The room went silent waiting for the bad news they all sensed was coming.

"Seems they found the guy dead. Shot behind the windmill. A couple of homicide inspectors are on the scene now."

For several seconds no one spoke. The Lieutenant put his hands on his hips. Wong tried not to notice the hourglass stains of perspiration under each of Donaldson's arms. It happened so consistently that as a rookie he had been nicknamed "Dripping Don." With his promotion came another moniker. Although none of his squad ever called him this to his face, some wag had hit upon "Hot Pits" Donaldson. Naturally it had caught on and was shortened by some to "Pits" and "Pittie."

"I'd like you all to stay a couple of minutes so I can bring you up to date on the latest developments," Donaldson said, "and on tomorrow's funeral arrangements for Officer Spencer."

While the others pulled up chairs or sat on the edges of desks,

Mark noticed Jack Bassetti make a quick phone call. You didn't have to be a crack detective to deduce that his wife was the homicide inspector at the scene and since he, too, was tied up the third in line was being asked to perform the royal pickup duty.

Without any preliminaries, Donaldson launched into what details he knew about the murder of Junior Johnson, a man with whom the Vice Squad was very familiar. Junior represented the real underbelly of San Francisco's criminal society. In fact, he had been their number one choice for Sarah Spencer's murderer. Although most seemed relieved that he was off the streets, his death brought up other question. If he had murdered Sarah, who had killed him and why?

Halfway through the Lieutenant's briefing, the squad door cracked open and a tough-looking character wearing Levis and a T-shirt let himself in. It took Wong several seconds to realize that the scraggly Abraham Lincoln beard camouflaged the face of Officer Tim Moran. If it hadn't been for his bright blue eyes and the word MOTHER on his knuckles, Wong wasn't sure that he would have recognized him at all.

"What you doing here?" Donaldson asked gruffly. "Aren't you supposed to be someplace?"

Moran's face froze into an angry mask. "We need to talk," he muttered.

"Later, Moran. I'll talk to you later," Donaldson said, ignoring Moran's fiery eyes fastened on him.

If looks could kill, Mark thought, scarcely hearing what the Lieutenant was saying.

"I'll see you all tomorrow then at St. Mary's Cathedral for Officer Spencer's funeral. Nine-thirty sharp," he said, then motioned Moran to follow him into his office.

From the bang of the door, Wong knew that the meeting was going to be stormy.

"If you ask me, partner, the streets figure to be safer tonight than a meeting with Pits," Brian Dineen said, his eyes twinkling.

The room exploded in laughter that stopped abruptly when the door to Donaldson's office flew open. Without a sideward glance, Moran stormed out of the Section. It didn't take long for the place to clear out.

❧❧❧

"What now?" Dineen asked as he drove toward the Tenderloin. Although it would be light for another couple of hours, the neighborhood was beginning to come alive. Bars and liquor stores were already doing rapid business and there was an un-settling kind of electricity in the air. Prostitutes emerged from the old hotels in twos and threes, laughing and gossiping as they sauntered toward their corners. A group of working girls waved to Wong and Dineen. "Hi, fellas," one called. "Isn't it a beautiful night for a stroll?"

"As long as you just keep on strollin'," Dineen called out and the women giggled.

"Slow down. Let's see if we can find Olivia," Wong said, straining to look down the alley that Dineen was passing.

"My thought exactly," Dineen agreed. "If anyone has the skinny on Johnson, it'll be our girl, Olivia."

It didn't take long for the officers to spot her. Olivia's plati-num hair was a beacon. Dressed in a black lace teddy and snug, black velvet shorts, she was leaned against a lamppost, her hand on her hip. Her knee-high black boots were laced with a silver cord and she played seductively with several long silver chains around her neck. Her broad shoulders, thin body, and shapely legs gave her a youthful look. To tell the truth, Wong thought, it wasn't until you actually looked at her face that you realized she was middle-aged.

"Olivia!" Wong called, getting out of the police car.

Her brown eyes hardened as she turned toward him. "Not you

two, again," she screeched. "Get the hell away from me or I'll report you for harassment."

"Harassment?" Wong asked. "After we bought you dinner last night?"

"Big deal!" Olivia sneered and tried to walk away from him, but Wong caught her arm.

"Is there someplace we can talk?" he asked, noticing that several of the other girls were gathering around, willing to protect Olivia if she needed it.

"Is everything all right, sweetie?" one of them asked.

"You need help, sister?" another voice called.

"We got rights," a tall blonde cross-dresser protested.

Olivia looked around wildly. Slowly Dineen pulled his large frame from the car. The sight of the big man seemed to calm down the situation immediately. *Thank goodness*, Wong thought. What they didn't need tonight was a riot in the Tenderloin.

"Let's get out of here," Dineen said, helping Olivia into the backseat of the police car.

"What did I do?" she screamed. "I didn't do nothing!" Dineen slammed the door on her. "Help!"

"We just want to talk to you and you look as if you could use a cup of coffee," he said.

"I don't want no coffee! That coffee they got around here is killing my stomach," she said. "What I need is a chocolate milk shake. A milk shake is soothing."

Although it took a little time to find a place that served milk shakes, they finally did. Fortunately it was in the neighborhood so Olivia didn't look too out of place in her black teddy and shorts.

"What do you want now?" she asked once they were settled in a back booth and Dineen had ordered the chocolate shakes.

"First, let me ask you," Wong began, "have you heard anything more about Junior Johnson? Anything after you talked to us yesterday?"

Olivia pretended to think. "Yeah, I guess it was after I talked to you two guys. Who should pick me up on the corner but himself in that show-off pink Cadillac of his. We rode around the 'hood for ten or fifteen minutes."

"What did he want?" Wong asked, taking a swallow of chocolate shake. Olivia was right. It was soothing.

"He wanted me to give his Auntie Geraldine a message."

"Which was?"

Olivia shrugged. "It was in code, I think. He said to tell her to meet him at the kiss."

"Kiss? What is the kiss?"

Olivia looked genuinely baffled. "Damned if I know. Like I said, I think it's a code. Anyway Genie seemed to know exactly what he meant."

"What time did you talk to Junior?"

"About two o'clock," she said.

"What time did you give his aunt the message?"

"By the time I found her at the Refuge it was almost closing time. About three. Why so many questions? Why don't you ask Junior?"

The two men stared at her. It never occurred to either one of them that streetwise Olivia didn't know.

"You didn't hear?" Wong asked gently.

"Hear what?" Olivia's eyes jumped nervously from one to the other. "Hear what?" she demanded, her face tightening.

"That Junior is dead. Shot."

It took a few seconds for her to realize what Wong had said. When she did, Olivia blanched. Tears sprang into her eyes. She moved her mouth but no words came out. She seemed unable to catch enough breath to speak.

"They found him in Golden Gate Park by the windmill," Dineen said.

Moaning, Olivia leaned her forehead into the palms of her hands and sobbed.

Dineen and Wong looked at one another, wondering what to do. It was obvious that Olivia was in shock and that she didn't know nearly as much as they had thought she might.

"Maybe it's best if we leave her alone," Dineen whispered to his partner. "She'll probably feel better after a good cry."

Wong nodded and the two officers left Olivia in the booth with her sadness.

For several blocks, they rode in silence. "I guess we have a frame of about thirty minutes in which the crime could have been committed," Dineen said.

Wong agreed, frowning.

"What's bothering you, partner?" Dineen asked.

"How did Geraldine know where he was? The word Olivia used was 'kiss.' How do you translate 'kiss' into the Dutch Windmill in Golden Gate Park?"

Slowly Dineen turned the corner. "Kiss, kiss," he repeated obviously searching for the connection. "Tulips!" he said with a triumphant laugh. "Kiss. . . . two lips . . . tulips . . . Dutch . . . Dutch Windmill! Elementary, my dear Watson!"

"Ah, if everything would work out as easily," Wong said, listening to an incoming call.

Silent now, they flew down the street, siren blaring, heading for a dilapidated hotel on Jones Street. Wong's stomach knotted. There was nothing he hated worse nor that he considered more dangerous than answering a call to domestic violence.

❦❦❦

The evening fog had already blotted out much of Geary Boulevard when Inspector Kate Murphy finally pulled up in front of her home. The lights from her living room windows shone like beacons out onto the wet street. The window nearest the front door framed the small, round face of her son John. With an ache of love, she watched him smile and wave when he saw her car pull up in front. It was amazing how the sight of that cherubic face and those melting brown eyes could set even the most horrific day right.

"Hi, Mom," she heard him calling.

"Hi, John," she called back and waved. Kate was so happy to be home at last that she almost missed her mother-in-law's car parked in front of Jack's. *What in the world is Mama Bassetti doing here?* she wondered. After a day like today, she didn't need any more aggravation.

Driving home from the Hall of Justice she had envisioned a quiet cozy evening with the two favorite men in her life—an evening when she could try to forget her daytime reality.

Mounting the front stairs, Kate struggled to control her disappointment. The poor woman had been so good to them and all she wanted really was a little love in return. Was that too much to ask? Of course not, Kate thought, waiting for John to swing open the front door and greet her with hugs and kisses. With him came the delicious aroma of bubbling marinara sauce.

"Poor girl! It's about time you're home. You must be dead." She heard her mother-in-law's steady voice coming from the kitchen. "Jackie, hand me that potholder and fix your wife a drink. What kind of man, I ask you, lets his wife work longer hours than he does? Your Papa, God rest him, is probably rolling over in his grave! No! No! More ice, Jackie, more ice. And don't forget a slice of lemon."

Kate had scarcely finished hiding her gun on the top shelf of the hall closet and hanging up her coat when her husband arrived bearing her tall vodka tonic in one hand and a short bourbon for himself in the other. "Your Coke is on the kitchen table, buddy," he said to John and the youngster ran into the kitchen.

"Want me to help?" they heard him ask.

"Of course, my darling, I'd love you to help," Mama Bassetti answered. "Hand Nonie that big spoon, please."

"The kid will probably grow up to be a chef," Jack remarked, handing Kate her glass.

"Maybe that's better than being a cop." Exhausted, Kate sank into the overstuffed living-room couch. "Looks as if you and your mother have made up," Kate whispered. "Is that why she came over?"

Sitting down beside her, Jack smiled sheepishly. "Not really," he said. "Donaldson, who by the way had the good grace not to refer to his conversation with my mother, asked us to stay after our shift for a few minutes. I was afraid that John might be upset if I didn't pick him up on time. So I called my mother and asked her to do the duty. I fully intended to pick him up from her house." He sipped his drink. "I should have realized that nothing with Ma is that simple.

"From picking him up, she jumped right into feeding him and us, too, of course. She rambled on about eating properly, quoting some nutrition program she'd heard on television. By the time she finished she made us out to be prime candidates for rickets—which, of course, her spaghetti and meat sauce would instantly combat. When she finally paused for breath, I surrendered."

"If you hadn't, you'd probably still be on the phone," Kate said.

The two sat quietly for a few minutes relaxing, each hoping to let go of the day. "To be honest," Kate said finally, "it does smell delicious. I'll bet we are the only people in San Francisco who complain about somebody making them dinner."

"Right," her husband agreed. "Maybe in the whole state of California."

They heard small footsteps hurrying down the hall. "It's almost ready," John announced from the doorway. "Nonie says there's just time for another drink, so come on, Dad."

"Here I come," Jack said, heaving himself up from the couch and taking Kate's glass.

"Thanks," she said, watching him go. It always amazed her that he was so patient and good-natured about his mother's nagging. *It must be a special gene*, she thought, *one that I'm missing.* Kate closed her eyes. They burned. Probably from the salt water at the beach, she thought, trying to block the scene behind the windmill from her mind.

"Beware of the garlic bread," Jack said when he returned from the kitchen with their drinks. "My mother is letting the kid make it."

Kate smiled. "Which is more than she lets you and me do."

"Go figure!" Jack raised his glass. "Salute!"

"Salute!" Kate answered, still struggling to keep the grisly discovery at the park at bay, resolved not to let it invade her at home.

"You okay?" Jack asked.

Kate nodded, but he wasn't fooled.

"Much as I hate to agree with my mother," he said, "you really do look beat. From what Pits told us I gather you and Gallagher are the two who caught the Junior Johnson homicide."

"Yeah," Kate said, wishing that will power alone could banish the haunting memory. "Somebody shot him," she said simply, "in the head. From the look of it, Gallagher and I think it might be the same perp as shot Sarah Spencer."

"What makes you think that?"

"The size of the bullet wound and the fact that we didn't find any shells. We will have to wait until we get the forensic report to be sure."

"Any idea who the perp could be?" Jack asked.

"None whatsoever," Kate said. "I was kind of favoring Junior Johnson." She gave a half smile. "Obviously, it wasn't he. Unless he was in on it with someone else and there was a falling out among thieves. Anyway, with every cop in the city on a mission to find the perp, he doesn't have a prayer. We'll get the bastard."

During dinner the conversation was light and pleasant. Little John talked about his day at nursery school and what went on at daycare with his pals and Sheila, the babysitter. Mama Bassetti talked about what her neighbors said and thought. If she could be believed there was scarcely a subject from the mayor to the Muni on which they didn't have a strong and vocal opinion. Loretta Bassetti was still annoyed about her conversation with Lieutenant Don Donaldson. "Sassy," she had called him, and she said it again as she served chocolate biscotti and coffee.

Stirring in a few drops of cream, Kate wondered what adjective *she'd* use to describe the man.

At the mention of Don Donaldson, Jack, who seemed to have tuned out, re-joined the party. "One reason I was late," he said, then rushed on before his mother could comment, "is that Donaldson wanted to make some announcements about the service for Sarah Spencer tomorrow."

"Where is it?" Loretta Bassetti asked.

"St. Mary's Cathedral. We need to be there at nine-thirty," he said.

Kate was glad when little John asked to be excused. He was awfully young. She wasn't really sure how much he understood about death and funerals or what was the right age to try to explain them to him, but she was relieved that tonight wouldn't be the night that she'd have to make that decision. The familiar music from *Wheel of Fortune* floated in from the living room.

"Do you think the kid has a thing for Vanna White?" Jack asked.

His mother's eyes flashed. "Shame on you!" she said. "What a thing for a father to say! He is a very intelligent little boy. He likes to see if he can read the words."

"Just kidding," Jack said.

"Not funny!" his mother snapped back and rose from the table, starting to clear it.

"No, Loretta," Kate said more emphatically than she intended. "Jack and I will clean up. You have done enough. Sit down. Let me warm your coffee."

To Kate's amazement Loretta Bassetti did as she was told. "What time did you say that you have to be there tomorrow? Nine-thirty?" she asked.

Jack nodded.

"Why don't I take John home with me tonight? That way you can be free in the morning."

"What about nursery school?" Kate said.

"It's summer," her mother-in-law reasoned. "What about a day off?

Kate must have looked a little dubious.

"Millions of kids never went to nursery school at all," her mother-in-law said, "and they lived long and productive lives. Did Einstein go to nursery school?" Her brown eyes searched both her son and her daughter-in-law for an answer. "Did Michelangelo? Did Pope John XXIII? As a matter of fact, did either of you?"

"Ma, I think you've made your point," Jack said finally.

"Well?" his mother asked.

"Maybe it's a good idea," Kate said. "Tomorrow morning will be a big rush."

❧❧❧

Thirty minutes later, carrying a small overnight bag, John kissed them both and took his grandmother's hand. "Nonie, do you still have Rocky Road ice cream at your house?" Kate heard him ask hopefully.

As Kate cleared the table, Jack began to load the dishwasher. They were finished in less than twenty minutes. "Talk about teamwork," Jack said.

Without asking he poured two brandies and took them into

the living room. Kate followed and they settled on the couch. The room was warm from the kitchen heat. The delicious aroma of Italian spices still hung on the air. With only one lamp on, the room was dim and cozy. Kate liked it that way. She pulled her feet up under her and sipped her brandy.

"Feeling better?" Jack asked.

Kate nodded. "Better," she said, "but I still can't seem to shake this afternoon." Without warning, and without really wanting to tell her husband, the awful scene tumbled out—Junior's skull shattered by a single bullet, the horror of finding bits of his brain on the tree branch, Geraldine's eerie keening. It was as if she needed to purge herself. When she had, she actually did feel better.

"Thanks for listening, pal," she said, putting her head on his shoulder.

"My pleasure," Jack said, gently kissing the top of her head.

"I don't know what I'd do without you," she said and she meant it. And I hope I never have to find out, she thought, a sudden chill racing over her body.

❧❧❧

Over and over on the drive from Ocean Beach to Mount St. Francis Convent, Sister Anne wondered what had ever possessed her to think that Sister Mary Helen and she needed to solve this murder *together*. She had uttered the statement less than four hours ago—big bravado: "I think we need to solve this"—dramatic pause—"together!"

The shocked expression on the old nun's face should have given her a clue. Already she wanted out. Anne stopped at the signal on Fulton and Stanyan Street and switched on the headlights. She didn't have the stomach for it, as poor Inspector Gallagher could attest. Anyone who throws up on the murder scene clearly isn't cut out for the job. No one had actually said so, but you didn't need to be a rocket scientist to figure it out.

"Why so quiet?" Mary Helen asked at last. When Anne didn't answer, Mary Helen ventured a guess. "Are you dreading what will greet us when we get home?" she asked gently.

Anne's mouth went dry. She hadn't even considered that yet. She could just imagine the other nuns—some slightly disapproving, some very curious, all wanting some explanation. And there was none. None that Anne could think of. Why had a young undercover police officer and a known felon both been murdered in almost the same way? There must be some connection, but Anne was hard pressed to figure out what it could possibly be.

"Did you hear me?" Mary Helen asked. Anne had to admit that she hadn't. She hadn't even been aware that Mary Helen was speaking. She must have been in shock. Who wouldn't be after seeing what they had just seen?

"I said," Mary Helen repeated distinctly, "that in a few short blocks we'll be home. Our best defense, as the old saying goes, is a good offense. Obviously we've missed dinner. I suggest that we burst into the Sisters' Room." She checked her wristwatch, "Most of them will be glued to the news. And that we declare how upset and overwrought we are."

"Isn't that the truth?" Anne muttered.

Mary Helen gave her a sharp glance. "I wasn't suggesting that we don't tell the truth. Just take the offensive."

"Right," Anne said, feeling suddenly exhausted. It took all her strength to turn the steering wheel into the driveway and start up the college hill.

Near the top, Mary Helen sat up, rigid in her seat. "What's that?" She pointed toward the front door of the convent. "It can't be!"

Anne sucked in her breath. TV vans circled like covered wagons around cameramen and anchorwomen with microphones. "The eleven o'clock news," she groaned.

"Reverse the car!" Mary Helen shouted, but it was too late to back down the hill. They had been spotted. Before Anne had even turned off the ignition, men and women swarmed around the car, asking questions, pushing microphones in their faces, all shouting at once. Anne covered her ears and climbed out of the driver's seat, wondering how they would make it inside. She looked around for Sister Mary Helen, who seemed to have been swallowed up in the crowd.

"This way, Sisters." Anne heard a familiar, deep voice. It was Sister Patricia, the college president. The Cavalry, she thought, tension lifting from her shoulders as she caught sight of the tall, square woman, her white hair bright against the dark convent front door.

Head down, Anne push through the crowd. She was relieved to hear Sister Mary Helen beside her muttering, "Good night, nurse!"

Once inside the convent, the sudden silence was startling. "Are you all right?" Patricia asked, her dark eyes worried.

"Fine, thanks," Anne managed to say as Patricia led them to the Sisters' Room. A small game table near the windows was set and the dinner that had been kept warm for them arrived almost as quickly as they sat down. Without even asking, old Donata poured Anne a glass of deep red wine, then turned to Mary Helen.

"Well, you really got your foot in it this time, old girl," she said, filling Mary Helen's glass to the brim.

Mary Helen took a bite of baked chicken, a few oven-browned potatoes, and a taste of zucchini. "Delicious." She raised her glass to Donata. "To be honest, we really don't know what we got into."

Anne thought Donata looked skeptical, but she didn't say anything. Therese, on the other hand, was very vocal. "What do you mean?" she sniffed in disbelief. "What Donata is talking about is the murder that they just showed on the television. The reporters said that the authorities supposed it was connected to the one outside the Refuge." She spat out the next few words as if they were sour. "Your names, of course, were mentioned."

Anne's stomach somersaulted. "On television?" she asked.

"Yes, on television." Therese's voice rose at least an octave.

"What did they say?"

"Nothing too much." Patricia tried to sound comforting. She shot Therese a look which Anne figured anyone could decipher. Anyone except Therese, who must have missed it, since she didn't slow down for a minute.

"The reporter on the television said that a body had been found in the park near the Dutch Windmill and that two nuns stumbled upon it. They promised more details on the eleven o'clock news."

"Which is why those reporters have descended on us," Patricia said.

"But we don't know anything that they don't know," Anne seemed to be stuttering. "Actually Geraldine found the body. We just heard her scream and went to help her."

Therese's eyebrows shot up. "Why in the world would you do that?" Not waiting for an answer she went on. "Don't you know it's dangerous for nuns to be finding dead bodies?" She sounded outraged.

"We didn't want to find a body." Anne caught herself before she said, "It wasn't our fault." Even to her, it sounded too much like a whine.

Picking at her food, Anne was glad to hear Mary Helen clear her throat. With any luck at all, she was about to take over.

Deliberately, Mary Helen set down her fork and leaned back in her chair. Her hazel eyes scanned the room like searchlights taking in the assembled Sisters. A tense hush settled over the group. Even old Donata and Therese were quiet.

"Sister Anne and I," she began in a soft, strained voice, "have just had one of the worst afternoons in our lives. Less than three hours ago we found a man whose skull was shattered by a bullet with bits of his brain clinging to the branches of a tree."

Anne heard someone gasp and several muttered "Oohs."

Mary Helen adjusted her bifocals on the bridge of her nose. "We comforted his grieving aunt, called the police, and spent time answering their questions only to come home to a horde of media people who acted as if they would like to tear us apart. But for the intervention of Sister Patricia, they might have." She nodded graciously toward Patricia.

"In addition to being emotionally exhausted, we are, as you may imagine, physically tired and hungry. I know I was delighted and grateful that you kept our dinner warm." Anne nodded in agreement. "Which, by the way, is delicious. Please now may we have a few minutes to relax and eat? Then we can talk."

After a moment of embarrassed silence, Ursula spoke up. "How thoughtless of us! Mea culpa!" she muttered piously and rushed for the coffee. Patricia set a plate of homemade chocolate chip cookies on the table. The rest of the group quietly dissolved, although Anne noticed that they didn't move too far away.

Old Donata brought back the wine bottle and re-filled their glasses. "I know an academy award performance when I see one, old girl," she said in a stage whisper.

Anne noticed Mary Helen's eyes twinkling. "On our way home, I was explaining to little Sister here"—she pointed her fork toward Anne—"that a good offense is the best defense."

"I'm sure your last performance made the point abundantly clear," old Donata said and chuckled. "As the saying goes, you are a class act."

Both sets of eyes turned toward Anne. They seemed to be waiting for her to say something. She felt her cheeks grow hot. "This murder business is not for me," she said finally, "and the sooner I'm out of it the better."

Officers Mark Wong and Brian Dineen were in the second car to arrive at the hotel on Jones Street. A woman with a black eye and a bloodied lip was shouting obscenities. At first Wong wasn't sure exactly whom she was reviling, her husband, who most likely had battered her, or the patrolman who was dragging the man away in handcuffs. That is, until the woman kicked at the officer and his partner moved in to restrain her.

"That's what I hate most about these calls," Wong said, watching the struggle. "You almost always end up the bad guy."

"Yeah," Dineen nodded. Then he added philosophically, "The one time in a dozen that you really do save somebody from having the crap beat out of her makes it worthwhile—almost."

Back in the squad car, Dineen yawned and checked his watch. "Two-fifteen," he said. "You'd think these married types would be asleep by now."

"You'd think," Wong said, pulling out from the curb. The bars had just emptied out their crowds. The two officers cruised along the street knowing that the sight of them would deter at least a few crimes.

"Where to now?" Wong asked.

"Look! Is that who I think it is?" Dineen said, pointing.

Wong squinted and peered into a darkened doorway, but all he could make out was the tall, muscular man in the shadows—probably white. "Who do you think it is?" he asked.

"Go around the block!" Dineen ordered. "It looks like Tim Moran. I wonder what he's doing here."

Quickly Wong turned the corner, ignoring the shouts of several slightly woozy pedestrians on their way home. By the time he had circled the block, Moran, hands in pockets, was walking briskly along the sidewalk. Hunched forward, he seemed to be checking his reflection in the store windows as if making sure that he wasn't being followed.

Wong rolled up the car beside him. Startled, Moran shied away. "Hop in," Dineen invited.

Moran hesitated, checking to see if he was being observed. Then he gave them a little lip just in case anyone was watching. Finally he climbed into the backseat. "Thanks," he said and wiped his forehead. Despite the chilly night, the man was perspiring.

"What are you doing out here so late?" Dineen asked. "Shouldn't you be home in bed?"

"I was, but I couldn't sleep." Tim pulled nervously at his beard. His blue eyes jumped from them to the street. "I just can't get Sarah Spencer out of my mind. Poor kid! I thought maybe I'd run into somebody who knew something. But so far, no luck!"

Wong said nothing, although he wondered if Moran's insomnia could be blamed in part on his stormy meeting with Lieutenant Donaldson this afternoon. He was curious about what had brought on that confrontation, but he was hesitant to ask since clearly it was none of his business.

"Pits was acting like he had a pickle up his ass," Dineen said.

"You can say that again," Moran laughed bitterly.

"What was his problem?" Obviously Dineen had no such reservation.

"You know how he is," Moran muttered. "Acting like it was my fault that my cover was blown. Like I could stop somebody from killing that girl. Or that I could stop that nun, Helen something, from seeing and hearing. And what is worse in Donaldson's mind—thinking." Moran slammed his fist into the car seat.

"What exactly was his beef?" Dineen asked.

Wong was glad for the question. It wasn't quite clear to him either.

Tim Moran shifted nervously in his seat, still checking out

the side window as they drove along. Wong could smell the tension.

"You know Donaldson," Tim said with a hollow laugh. "If he's got an undercover deal going he wants it to look good in front of the brass."

"That's our Pits," Dineen agreed.

"Yeah," Moran grumbled. "I was a plant in that tattoo parlor. Chosen for obvious reasons." He pointed to the tattoo on his hand.

"What were you looking for?" Dineen asked.

Tim shrugged. "No big deal. Just a neighborhood prostitute ring. What I didn't know was that Sarah was working on the same case, only from another angle. At least, I think she was."

"Don't you know?" Dineen sounded surprised.

"I don't." It was obvious from his tone of voice that Moran was hedging.

"And that's what got her killed?" Dineen clung to the subject like a bulldog to a bone.

"Geez, Dineen, how the hell do I know?"

Moran sounded angry, but Wong was sure it was more fear than anger. Who could blame him? What was stopping whoever shot Sarah Spencer from shooting him?

"What kind of prostitute ring kills a cop?" Wong knew from the tone of voice that his partner was thinking out loud. "Wouldn't it be safer just to move the action to another location?"

"Yeah, you'd think so," Moran said, calming down a little. He moved up to the edge of the backseat. "Thanks for the ride, fellas," he said. "You can let me out anywhere along here."

"We were thinking about taking a coffee break," Dineen said. "Want to join us?"

"Coffee!" Moran laughed. "I ain't got enough trouble sleeping? Anywhere along here," Moran repeated. "I can catch the Muni."

"What do you make of that?" Dineen asked when they had dropped Moran on Market Street and pulled away from the curb.

"Obviously the guy knows more than he's telling us," Wong said.

"Did he seem awful jumpy to you?" Dineen drummed his finger on the dashboard.

"Yeah, but you can't blame him." Wong turned down Jones again. By now it was nearly deserted. "A fellow undercover cop gets shot right in front of the shop he's hanging out in—maybe he thinks the bullet was intended for him. And it could have been."

"Right," Dineen conceded. "Or maybe, he saw something that's got him worried."

"That too, but if he did see something wouldn't he tell Donaldson or the guys from Homicide about it?"

"I guess." Dineen sounded as unsure as Wong felt.

"Unless, of course, it was something he didn't want them to know."

"And what the hell would that be?" Dineen asked.

"I only wish I knew," Wong said, feeling suddenly tired. "Were you serious about a coffee break?"

"Is the Pope Catholic?" Dineen answered.

"I take that to mean yes," Wong said, glad that they'd be off the streets in just a couple of hours. He had a real funny feeling about Moran and he sure didn't want it to be played out on his shift.

❧❦❧

Something woke Sister Mary Helen in the middle of the night and she could not fall back to sleep. Was it a dream? A loud bang? A siren? She wasn't sure. The only thing she was sure of was that when her eyes popped open, her mind clicked on.

The events of the day flooded in on her like muddy water

from a broken main. It was difficult to believe that so much had happened in just one day. What was it some English poet had said? At least, Mary Helen thought she was English.

It was good, it was kind, in the Wise One above,
To fling Destiny's veil o'er the face of our years,
That we dread not the blow that shall strike at our love,
And expect not the beams that shall dry up our tears.

Odd, she could remember the lines and not the poet's name. It would come, like everything else, when she least expected.

Mary Helen sighed. Was it only this morning—not yet twenty-four hours ago—that Father Adams had spoken about Saint Boniface whose life had been cut short by pagan warriors in retaliation for chopping down their tree god? Retaliation hadn't stopped with the end of tree worship. It seemed to be alive and well in twenty-first century San Francisco.

In one sense, the SFPD was retaliating for the murder of one of their fellow officers by sweeping the neighborhood, rousting everybody they thought might be vaguely connected. Someone was retaliating for—Mary Helen knew not what, by savagely shooting Junior Johnson. Although not a sterling character by any stretch of the imagination, even he deserved better than that.

Mary Helen rose up on one elbow and punched her pillow, trying to make it more comfortable. In the distance she heard water running through the pipes. Someone else was up, too. *Misery loves company*, she thought, wondering who it was. No, she nipped the urge to get up and find out before it went any further. She was too exhausted.

Settling back on her pillow, she closed her eyes and tried to think of peaceful meadows and calming sunsets. Unfortunately at this moment all she seemed able to think about was poor Geraldine. Surely Geraldine was having a sleepless night. Imagine finding her nephew like that. Mary Helen shuddered at the very idea.

And what about Tim Moran? There was something about that man and his tattoo shop that caused the hair on the back of her neck to prickle. If she mentioned that to Inspector Gallagher surely he would say that there probably was a draft somewhere in the shop and that she ought to stay out of it.

The Inspector had always been a force to deal with when it came to her involvement in murder cases. Not that he hadn't been grateful in the past when she'd helped him solve a few. She smiled to herself in the dark. He'd be horrified to know that he was often more of a spur than a deterrent when it came to her involvement in these cases.

She pulled the covers up under her chin, shut her eyes, and breathed deeply. "Come, sleep. Come, sleep," she repeated over and over like a mantra. Unfortunately the only thing that came to her was the image of Tim Moran's face twisted in anger, the dragon around his neck undulating, as he stood amid the wreckage of the tattoo parlor. Although he was obviously the victim of the vandalism, there was something about him that just didn't sit right with her. For the life of her, she couldn't put her finger on it. Chances were that she'd be better able to identify the problem tomorrow if she had a good night's sleep.

At the moment her whole world seemed topsy-turvy. Oops! With everything that was going on today, she had forgotten to ask old Donata to look up the etymology of that expression. She'd do that first chance she had tomorrow.

Funny the things that pop into your mind in the middle of the night, she thought. Her body felt heavy all over, her limbs too weighed down to lift. But her mind still refused to surrender, pulling up pictures of Junior and the matted bush.

Lord, she prayed, fighting down an unexpected swell of nausea, *have pity on your people.* Mary Helen drew in another deep breath and let it out slowly. "Pity" was the last word Sarah Spencer had uttered. And Junior? What about Junior? *Only you, Lord, know his dying words, his dying words, his thoughts, his last agony. What else would a compassionate God feel toward his suffering creature,* she wondered, *but pity and love?*

But tonight in the stillness of her darkened bedroom even the Lord seemed oddly silent, as if He were teasing her, goading her, pushing her to figure out something just beyond her reach. *What is it?* she wondered. *What is it that I'm missing?* But again there was no answer.

Wednesday, June 6

❦❦❦

Feast of Saint Norbert, Bishop

Sister Mary Helen slept in. Last night, when Sister Patricia suggested it, she had brushed the idea off as unnecessary. "I'll probably be awake anyhow," she had said. When the alarm rang this morning, she couldn't push the off button fast enough.

Sister Anne and she were to meet at 9:15 at the side door of the convent. That should give them plenty of time to get to St. Mary's Cathedral for Sarah Spencer's funeral. Because parking might be a problem, they had decided to walk down from the college to Geary Boulevard, and hop the 38 Muni bus which ran right in front of the place. It was only a little over a mile away. From the college they could see the Cathedral of Saint Mary of the Assumption, as it was officially known. The innovative and controversial design, in which the four corners of the structure met, then curved gracefully upward, soaring to 190 feet and crowned with a 55-foot golden cross, caused some critics to refer to it as Saint Mary Maytag.

Surely we'll have time enough to find a seat, Mary Helen thought, walking slowly toward the shower. After all, the Cathedral's seating capacity was 2500. Just to be safe, she decided to wear comfortable shoes.

"Don't cut it too short," old Donata warned when Mary Helen suggested that they had time for a second cup of coffee. "Every policeman for miles around will be there," she said. "Corporal work of mercy, you know. To bury the dead."

Mary Helen noticed a blank expression on Anne's face. "Seven corporal works of mercy," she hinted. When Anne's expression did not change, she began to recite the old catechism answer counting them off on her fingers: "To feed the hungry; to give drink to the thirsty; to clothe the naked; to visit the imprisoned; to shelter the homeless; to visit the sick; and to bury the dead."

Anne still looked bewildered and Mary Helen remembered that Anne was too young to be a catechism-answer kid.

As the two nuns stepped off the bus, Mary Helen realized that Donata was right. The entire front of the massive cathedral was thick with blue uniforms. Literally hundreds of police officers wearing white gloves stood in silent respect. Nearby the mounted honor guard rose above them, holding their dark quarter horses in check. An imposing bay sidestepped beside a group of motorcycle policemen waiting on their shiny bikes.

In the crowd Mary Helen recognized the Chief of Police. Surrounding him were a group of older officers whom she supposed were ranking police brass. She spotted Inspector Gallagher and Kate Murphy and was surprised to see that they were both wearing their blue uniforms. She waved at them as she wove her way through the thickening crowd. Kate responded with a nod of her head. She recognized Officers Mark Wong and Brian Dineen. She had become acquainted with the two Vice Squad officers last year when Melanie, one of the refugees, had been found dead outside the Refuge. She noticed that Wong was talking to a young, good-looking Asian woman. Even at this distance the body language was unmistakable. She was smitten.

Moving along, Mary Helen scanned the crowd wondering if Tim Moran was there. Frankly, she was curious to know if he still had the blue dragon on under his blue uniform jacket. But she didn't find him. There were just too many blue jackets.

"Gold in peace. Iron in war," the insignias on each arm read in Latin. And very solemn in the face of death, Mary Helen reflected, mounting the Cathedral steps. These men and women couldn't help but take the death of a fallen colleague very personally, she thought. Although they probably didn't even admit it to one another, they couldn't help but think, *There but for the grace of God go I.* It must be on every mind.

A sharp wind rolled across the large granite entryway, turning small bits of paper and dirt into miniature tornados. Mary Helen shivered and closed her eyes against the grit. She had never thought about wearing something warm, although anywhere close to 2500 bodies in the Cathedral should provide plenty of warmth.

As always, once she slipped inside, the breathtaking beauty of the interior made her forget everything else. She stood on the red brick floor reminiscent of the early Missions while above it the rounded ceiling rose nineteen stories. At each corner of the Cathedral, vast windows looked out upon spectacular views of San Francisco. Over the altar a kinetic sculpture of aluminum suspended on gold wires was alive with reflected light. Its fourteen triangular tiers symbolized the channels of loving grace from God to His people and their prayers and praise rising to Him.

The Cathedral buzzed with hushed conversation as the last of the mourners gathered to offer the final Mass of Burial for Sarah Spencer. Mary Helen and Anne had just settled in a pew when the magnificent Ruffati organ came to life filling the Cathedral with a haunting melody from Taize, *"Jesus, remember me when you come into your kingdom.*" Over and over the last words of the Good Thief as he hung next to Jesus dying on the cross washed over the assembly. Mary Helen felt her eyes sting.

Rising, the congregation watched the casket, draped with a gleaming white pall, being rolled down the aisle. Behind it in solemn procession were a middle-aged couple that Mary Helen supposed were Sarah's parents, weeping silently, behind them a young man who seemed to be in shock.

"Eternal rest grant unto her," Father McKay, the chaplain for the police and fire department, intoned. "And let perpetual light shine upon her."

The Cathedral rang with a wholehearted, "Amen."

At the conclusion of the Requiem Mass, with the strains of *In Paradisum—May the Angels Lead You into Paradise* still coming from inside the Cathedral, the congregation filled the courtyard in sad silence. The honor guard of police officers readied a cortege to escort Sarah's body to its final resting place at Holy Cross Cemetery.

As she stood there, Mary Helen couldn't help but ponder what kind of funeral Junior Johnson would have. Would any of his companions take his death so personally? Would they pray for angels to lead him into Paradise? Were his last words, by any chance, the last words of the Good Thief on the cross? Mary Helen didn't know. The only thing that she did know for sure was that both of them, the young policewoman and the young career criminal, had met a merciful and loving God who would indeed judge them with pity.

"Sister Mary Helen," Anne's voice startled her. Mary Helen turned. "We better get to the Refuge," Anne said, her voice choked. "Our ladies will be waiting for us."

Obediently Mary Helen followed.

❧❦❧

Both Inspector Gallagher and Kate Murphy were quiet for most of the short ride from St. Mary's Cathedral to Holy Cross Cemetery in Colma. There was something very sobering about the death of a fellow police officer that Kate knew they all felt.

Quietly the long line of cars entered the ornate gates of the cemetery, and then snaked up the paved roads, following the hearse. Finally, near the enormous stucco mausoleum, it pulled to the curb and parked. Cars followed suit, forming a long line bordering the manicured green lawn. The slamming of car doors echoed in the silence. A crisp wind tousled the mourners' hair and sent one hat flying. It blew flower petals from the wreaths, which skipped over the grass like small chips of white and red and bright yellow paint.

The high, mournful notes of the bagpipers sent chills through Kate as they led Sarah's body to her final resting place. Although she had not really known the policewoman, Kate felt the tears sting her eyes. No one should die so young and so violently. Why did God allow these kinds of tragedies to happen? No one seemed to be able to explain it to her satisfaction. She'd have a lot of questions to ask when she finally got up there.

The prayers at the gravesite were brief. Although from where she stood, Kate could not hear Father McKay very well, it was a familiar ceremony. Too familiar, she thought ruefully as she said the final "Amen."

Slowly, almost as if they were waking from a dream, the crowd began to break up. Kate smelled cigarette smoke coming from those who could wait no longer. Here and there, a laugh rose above the hushed conversation. An engine revved. "Be right back," Gallagher said and move toward a tall man who Kate recognized as an old friend of Denny's—now retired.

"Hi, hon." Jack's voice startled her. She had spotted her husband at the opposite end of the gathering standing with some other officers from Vice. She hadn't expected that he'd be able to struggle through to her this quickly. Behind him were Mark Wong and Brian Dineen.

"Hi, pal," Kate said, scrutinizing the three men. The grave expressions on their faces told her that this wasn't just a social call. Something important was on their minds. "What's up?" she asked, almost afraid to find out.

Jack shrugged. "It may be nothing, but Mark and Brian were just telling me about meeting Tim Moran last night." He turned toward the two men. "Why am I doing the talking? You tell her."

In hushed tones, Wong related their brief meeting with Moran on the streets. "You didn't have to be Sigmund Freud to figure out that something was really bothering him," he said. "When we went off duty this morning, the detail was pretty deserted." He lowered his voice still further. "So we took the opportunity to look at the log for Sarah Spencer— to check if she was on surveillance."

"And?" Kate's heart quickened. Sarah's activities should be recorded. Could this be the breakthrough that Gallagher and she were looking for?

"And, nothing." Dineen's low voice was gruff. "Nada. Zip."

Kate's stomach dropped and her gaze jumped from Dineen to Wong and back again. "Are you sure?" she asked.

The annoyance on Dineen's face made her wish that she could take the question back. "Sorry," she muttered. "Sure you're sure." She stood there awkwardly and was very glad when she felt Gallagher move in beside her.

"What's up?" he asked.

Quickly Wong filled him in on the surveillance log.

"Nothing there? Jeez!" Gallagher took off his cap and ran the palm of his hand over his bald crown. "What the hell happened to it?"

Wong shrugged. "That's exactly what we want to know."

"Could that be why Moran was so upset?" Gallagher asked.

"There's one way to find out," Kate offered. "Let's ask him." Frowning, she scanned the crowd, which was beginning to disperse, but she didn't catch sight of him. "Not here," she said wondering suddenly if he'd been to the funeral at all. "Did any of you see him this morning?" she asked.

They looked at one another but no one spoke. "As a matter of fact," Jack said finally, "I was looking for him at the Cathedral but I never did find him."

"Odd," Dineen said. "He was so broken up when we met him on our shift I would have bet money that he'd be here."

"It was a pretty big crowd," Wong said, reasonably "and with us all in uniform, it would be easy to miss him." He yawned and Kate realized that both he and Dineen hadn't yet been to sleep.

"Thanks, guys," she said. "You two must be exhausted. Why don't you go home and let Gallagher and me get on this."

"One more thing." Wong yawned again. "I was talking to someone from the Chief's office and this person mentioned hearing rumors of an alleged brothel in the neighborhood."

"The neighborhood Sarah was staking out?" Kate smiled. "Why doesn't that surprise me?"

"What will surprise you," Wong said with a knowing grin, "is that rumor has it that the alleged brothel is frequented by a number of affluent and influential San Franciscans."

Kate's stomach lurched. *He's got to be kidding*, she thought, scarcely aware that her husband was talking to her. "What?" she said.

"See you tonight at home," Jack repeated.

"Yeah, thanks," she muttered, watching him follow Wong and Dineen to their parked cars.

"Don't forget it's your turn to cook," she called after him. She wasn't really sure whose turn it was, nor at this moment did she really care, but it was worth a try.

Beside her, she heard Gallagher snort. "Did you hear that Wong? Talking to somebody at the Chief's office! Who does he think he's kidding? He's talking to Susie Chang. Jeez! It's common knowledge that they're a number! Did you see them talking in front of the Cathedral? Even a blind man would have noticed them flirting."

Shaking her head, Kate stared at him dumbfounded. How had she missed it? She was busy wondering what else had slipped by her when she felt Gallagher touch her shoulder. "Don't look now, Katie-girl, but the Chief just called Lieutenant Donaldson aside."

Pretending to study the cumulus clouds piling up against the brilliant blue sky over the San Bruno Mountains, Kate took in the Chief and Donaldson. The Chief's face was the color of raw beefsteak—a sure sign that he was angry. Lieutenant Don Donaldson hunched his shoulders defensively as if to ward off the mounting wind.

"What do you figure that's about?" Gallagher whispered.

"Beats me," Kate said. "Maybe we ought to get back to the city and see if we can find out." Turning on her heel, she made her way to their parked car.

"Jeez, Kate," she heard Gallagher muttering behind her, "that's all we need—a case where the city's big kahunas are involved."

Little shivers skittered over her skin. "But you know, Denny, it does make sense."

"Whoa!" Gallagher's voice rose. "Don't even go there! Or if you do let's make sure we've checked out every other possibility. Right?"

"Right," Kate agreed. "Where do you think we should start?" Car doors slapped along the curb.

"My gut's telling me Tim Moran is as good a place as any," Gallagher turned the key in the ignition. "Let's try the tattoo parlor and see if he's there."

"Good idea," Kate said, wondering just how happy Moran would be to see them. Well, they'd soon find out.

Gallagher pulled away from the curb. "And let's hope that there's a logical explanation for the missing pages in the surveillance log and that there's no connection between the alleged brothel and the San Francisco bigwigs."

"That's a lot of hope," Kate mumbled as her partner merged onto El Camino Real.

"Isn't that damn stuff supposed to spring eternal?" he asked.

❧❧❧

When Sister Mary Helen and Sister Anne pulled up in front of the Refuge, a small crowd of women was already gathered at the front door. "If I didn't know better, I'd say we were being picketed," Mary Helen remarked, taking in all the unhappy faces.

Anne smiled and pulled into the parking lot. "You're right. The only things that seem to be missing are the placards," she said.

"Where you been?" Venus demanded as the two nuns rounded the corner. Her dark eyes narrowed as she waited for an answer.

"Have you been waiting long?" Anne asked sweetly.

With a look of disgust, Venus ran her long fingers through her hair which, crazily, always reminded Mary Helen of black broccoli. "Yeah, we all been waiting long." She stomped her feet trying to get warm.

"Didn't you see our sign?" Anne turned the key in the front door and pulled it open.

"I seen it," Venus said. "It say you going to a funeral. It be nearly lunchtime. How long a funeral take?" she asked accusingly.

"Oh, hush your mouth, girl," Sonia said grinning at Mary Helen.

Poor Sonia looked especially pale this morning. Her sickle cell anemia must acting up again.

"Who you telling to hush, girl?" Venus challenged.

For a moment, Sonia looked as if she might pick up the gauntlet.

"Don't be acting the fool," Miss Bobbie said. The scar around her right eye twitched dangerously.

Venus whirled to face her. "You calling me a fool?" she asked, her voice low and threatening.

"If I is, it's 'cause you are." Miss Bobbie didn't seem as if she was going to back down.

Mary Helen felt the muscles in the back of her neck tense. Where was this going?

"I'll get the coffee on as quickly as I can," Sister Anne said loudly, obviously trying to distract the two women.

"And I'll put out the doughnuts," Mary Helen added. "I think I saw some apple fritters in the box."

Thankfully, the mention of food worked. Without any further fussing, the women filed into the Refuge, wrote their names on the sign-up sheet, and found places at the tables.

"Bring me a doughnut, Peanuts," Miss Bobbie commanded as soon as Mary Helen had set the tray on the serving table.

The diminutive woman pulled herself up to her full height. "If you asks a little sweeter, I may bring it," she said.

"Then I guess I be getting it myself," Miss Bobbie shot back and the room burst into laughter.

"Thank goodness," Mary Helen thought. They needed some comic relief.

Once she had seen to it that everyone had coffee and doughnuts, Mary Helen sat down across the table from Miss Bobbie.

"How you doing, girlfriend?" the old woman asked, although she didn't look up from her chocolate cake doughnut. "How be the funeral?"

"Sad," Mary Helen admitted. "It is always sad when someone so young dies. They say that only the good die young, but that doesn't help very much."

Miss Bobbie pursed her lips. "Not always," she said.

"Not always what?"

"Not always the good die young," she hissed. "Look at Junior Johnson. He be young, but he be a bad one."

How do I reply to that? Mary Helen wondered. "He must have some redeeming qualities," she suggested.

"Say what?" Miss Bobbie stared at her.

"There must be something good about him. Nobody is all bad."

The old nun felt Miss Bobbie's brown eyes studying her while she, no doubt, decided how to respond. "You better wise up some, girlfriend," the woman finally said, not unkindly, "or you not going to make it in this neighborhood."

At first Mary Helen was taken aback. It had been years since anyone suggested that she wise up. She wasn't sure just how to react. What was it Eileen always said? "The wise one keeps a shut mouth." Meeting Miss Bobbie's gaze, it seemed, indeed, the wisest thing was to keep still.

Without warning, the front door flew open and Crazy Alice's high giggle floated above the conversation in the room.

Miss Bobbie rolled her eyes heavenward. "That all we needing! Don't we got enough on our nerves without Crazy Alice playing the fool?" she asked, her question addressed to no one in particular.

Although Mary Helen doubted if the woman heard Miss Bobbie's remark, her giggling stopped abruptly. With a sweeping glare she took in the whole room. Her eyes narrowed and Mary Helen held her breath, anxious about what was coming.

"Hello, Alice," Mary Helen heard Anne greet the woman. "You look as if you could use a cup of coffee."

Before Crazy Alice could answer, the door swung open behind her, almost hitting her. Unaware that she'd had a near accident, Geraldine stormed into the Refuge.

Startled, Alice studied her without speaking. Then for no apparent reason, she began in a singsong tone of voice,

It's like a lion at the door;
And when the door begins to crack,
It's like a stick across your back;
And when your back begins to smart,
It's like a penknife in your heart;
And when your heart begins to bleed,
You're dead and dead and dead, indeed.

Geraldine's face lost all its color. The room was so still that Mary Helen could hear the hum of the fluorescent lights. She felt the hair on her arms stand up.

"What you talking about, you crazy fool?" Geraldine asked, her voice shaking.

Without answering Alice turned and left as quickly as she had come in. To be honest, Mary Helen was glad. Emotions were running high enough today. They didn't need Crazy Alice in the mix.

Without another word, Geraldine settled at a table in the corner of the room, her back to the crowd. *Greta Garbo couldn't have made it any more clear that she wanted to be alone*, Mary Helen thought, going to the kitchen for more napkins. *Sometimes we're not the best judges of what we need*, she reasoned. Although she had to admit, Geraldine looked terrible. In fact, Mary Helen could not remember ever seeing her look this bad. Her gray hair was tangled, almost matted. Deep lines cut into her face as if she hadn't slept. Dark half-moons had formed under her eyes and her shoulders were hunched with sadness. She'd let Geraldine relax for a while, sip her coffee, think her thoughts, and then she'd approach her and find out if there was anything she could do to help.

Surely Geraldine must still be in shock from finding her beloved nephew in the park. Mary Helen expected to have nightmares herself about Junior for a long time.

"Sister, it's my shower time. Can I have my towel and stuff?" Peanuts's voice brought her back to reality.

"I need a toothbrush and some toothpaste," Venus said, pointing to her missing front tooth.

"Do you have a plastic bag?" someone else asked and Mary Helen was off and running.

A little past one o'clock, Louise, the volunteer for Wednesday afternoon, arrived. Mary Helen was very glad to see her. Frankly she was bone tired. And who wouldn't be at her age? After all, she was seventy-eight—or was she seventy-nine? Not that it mattered.

Discovering a dead body, dealing with the police and the nuns, and attending a funeral—all within twenty-four hours— would weary the heartiest of souls at any age.

By two o'clock, she was even toying with the idea of asking Sister Anne if she could have the rest of the day off. A nap sounded so tempting. She could hop the Muni and be in her bedroom at the convent in thirty minutes.

She had all but made up her mind when she noticed Geraldine, a half-full cup of coffee and a half-eaten doughnut on the table in front of her. Poor thing had fallen asleep. Although it seemed too cruel to wake her up, Mary Helen wanted to offer her assistance if Geraldine needed it. She'd leave a note.

Quietly, so as not to startle the dozing woman, Mary Helen put the slip of scratch paper beside her arm. Despite her best efforts at being quiet, Geraldine started awake. "Oh, it's you," she said in a groggy voice. "What you want?"

"I was just leaving you a note." Mary Helen adjusted her bifocals on the bridge of her nose and slid the paper toward Geraldine. "If there is anything I can do for you . . ."

Geraldine's brown eyes filled with tears. Mary Helen watched one slide unheeded down her cheek. "Nobody can do what I need. Nobody can bring back Junior." She fumbled in her pocket and finally found a tissue.

"Maybe we can help the police find the person who took his life," Mary Helen said gently. "Tell me honestly, Geraldine, do you have any ideas?"

Geraldine's face hardened and her eyes snapped angrily. "All night I be talking to Junior's friends. They be telling me that it ain't nobody they knows who killed Junior."

"Are you saying they have no suspects?"

Geraldine gave a hollow laugh. "Oh, yeah. They got suspects. But they be the kind nobody can touch."

Mary Helen was puzzled. *What kind of suspects can no one touch?* she wondered, thinking of all the mystery novels she had read and all the crime television programs she had seen. International agents, spies, the Mafia, high government officials— surely none of these would have much reason to murder Junior Johnson, a petty criminal from San Francisco's Tenderloin. "And do you know who these untouchables are?"

Geraldine stared at her, her jaw stubbornly set. "Better I don't say nothing to you or to anybody. No, ma'am, Sister." She wagged her head sadly. "Don't want nobody finding us in the park with a bullet in our head. No way!"

Sister Mary Helen knew by the intensity of her voice that Geraldine was deadly serious. "If you want, I can talk to Inspector Kate Murphy. She's a friend of mine," she began, hoping to make Geraldine feel better.

The palm of Geraldine's hand shot up. "No," she said as if she were speaking around a lump of fear in her throat. "Don't be talking to no police!" She rose so quickly that her chair clattered backwards onto the floor. Several women turned to see what was going on.

"What's happening, Genie?" Miss Bobbie asked, using Geraldine's street name.

Ignoring her question, Geraldine stiffened, gathered up her purse and her plastic bags and nearly ran from the room.

"Look like the devil himself be chasing her," Peanuts quipped, "and she giving him a run."

Several women gave a halfhearted laugh. All at once, any thought of a nap left Sister Mary Helen's mind. The woman was scared—scared to death. Of the police? Mary Helen couldn't believe it. Why? Why would she think that the police were involved in Junior's murder?

Geraldine had mentioned a house of prostitution in the neighborhood and indicated that the police knew about it. At the time she had even hinted that they might be looking the other way. What was it she'd said? "For a smart woman, you be awful dumb."

Well, Mary Helen didn't intend to be dumb anymore. If the police were involved in any way, she wanted to know it and then pass on the information to Kate Murphy and Inspector Gallagher.

Where to start? she wondered. Where better than with the undercover policeman down the street—Tim Moran. She hadn't seen him at Sarah Spencer's funeral. He had probably been on duty at the tattoo parlor. She'd go down there this minute.

She wasn't sure Sister Anne saw her wave as she went out the front door of the Refuge. No problem. She'd be back before Anne even missed her.

❧❧

Officer Mark Wong turned the key in the ignition of his car and listened to the motor rev. It was almost as if he, too, was revving up. During Sarah Spencer's funeral he had felt as if, without toothpicks to hold them open, any minute his eyes would shut. Then he had run into Susie Chang. When she had suggested that they meet for lunch at Joe's of Westlake on John Daly Boulevard his adrenaline had started to pump again. He definitely had his second wind.

Surprisingly, he found a parking space in the nearly full lot. When he walked into the crowded foyer, Susie had already given her name to the maitre d'. She was perched gracefully like a tiny sparrow on the edge of a padded bench waiting for him.

"It's about a ten-minute wait," she said, motioning him to sit next to her.

"Not bad," he said, and it wasn't. Day or night, no matter what the time, there was always a wait at Joe's of Westlake. Sometimes it was the better part of an hour but the delicious aroma of Joe's Italian sauces was reason enough to endure it.

Mark sat beside Susie on the bench. "How about a drink?" he asked, checking to see how crowded the bar was.

"No, thanks," she replied. "I have to get back to work. But you have one if you'd like."

"If I have one I'm afraid I'll go right to sleep," Mark said, and then stopped.

"Oh?" Susie's eyes danced with humor.

"I didn't mean the company," he sputtered.

Listening to her tinkling laughter, he felt the heat move up his neck. How was he going to get his foot out of his mouth this time?

"Chang," the maitre d' called, "party of two."

Saved, Mark thought, jumping up without ever considering that there might be another Chang in the place.

Comfortably seated across from him, Susie perused the menu. Trying not to stare, Mark studied her round cheerful face and the way her eyelashes played against her cheeks. He watched her mouth form a small red "O" as she silently read through the selections. He noticed the light from the west window touch her raven black hair and through some trick fill it with sunshine.

"What are you having?" she asked, looking up so quickly that she caught his eye. Mark felt his face flush. Had she felt his eyes on her? Did she mind? "Veal scaloppini," he said without thinking. He always ordered the scaloppini at Joe's.

"Me, too," she said.

Mark gave their order to the waiter. Once again, he was glad that even though she probably weighed less than ninety-eight pounds soaking wet, Susie had a hearty appetite. He hated to eat with women who ordered a toothpick and a glass of water and couldn't finish either.

"That was so sad this morning," Susie said, playing with the edge of her napkin.

Mark nodded and slowly they began to talk about Sarah Spencer's funeral and the circumstances leading up to it. Mark admitted that Dineen and he had tried all night without much success to find someone who could give them a lead.

"Nobody?" Susie's almond eyes were wide.

Mark shook his head. "And we don't seem to be the only ones who are banging against the brick wall." He told her about Dineen and himself picking up a distraught Tim Moran.

At the mention of Moran's name, Wong notice Susie frowning. "You know, the oddest thing happened yesterday," she said. "Your mentioning Tim Moran made me think of it."

Although he wasn't sure why, Wong's shoulders stiffened. "What odd thing?" he asked, hoping not to sound as if he was interrogating her.

Susie laughed that tinkly laugh again. "It was just something silly," she said.

Wong waited, watching her decide just how much to tell him.

"I was at my desk when I looked up and saw Lieutenant Donaldson." She glanced at Wong checking his reaction to the mention of his boss's name. When he gave none, she went on. "He said that he was playing a little joke on Moran and he asked me to put on a Chinese accent and to pretend that I was from the Asian Market up the street from the building where Moran is on stakeout."

Wong felt his jaw tighten. "What did he want you to say?"

Susie shrugged and waited while the server put down their

salads. "Nothing much," she said. "He just wanted me to act as if we had prepared Moran some lunch and we wondered if he could come up the street and get it because we were busy." She started to eat.

"That was a joke?" Wong asked, wondering if that was what had upset Moran.

"I guess so. The Lieutenant mumbled something about getting back at him for pulling a dirty trick on him. I wasn't really listening. I just called the number he gave me and hoped that the Chief wouldn't come in and catch us. I have the feeling he wouldn't think that it was very funny, especially coming from his office during working hours."

"So, I take it that Donaldson had never asked you to do anything like that before." A vague uneasiness rolled through Wong.

"No," she said, her eyes dancing as the waiter put down large, hot plates in front of them. "And I hope he doesn't again. It was all I could do not to tell him how juvenile I felt it was."

Let's hope it was only juvenile, Wong thought, studying Susie, whose eyes were already devouring her scaloppini. Without another word she began to eat.

"Delicious," she said, buttering a crusty piece of sourdough French bread. "This will be lunch and dinner."

Wong nodded his agreement. "Delicious," he said, although at the moment his thoughts were miles away from Susie Chang and veal scaloppini.

❧❧❧

Stepping out of the Refuge onto Eighth Street, Sister Mary Helen was surprised to see that the day had turned warm. Sunshine and the cloudless blue sky made everything sparkle, she noticed. Even the neglected buildings along the street looked better in this light.

People, too, seemed to relax and open up when the sun shone. Several passersby smiled. One or two nodded and said hello. And the homeless folks shuffling along the sidewalks? Was it her imagination or did some of them lift their chins a little higher and grasp their coats a little less tightly?

Mary Helen felt the tension in her own shoulders ease as she strolled down the block. A line from a long forgotten poem jumped into her mind. " 'And young and old come forth to play, on a sunshine holiday.' "

Milton, she thought, was the poet but somehow it didn't seem gloomy enough for Milton. She would have to get old Donata on that one, too.

Approaching the New You Tattoo Parlor, Mary Helen wondered if it was open. The lights were on but there didn't seem to be much activity inside. Cupping her hands against the glass, she peered inside. From what she could see, it looked deserted. Maybe Officer Moran had gone home and forgotten to turn off the lights. It happens, she thought, testing the door.

Surprisingly it was unlocked. She pushed it and was startled by the tinkle of the small bell at the top of the door jamb. "How do?" she called, cautiously stepping inside. Her voice echoed in the stillness. Could it be that he had forgotten both the light and the lock? *Unlikely*, a small voice inside her challenged. Mary Helen ignored it.

"Officer Moran?" she called again. Again she was greeted with absolute silence. Carefully she moved around the counter. The cash register was closed and seemed undisturbed. Good sign, she thought, edging toward the back of the shop. "How do?" she called louder this time. Again, nothing.

Her mouth went dry as a vague uneasiness began to grip her. Don't be foolish, she thought gulping in a few short breaths of air to calm herself.

Surely Officer Moran had simply left without remembering to turn off the overhead lights. *I've done that myself*, she thought.

And the door? What about the front door? the nagging voice continued. *Not likely that he'd forget to lock it after what just happened to his shop.*

Thank goodness he had left the place lit, Mary Helen thought, avoiding a chair that was pulled away from the wall. *I'd be bumping into things all over the place.*

Slowly she moved forward. *The office is on my right,* she thought, trying a final "How do?" When no one answered she eased open the partially shut office door. Its squeak startled her. The muscles in her arms tightened. Uncertainly she peered in. The small room, which was a mess the last time she'd seen it, was back in order. The lamp and the window shades had been replaced and even the philodendron, looking none the worse for wear, replanted. *Good for him!* she thought.

Taking in the room, everything seemed in order. It had just been a careless mistake. She would turn off the lights, lock up for him, and go. Nothing was wrong, nothing that she could see. She sniffed. Except . . . She sniffed again—that odor—that unmistakable sweet odor.

Her stomach jumped as she quickly took a clean handkerchief from her pocket and covered her mouth. *It couldn't be,* she thought. Warily she peeked behind the wooden desk. "No!" she said, feeling lightheaded. "No! No! No!" She leaned against the wall to keep from falling, and then forced herself to look again.

Crumpled on the floor, frozen in a fetal position, lay Tim Moran. His blue jeans and wool shirt were soaked in blood. His left arm, the one that had MOTHER tattooed across the knuckles, was flung out to his side.

Using all her will power, Mary Helen crouched down beside the man. "Let him be alive," she chanted over and over, feeling for his pulse. The moment her fingers touched his wrist, she knew she was too late. Her heart sank. "Eternal rest grant unto him, O Lord," the ancient prayer sprang to her lips and she fought back a sob. "Let perpetual light shine upon him."

Like a sleepwalker, Mary Helen studied Tim's face, at least, the half of it that she could see. Milky blue eyes stared at her vacantly. His straggly beard was stained with blood.

In fact, the entire area behind the desk was puddled with blood. It was as if Tim had not died instantly, as if he had moved. Toward the phone? Toward the door? It was hard to tell. There were smears of his blood everywhere.

Noticing her own footprint in the sticky blood, Mary Helen backed up quickly. As she did, she saw something primitively drawn on a small relatively clean patch of the linoleum over Moran's head. *With the last of his strength he reached up*, she thought with a shudder.

Shoving her bifocals up the bridge of her nose, she moved forward, avoiding the blood. *Don't disturb the evidence*, she reminded herself. *Careful, do not touch anything.*

Pensively she studied the floor. It looked as if Moran had drawn something—were they letters?—with his finger dipped in his own blood. What was he trying to say? Could he be naming his killer? Mary Helen moved around trying to make some sense of the scrawl.

Her heart roared in her ears. Were they letters? Taking a deep breath, she focused on them. A "d." An "I" or was it a "1"? An "L" with a long leg or maybe an upside down "T"? And then a stick figure or a wobbly, upside-down "Y."

The scream of the telephone jarred her into reality. Backing away from the body, she began to shiver uncontrollably. Was that a noise she heard in the front of the shop or was it outside? All at once the hum of the fluorescent lights in the hallway sounded ominous. Had someone moved the chair or had it been there when she passed?

With a cold, shaky hand, she picked up the telephone receiver. Without saying a word, she hung it up again. Then quickly before whomever it was could call back, she dialed 911.

Still shivering, she chose to wait for the police outside the tattoo parlor. Eyes closed, Mary Helen leaned against the building. Although she felt the sun on her face and shoulders, she realized sadly that all the sunshine in the sky would not be able to warm her today. The cold she felt was a cold no fire could warm. It was the penetrating icy cold of absolute horror.

❧❦❧

All at once, Sister Anne realized that she had not seen Sister Mary Helen for at least ten or fifteen minutes. Strange! Could she be in the kitchen? "Sister Mary Helen," she called from the doorway, but the kitchen was empty.

Quickly she checked the supply cupboard, the office, then tapped on the bathroom door. No answer.

Although she knew better, she began to feel a little anxious. Maybe Mary Helen had gone to the basement for supplies.

"Mary Helen," she called down the stairs, but there was no answer. Remembering that the old nun was getting a little hard of hearing, Anne walked halfway down, then realized that the basement was dark. She surely wouldn't be in a darkened basement.

Back in the gathering room, she sidled up to Miss Bobbie. If anyone in the room knew where Sister Mary Helen was, she did. Miss Bobbie's dark eyes never missed a trick.

"You didn't happen to see where Sister Mary Helen went, did you?" Anne asked, trying to sound nonchalant.

"You be looking for her?" Miss Bobbie asked, studying Anne for any signs of concern.

Anne nodded, feeling herself growing impatient. She clenched her jaw hoping she didn't show it. She should have known better than to think she'd get a straight answer right away.

Miss Bobbie paused, her scar twitching. Then, acting as though she was imparting a carefully guarded secret, she said,

164

"She be an old woman, you know. You all should keep an eye on her. Make sure she be all right."

At the moment, Anne did not need a lecture on the care of Mary Helen. What she needed was to find the woman. *Calm down!* she reminded herself. Mary Helen probably just stepped out for a minute to walk. Fighting down her frustration, Anne felt her fingernails pressing into the palms of her hands. She should have guessed that her clenched fists were not lost on Miss Bobbie.

"She gone missing?" the older woman asked. "Like Junior Johnson?"

At the thought of Junior, Anne's stomach roiled. She refused to even dignify the remark with a response. "She was just here," Anne tried to keep her voice steady.

"Who you be looking for?" Peanuts asked.

Anne whirled to see the tiny woman behind her.

"I scare you?" Peanuts asked, looking somewhat pleased.

" 'Startled' is a better word." Anne forced a smile. "I didn't hear you come up behind me."

"Well here I is!" Peanuts's bright eyes sparkled. "Who you be looking for?"

"Sister Mary Helen." Anne grinned nervously and shrugged. "She has to be here someplace."

"No, she don't," Peanuts said.

"What?" Anne wasn't sure that she'd heard her correctly.

"No, she don't," Peanuts repeated.

"What do you mean?"

Peanuts shook her head in exasperation. "I means she don't got to be here, because I saw her leaving."

"Where did she go?"

This time Peanuts shrugged. "Outside someplace. She went out just after Geraldine got running out of here like she had the devil on her tail."

"And Mary Helen ran out after her?"

Peanuts nodded and Anne felt fear run down her spine. Could she have followed Geraldine to God-knows-where? Surely she wouldn't go too far without telling someone.

"How long ago?" Anne asked, but she didn't wait for an answer. She didn't want to waste another minute. Pushing open the front door of the Refuge, she burst into the sunlight. Its brightness bouncing off the glass windowpanes was almost blinding.

She stood for a moment blinking, trying to decide which direction to go. There was no guarantee that either would be the right one.

Glancing down the street, her heart stopped. Was that . . . ? Relief washed over her as she realized that the person leaning against the building was Sister Mary Helen. There was no mistaking that short stocky frame, the close-cropped gray hair, and the Aran sweater.

But what was wrong? Why wasn't she moving? Why was she just leaning against the building? Without another thought, Sister Anne half-walked, half-ran down the block. "Are you all right?" she called when she was close enough to be sure that the old nun heard her.

Mary Helen stared at her blankly from a face pinched with pain.

"What is it? What happened?" Anne's own heart pounded. "Are you all right?"

Mary Helen nodded. Her hazel eyes flooded with tears. "It's Tim Moran," she said. "He's . . ." She stopped, struggling for breath.

In the distance Anne heard the wail of the police siren. Mary Helen didn't need to explain any further.

❧❧❧

His adrenaline still pumping, he circled the block—once, twice, wondering whether anyone would walk into the tattoo parlor.

Chances were pretty good that Tim Moran could lie there for hours, even overnight, before anyone stumbled on him.

Tim had been the toughest of the lot, he thought, his palm still slippery with perspiration. Hell, they'd known each other for years. Although he had to admit that it was getting easier. Funny how anything, even homicide, gets easier with practice. He had walked up on Tim who was clearing his things out of the office. He had kept his hand in his windbreaker pocket. He wasn't even sure if Tim realized he had a gun in it.

For a minute Tim had even looked happy to see him. Undercover work can get lonely. When his eyes had fastened on the gun, when he realized it had a silencer, a look of understanding had come into them.

"You!" Tim had said, not so much in fear as in disbelief. "You!" he had repeated and started to laugh. "Of course, it had to be you. Who else could get hold of the surveillance log?"

Poor Tim really never knew what hit him. He had hurried from the office leaving the crumpled body on the linoleum. Somehow, he knew he'd never forget the sound of that dry, humorless laugh. But wasn't there something about, "He who laughs last, laughs best"? For sure, he'd have the final laugh.

He was just about to congratulate himself on the job well done, when he saw the old nun approaching the building. Damn it! He hit the butt of his hand against his steering wheel. The bitch turned in!

He couldn't wait around to see what happened. He felt his whole body grow sweaty. He needed to be the hell out of the area. Where would he go? Back to work? Sure. Why not be where lots of people could see him? As soon as he'd stopped shaking, he'd head back to work. His absence would be easy to explain if anyone bothered to ask him where he had been—which he doubted they would.

The whole thing was picking up speed. A couple of weeks ago he was just a guy doing a little work on the side, making a couple of extra bucks. Hell, he needed it for alimony and child support. Now he was damn near a serial killer. *Did three homicides make a serial killer?* he wondered. He'd be afraid to ask anyone.

These days he hated to pick up his telephone for fear that that familiar voice would be on the other end of the line asking, "What about our cover? Is it secure?"

Hell, the department wasn't stupid. Someone would start putting two and two together soon.

Maybe he'd be just as glad when it was all over. A pain shot through his chest. What would his family say if this ever came out? Thank God his father was dead and his ex-wife and kids had moved to Oregon. Maybe the story wouldn't hit the papers in Oregon. He could see the look in his mother's eyes.

He'd tried to shake off the feeling of impending doom. Maybe he'd get lucky and after a few weeks the whole thing would go into a dead file somewhere with all the other unsolved homicides.

He stopped at the red light and watched the pedestrians cross Bryant Street. Was it his imagination or were they all staring at him through the windshield? Their eyes almost burning him with their intensity. *I had to do it,* he wanted to shout at them. He covered his face so they couldn't see him. *I had to do it.* His head throbbed and his throat tightened until he felt as if he might choke. *If anyone had found out it would have ruined my life.* Why didn't Sarah understand that?

How much more of this can I take? he wondered, his body soaking wet. If she didn't stop looking at him, everywhere he turned, he would surely go crazy.

❦❦❦

Inspectors Dennis Gallagher and Kate Murphy were quieter than usual on the drive from Colma to downtown San Francisco. Although neither mentioned the missing surveillance log or what it could mean, Kate guessed that both of them were thinking about it. One look at Gallagher's grim profile and granite jaw left no doubt in her mind that she had guessed correctly.

For her part the speculation was making her a little sick to her stomach. Stumbling on a crooked cop was the last thing she wanted to do, although she would forge ahead if it meant solving Sarah Spencer's murder. In the entire history of the San Francisco Police Department only one officer's homicide had gone unsolved. She surely didn't want Sarah's to be the second.

When they drove up in front of the New You Tattoo Parlor on Eighth Street, Kate was surprised to see two black-and-whites parked in front.

"What the hell?" she heard her partner mutter as he jumped out of the car.

"Hi, Inspector," a young patrolman, his face solemn, opened her door. "Looks like we got another homicide," he said, slapping it shut.

"Another homicide, Officer . . . ?" Kate knew the face but waited for him to supply his name.

"O'Reilly," he said, "John O'Reilly."

"Another homicide?" she repeated. Her scalp prickling, she hesitated, reluctant to ask him if the body had been identified for fear of the answer she was sure would come.

"Yes, ma'am," he said, nodding his head. "My partner is in there securing the scene and I was just about to call it in." He gave a curious smile. "How did you manage to get here so soon?"

"Coincidence," Gallagher said, coming around the car. "Who was it called you, Officer?" he asked.

Smiling, O'Reilly pointed toward the wall. "That old nun," he said, a note of sympathy in his voice. "Poor lady is really shook up."

"Yeah, right," Kate heard Gallagher grumble. From his tone of voice, she knew without looking that the old nun must be Sister Mary Helen.

"Don't waste too much sympathy on that old bird," Gallagher mumbled walking toward the entrance. "She's as tough as they come."

Officer O'Reilly looked shocked but prudently said nothing.

Kate followed her partner, but not before she noticed that Sister Anne was standing beside Mary Helen. *One isn't bad enough*, she thought, entering the brightly lit tattoo parlor, *there has to be two of them*.

Cautiously Gallagher and she made their way to the back room. Even as they approached the door the odor was sickening. Kate, her stomach jumping, tried to hold her breath until she was able to pull a handkerchief from her pocket and cover her nose.

They stopped at the doorway where O'Reilly's partner had strung the yellow tape. Looking inside at the blood-covered linoleum, Kate felt lightheaded, as though the room was moving around her. She leaned against the doorjamb to keep her balance.

Beside her she heard Gallagher swearing softly. "Have you ever seen so goddamn much blood?" he asked.

Kate did not trust herself to do anything but shake her head. Once she was sure she was steady, she followed her partner into the room. Just as she had feared, the crumpled body of Officer Tim Moran lay on the floor, one arm stretched out as though he were reaching for something.

Careful not to step in any of the blood, she trailed Gallagher, the two of them staying as close to the wall as possible.

Gallagher pointed to a footprint in the blood. "Maybe we got lucky," he said.

"Maybe," Kate agreed looking closer at the print. The small size, the flat heel, the plain sole looked suspiciously as if it might belong to one of the nuns standing outside. For the present Kate thought it more prudent to keep this opinion to herself.

"No shell casing," Gallagher said, "at least, that I can see."

He pointed to some scrawl, on a small relatively clean spot of linoleum. "What's that?" he said. "Looks like the poor guy reached up and tried to draw something."

"In his own blood?" Kate asked weakly.

"What does it look like to you?" Gallagher asked.

Kate squinted and studied the scrawl. "I'd say it looks like an "L" with a long foot, the number "1" or an "I," a small case "D," and an upside down "Y." Lidy? Who or what is lidy? Or maybe the "Y" isn't a "Y." Maybe it's the beginning of a stick figure. Lid fellow? Lid man?"

"We'll have forensics take pictures of that from every angle," Gallagher said. "If the guy spent his last moments on earth doing it, it's got to be important."

Kate agreed and was glad to hear the forensic team and the coroner arriving. She wasn't sure how much longer she'd be able to stay in the room with Moran. It was bad enough when you didn't know the victim. But when you did . . . She pushed past Officer O'Reilly and out onto Eighth Street.

Blinking, she was surprised to see that the street was bathed in sunshine. Somehow in the blood-spattered, foul-smelling room she hadn't remembered that the sun was shining.

Cars slowed as they passed the tattoo parlor, their drivers curious about the police vehicles and all the commotion. Angry horns and screeching brakes added to the confusion.

"You-hoo, Kate." She heard the familiar voice of Sister Mary Helen. Speaking of confusion, she thought. Kate had nearly forgotten about the two nuns leaning against the building. Now there was only one.

"What happened to Sister Anne? she asked.

"She went back to the Refuge," she explained. "It isn't wise for both of us to be outside."

Now you start being wise, Kate thought. "I suppose you stayed and she went because you are the one who discovered the body?" she asked.

Mary Helen brightened. "Exactly right. I came down to see Officer Moran."

"And what was it that you wanted to see him about?"

To Kate's surprise, the old nun hesitated. She noticed that Mary Helen seemed to be struggling with her answer. That wasn't like her at all. Obviously, whatever she was about to say was difficult for her.

"Would you like to sit down somewhere?" Kate asked. "You must be getting tired standing."

"That would be nice," Mary Helen looked relieved. "These old legs are beginning to feel numb."

The two women slipped into the front seat of the unmarked police car. "Much better," Mary Helen said rubbing her thighs. "Much better, indeed." Again she paused as though she were struggling with how to tell Kate what was on her mind.

"This is very difficult for me to say," Mary Helen admitted at last, "but I learned long ago that the best way to tell someone something difficult is quickly."

Where in the world is she going with this? Kate's scalp was beginning to prickle again.

Resolutely pushing her bifocals up the bridge of her nose, Mary Helen's hazel eyes leveled at Kate's face. "Some women at the Refuge have hinted that the police know about a house of prostitution in the area but that they do not shut it down." She took another breath and plunged ahead. "And that Junior Johnson's death is somehow involved. It is as if the women believe that the police are responsible for his murder." By now Mary Helen's eyes were wide with indignation. "Imagine!"

Kate couldn't believe that the old nun had named her own fear.

"So I was coming down to talk to Officer Moran about it," Mary Helen said. "If there is any truth in what they are saying, as an undercover policeman he should know. And if it is true, then, again as an undercover policeman, he should put a stop to it. There you have it." Looking relieved, she turned to Kate and waited for her to speak.

The image of Tim Moran's blood-soaked body flashed through Kate's mind. Her mouth felt furry and, all at once, she was at a loss for words. In the silence, the roar of the commuter traffic seemed louder; the blare of car horns more strident; Mary Helen's frank stare more piercing. It couldn't be one of us, Kate thought. She felt sick. Mind reeling, she was relieved to hear the front door of the tattoo parlor swing open and to see Dennis Gallagher emerge from the building. She would leave the whole thing to him.

❧❧❧

Gallagher, too, was blinded as he came out of the storefront into the sunlight. His bald crown was shining with perspiration and his tie hung like a noose down his shirt front where he had been tugging at it.

Kate held her breath waiting for the explosion when he saw Sister Mary Helen. To her amazement, none came. In fact, he acted as if he scarcely noticed the old nun. His blue eyes were watery and distracted. At this moment he looked every bit his age.

Mary Helen must have expected a barrage from the Inspector, too, because at the sight of him Kate noticed the old nun's back stiffen and her chin jut forward.

Gallagher came over to the car and leaned in. "Why don't you go back to your place, Sister?" He sounded as if his mind was far away. "I take it from what the patrolman says that you discovered the body."

"Yes, Inspector," Mary Helen looked as though she was about to say more, but he cut her off.

Opening the car door, he offered her a hand that she reluctantly took. "If we need you, we know where to find you," he said climbing into the seat she'd vacated. "Kate, you drive."

Quickly Kate pulled away from the curb leaving a tired and confused looking Sister Mary Helen standing on the sidewalk. She looked so forlorn that Kate almost felt sorry for her. Almost.

"What was that all about?" she asked. "But first, where to?"

"Back to the Hall," Gallagher said. "And what was what all about?"

"Under ordinary circumstances, you'd have a fit when you finally had a chance to talk to Sister Mary Helen."

"These aren't ordinary circumstances," Gallagher said grimly. Kate sensed the fury he was struggling to control. "Another police officer has just been brutally murdered and my gut tells me that something more than a coincidence is involved here.

"Too many unanswered questions," he said. "I got a real bad feeling about this one, Katie-girl." He drummed his fingers on the dashboard. "Real bad."

Still reeling from Mary Helen's revelation, Kate stopped for a red light on Brannon Street, and turned toward her partner. She shared his uneasiness. "What do you think?" she asked, not sure she wanted to know.

"First of all, it looks like the same person killed all three victims."

As much as Kate would have liked to blame Junior's death on an isolated dispute between drug dealers or pimps, she, too, felt certain there was a connection with the deaths of the two police officers. The three homicides were too similar. Each was killed by a single bullet—her stomach knotted as the image of Tim Moran lying in a pool of his own blood flashed through her mind; she took a deep breath wondering how long the scene would haunt her—and no shell casings were left at any of the scenes. Their perp was a very careful killer. He—or she, Kate thought. It could have been a she. No real strength was needed to shoot a person in the head, only good aim.

Kate pulled into the parking lot of the Hall of Justice and

turned off the ignition. "Did Mary Helen tell you why she happened to stumble on the body?" Gallagher asked.

Cracking the car window to let in a little air, Kate faced her partner. "Her story is that she came to see Tim Moran to clarify some very unsettling rumors that she had heard from the women who drop in to the Refuge."

Gallagher waited.

"The women are saying that the Department is somehow involved in a cover-up of a house of prostitution."

"Even if the cover-up means murdering one of our own?"

Kate nodded.

Tension filled the car like heavy air as the partners stared at one another. Softly Gallagher began to swear. For some inexplicable reason, it made Kate feel better.

"What now?" she asked when she was sure he'd said his final "damn."

"First," he opened the car door, "we need to find out who's going to notify Moran's next-of-kin," he said.

Ever practical, Kate thought. "I think he's divorced," she said, following him across the parking lot. "That will be in his personnel file, which Lieutenant Donaldson should have."

"Which will lead us to our next move. Lieutenant Donaldson. There are some unanswered questions we need to ask that guy about."

"And what if the old Pits decides he doesn't want to answer our questions?" Kate had a sinking feeling.

"He'll answer, all right. Mark my words, Katie-girl, he'll answer," Gallagher said with a fierceness she had rarely heard before.

❧❧❧

Slowly Sister Mary Helen made her way down the block toward the Refuge. She was scarcely aware of the police officers busy about the crime scene or the cars streaming along Eighth Street on their way to the freeway, or even the people pushing past her on the sidewalk. It was as if she were sleepwalking. Could she really have stumbled on the gruesome scene at the tattoo parlor or was it all nothing more than a bad dream? Would she wake up soon, cozy and safe in her own bed?

In a fog, she pushed open the door of the Refuge and was surprised to find the place empty. She checked her wristwatch. Of course it was empty! It was nearly four o'clock—way past time for everyone to have gone in search of a night shelter.

"Where have you been?" Anne asked, stepping out of the sleep room. Her voice was as close to a whine as Mary Helen could stand. "I was just about to go after you," she said, her forehead wrinkled in a worried frown.

"No need," Mary Helen said, trying to sound nonchalant, but not so nonchalant as to be insulting, "I was with the police. I couldn't have been safer."

"Police?" Anne's voice rose an octave. After studying Mary Helen's face, she pulled out a chair. "You look exhausted," she said. "Sit down." Her own worry apparently forgotten, she said, "Now tell me what happened. Were you with Inspector Gallagher and was he terribly upset?" Mary Helen noticed the color drain from Anne's face while she waited for the answer.

Poor child is terrified of Gallagher's bark, Mary Helen thought, while she herself much preferred it to the cold, unspoken fury she had just witnessed in his demeanor.

"The Inspector isn't upset with us," she said, reaching over and patting Anne's cold hand. "Understandably, he is very upset about Officer Moran's murder."

Although Mary Helen hadn't thought it possible, she noticed that the young nun's face became even paler. In fact, to recoin an old phrase, she looked like death warmed over.

"Murder!" Anne's voice was so soft that Mary Helen scarcely heard the word. "Was he shot like Junior Johnson?" Anne shivered and for a moment, Mary Helen was afraid that she might get sick all over again.

"He was shot like Junior," she said. "One bullet to his head. That part is the same." She stopped. Best not to go into any more detail. "One thing, however, was very different," Mary Helen said. Anne seemed genuinely relieved to get onto another subject.

"What was that?" she asked, some color returning to her face.

"Officer Moran managed . . ." Mary Helen hesitated. How could she tell Anne about the scrawl without mentioning the bloody floor? Very carefully, she decided. Measuring her words, Mary Helen began. "He managed," she repeated, "to write down some letters or symbols—I'm not sure which—before he died."

"On a paper?" Anne asked.

"No, on the floor," Mary Helen said.

"On the floor?" Anne repeated sounding astonished.

Mary Helen nodded. "Above his head," she said. "It was as if he was conscious enough to reach out with his last bit of strength and try to tell us who his killer was."

Anne's eyes glistened with tears. "Good for him," she said, her words thick with admiration. "What did he write?" she asked anxiously.

Mary Helen sighed. "I'm not sure exactly," she said. "Please hand me a piece of paper so I can write down what I saw while it is still fresh in my mind. Maybe two of us can figure something out."

Slowly she traced the symbols as accurately as she could remember—the "d," the "I" or was it "1?" The upside down "T" or was it an "L" with a long leg? And finally, the stick figure. Extending the paper, she showed it to Anne who stared, but said nothing, only sucked in her breath.

"What do you think?" Mary Helen asked when she'd coped with all the silence she could handle.

Anne turned the paper upside down, then sideways. She

cocked her head. "I don't know," she said at last, "but it must be very important if he used his last bit of life to write it."

"I'm sure you're right about that," Mary Helen said.

Unexpectedly Anne looked up. "What did he write it with," she asked quietly, "a pencil? Doesn't it seem odd to you that he had a pencil handy?"

Staring over Anne's head at the clock on the far wall, Mary Helen pretended not to hear her question. Sometimes being a little deaf came in very, very handy.

"My, my," she fretted. "Look at the time. Dear me! We'd better get going on home before anyone starts to worry about us."

❧❧❧

Officer Mark Wong walked into the Hall of Justice a few minutes early for his shift. When he had finally arrived home after Sarah Spencer's funeral and his lunch with Susie Chan, as hard as he'd tried he hadn't been able to sleep. By all rights, he should be exhausted. Instead he was wired.

He couldn't get Susie's innocent story about Lieutenant Donaldson off his mind. Not that cops don't play practical jokes on other cops. They do. They almost have to in order to stay sane on the job. But why would old Pits ask her to call Moran and pretend she was from the Chinese restaurant? What was the joke? Maybe it was one of those things where you had to have been there.

Wong pushed the elevator button. Why did it sit wrong with him, he wondered. Donaldson was not the most congenial guy in the world, but he was a good cop. Why was his little gag making Wong so uneasy? Did it have something to do with Susie? He did not want to see her get into any hot water with the Chief. Maybe he was just being overprotective.

"Hold the door," Wong heard a familiar voice shout. Catching it just in time, he steadied it for the two homicide detectives who were hurrying across the entrance.

"Thanks," Inspector Dennis Gallagher said, his face like a thundercloud. Kate Murphy followed close on his heels.

"What's up, guys?" Wong asked as the elevator door slid shut behind them.

"We just found Tim Moran," Kate said, struggling to keep her voice steady. "Someone shot him."

For a minute Wong wasn't sure he had heard correctly. "Tim Moran?" he asked in disbelief.

When Kate nodded, Wong felt as though someone had sucked all the air from the elevator. He was stifling. "Where?" he asked, running his finger around his shirt collar.

"At the tattoo parlor on Eighth Street," she said.

The elevator door opened and Wong welcomed the rush of cold air.

"You okay?" Kate asked and he nodded.

"I just can't believe it. When did it happen?"

"We haven't got the coroner's report yet," Kate said, "but from what you told us it has to have happened between the time you and Brian saw him and early this afternoon, when an elderly nun who works in the homeless shelter a few buildings down found him."

"Does Lieutenant Donaldson know?" Wong asked, when he realized that Gallagher and Murphy were headed for the same Detail as he was.

"The way stuff gets around in this building, I'm sure he has been informed by now." Gallagher spoke for the first time. "I'll talk to Donaldson," he said to Kate.

When the three entered the Vice Squad room, Wong was grateful to find it nearly empty. He was in no frame of mind to do a lot of talking or even a little talking to a lot of people. To be honest, he felt sick to his stomach. He watched Gallagher head for Lieutenant Donaldson's office, thankful that he'd only have to deal with Kate.

Barely acknowledging the two or three officers who were getting ready to leave, Wong motioned Kate to take a seat in the far corner where they had the best chance of being left alone. "We need to talk," he said in a low voice.

"What's bothering you?" Kate asked.

Mark Wong could feel his face redden. He detested sounding like a gossip. *Why did I ever get into this?* he thought, shifting uneasily in the chair. "I don't know how much this has to do with anything," he said, wishing he could think of a way to eel out.

"I understand," Kate's candid blue eyes studied him. "Anything you offer could be helpful," she sighed, "and, God knows, we need all the help we can get."

For the first time since she had stepped into the elevator, Wong really looked at Kate Murphy. "Worn out," was the first word that popped into his mind. "Frustrated," was the second. And why not? Two police officers had been murdered and there were no solid leads.

Without further hesitation, he told her about Donaldson approaching Susie Chang and asking her to play a joke on Moran.

"Odd," Kate said. "Although it's not against the law to have a weird sense of humor."

"Poor Tim," Wong was having trouble getting enough air. "God, Kate, I wish Brian and I had taken him home or something."

Kate looked as if she was about to comment when her partner came out of Donaldson's office. Wong was relieved. He didn't want to hear how it wasn't his fault or that he'd done what anyone else would have done. Whether or not it was true, it didn't stop him from feeling like hell.

"He's gone," Gallagher said, leaving no doubt who "he" was.

"To notify the family?" Kate asked.

Gallagher nodded. "I guess. I just hung up from Lieutenant Sweeney. He says for us to go home, get a good night's sleep, and we'll go full speed ahead in the morning."

"Sounds like good advice," Kate said, closing her notebook.

From the tone of her voice, Wong suspected that she didn't believe it.

"It's been a long day," she said, as if she were trying to convince herself to go. "See you, Mark," she called, following Gallagher out the door.

Officer Mark Wong sat silently, trying to realize what had happened even if he could not yet figure out the why.

"Howdy, partner." Brian Dineen's deep voice filled the nearly empty room. "What's wrong?" he asked the moment he had a clear look at Wong's face.

"I'll tell you in the car," Wong said. "I hope we can make some sense of this mess, even if we don't do anything else all night."

❧❧❧

Contrary to Sister Mary Helen's fear, when she and Anne arrived at the convent no one at all seemed to be worried about them. In fact, the entire community was glued to the television set in the Sisters' Room.

"Another unsolved police murder," she heard the anchorman say in grave tones.

"What is this city coming to?" the young, blonde co-anchor lamented in a high, childlike voice.

"What, indeed?" Sister Therese said, echoing the blonde's sentiments. "What, indeed?"

Only old Donata noticed Anne and Mary Helen slip into the room. She winked at Mary Helen, but said nothing. Apparently the segment on Officer Moran's murder was just starting.

Sliding into a vacant chair near the door, Mary Helen closed her eyes and hoped fervently that no reference would be made to her discovering a body.

She may as well have hoped that the sun wouldn't rise. There was about as much chance.

"Although at this time the San Francisco Police Department is not commenting, we have learned from the reliable source that there has been another undercover police officer shot to death," the high voice proclaimed. "The officer's name is being withheld until his next-of-kin is notified."

The Sisters' Room was unnaturally still.

"We go now to Cindy Sasaki who is on the scene."

The quick intake of breath in the room, plus a couple of "Oh, no's" told Mary Helen that the camera must have switched to downtown San Francisco, somewhere near the Refuge. Reluctantly she opened her eyes.

Sure enough, the reporter, her collar pulled up around her ears, was standing right in front of the place. All eyes were on the television screen except the ones that were on her.

Cindy Sasaki, who up to this point Mary Helen had liked, confided conspiratorially, "Reliable sources tell us that late this afternoon, one of the nuns who ministers at a homeless shelter in the area discovered the body. We have been unable to contact her for comment. We have, however, spoken with several women who frequent the homeless shelter. One has agreed to talk with us."

With a satisfied smile, Cindy pushed the microphone toward a homeless woman. "Can you tell us what you saw or heard here this afternoon?" she asked. The woman turned and faced the camera. Mary Helen couldn't believe her eyes. Of all the women on all the streets in downtown San Francisco, the reporter had picked Crazy Alice.

Crazy Alice smiled wisely into the camera. Then she paused as if she were weighing her words. Cindy Sasaki waited anxiously, anticipating an in-depth assessment of the situation. "This afternoon?" she prompted.

Mary Helen shifted in her seat, wondering just what Alice would come out with.

Staring into space, Alice stiffened, then without warning, she turned her burning hazel eyes toward the camera. "Murder may pass unpunish'd for a time," she announced solemnly, "But tardy justice will o'ertake the crime." Wheeling on her heel, she disappeared quickly into the crowd.

For a few seconds, even Cindy Sasaki was speechless. "And we hope that she is right," she finally managed. "Now back to you in our studio."

"Dryden," Sister Therese said in a stage whisper.

"What's dry?" Donata asked.

"Dryden. That's a quote from John Dryden," Therese said distinctly.

I hope the murderer knows that, Mary Helen thought, a strange fear creeping over her. Poor Alice may have sounded too knowledgeable for her own good. From what she said, the killer might surmise that she knows who he is. Or who she is—it could be a she, she reminded herself. On the other hand, what were the chances of someone killing another human being then sitting down to watch the six o'clock news?

Suddenly she was aware of a strange silence in the room. Glancing furtively around, she realized that she had become the center of attention.

"Well?" Old Donata asked.

"Well, what?" Mary Helen stalled, although she was perfectly sure she knew what they wanted.

"Tell us what happened." Old Donata left nothing to chance.

After taking some deep breaths, Mary Helen told the Sisters that, quite by accident, she had discovered Officer Moran's body in the tattoo parlor. Noticing a few faces pale, she decided to leave out as much as possible about finding him in the ragged-edged, sticky pool of blood on the linoleum floor.

"He did manage before he died to draw some lines—lines that looked as though he was trying to print letters," she said, deliberately omitting the *with what*. The grimaces on some faces let her know that they had guessed.

"What word did the letters spell?" Ursula asked.

"Unfortunately, they didn't spell anything," she admitted. "At least nothing I could figure out."

"Draw them for us," old Donata demanded. "Maybe one of us can."

Obligingly Mary Helen wrote down on a piece of scratch paper what she'd seen. *Wouldn't Inspector Gallagher have a fit if he knew what we were doing*, she thought, watching the paper go around the room.

"It has to mean something," Therese said, turning the paper every which way. And they all agreed, although no one could come up with exactly what.

Mary Helen noticed that Sister Patricia, the college president, didn't even try. "What I'd suggest," she said sitting up stiffly, "is that you two close down that place for a couple of days and we let the police do their work. It seems dangerous to me for you to go back down there until the killer is caught."

"Dangerous?" Anne protested, a little starch in her voice. "What makes you think that we are in any danger?"

"Really, Anne," Patricia's blue eyes sparked. "Officer Moran finds Officer Spencer's body, then he is killed. Sister Mary Helen finds Officer Moran's body, not to mention the both of you finding that criminal's body. And then . . ." she let the sentence trail off.

"That doesn't necessarily follow," Anne said, not giving an inch, Mary Helen noticed.

"Right," Patricia conceded, "but doesn't it makes sense not to take the chance?"

"Not that sense has ever been your strong suit," Therese snapped.

Mary Helen felt her blood pressure rising at the same time as she felt old Donata's hand on her arm. Obviously, Donata had missed most of the exchange. Lucky for her, Mary Helen thought, leaning toward her to hear what she was saying.

"I found the reference for "topsy-turvy" today," Donata said, her eyes twinkling. "On the Web."

With all the goings-on, Mary Helen had completely forgotten about Donata's research project.

"It's from "top" plus the obsolete "terven" meaning in Middle English to overturn. Usually means upside down, in a state of disorder or confusion." That said, she closed her eyes and, to those who didn't know better, she seemed to be taking a cat nap.

"What do you think, Mary Helen?" Patricia asked.

It took Mary Helen several seconds to realize that they were still discussing closing the Refuge for a few days. In fact, both Patricia and Anne had managed to dig in their heels and the room was quickly dividing. She was being called on to be the voice of reason. Each one, of course, thinking reason was on her side.

"For safety's sake," Patricia repeated, making her point.

"We are not in any real danger," Anne countered, just as persistently.

Mary Helen cleared her throat. All eyes were on her. *Lord, how did I get in this mess?* she wondered. *And more to the point, how will I get out of it?* "I think," she said slowly without looking at either Patricia or Anne, "the decision whether or not to close the Refuge is Anne's. She is the director." She paused. "However, Patricia has a valid concern. We may well be in danger. But danger or no danger, in my opinion, after this week we both could use a break." She smiled and waited.

"You're right about that," Anne agreed quickly. Too quickly, to Mary Helen's way of thinking. Maybe she was frightened and just didn't want to admit it. *She has every reason to be*, Mary Helen thought, watching the relief wash over Patricia's face.

Without any further discussion, the decision was made for the whole community to sleep in later in morning. After all, a little rest would be good for them all.

Old Donata's eyes shot open. "Wise move, Mary Helen," she said.

"Dumb luck," Mary Helen said with a smile.

"A good combination," Donata conceded, handing her back the paper with Moran's scribbling on it. She flicked a crooked finger toward it. "Now, let's see what you can do with this."

This, Mary Helen thought, examining the paper, is going to take more than luck or wisdom. Even if she were lucky enough to figure out what Moran was trying to say, it would take the wisdom of Solomon in all his glory to figure out the why.

❧⟡❧

Inspector Kate Murphy scarcely noticed the traffic as she drove from the Hall of Justice to her home in outer Richmond. She was so preoccupied that had anyone asked her whether or not the fog had rolled in, she wouldn't have known.

In fact, it had not, which was unusual for a June day in San Francisco. But, all-around, today had been an unusual day!

Pulling up in front of her yellow peaked-roof house, she was glad to see her husband's car already parked in front. Jack was home and with any luck at all, he had started dinner. Or at least, he had figured out the menu. She was too exhausted to even think about what to fix.

Kate checked the front window looking for her son John's round eager face. He was usually there waiting and watching for her to come home. Tonight, oddly, the window was empty. Suddenly a strange, sinking feeling filled her—almost like panic.

Was it her turn to pick him up? Had she been so involved with this homicide that she had forgotten her own child?

"Jack," she called as soon as she pushed open the front door. "Did you pick up the baby from Sheila's?" She tried to keep her anxiety out of her voice.

"Relax, hon," Jack walked toward her wiping his hands on a dishtowel. "He's at my mother's. Remember?"

Kate felt as though the breath has been knocked out of her. Of course! How could she have forgotten? Her mother-in-law had taken him home last night because of the funeral. "Are we supposed to pick him up?" She noticed that she smelled nothing cooking. Perhaps Loretta wanted them for dinner. Kate sighed, wondering if she'd be able to stay awake through the whole meal.

Jack shook his head. "I just talked to the two of them. It seems that they are having such a good time, that my mother asked if John could spend another night."

"And how did he sound?" Kate asked, afraid he might be homesick.

"Like any kid his age would sound in a never-ending paradise of ice cream and candy and cookies with Disney videos at your fingertips and a grandmother who thinks you can do no wrong."

"Sounds good to me," Kate said, hanging her coat in the hall closet and putting her revolver on the top shelf. "Do you think we should go over, too? I could use a little TLC."

"Somehow," Jack said, "I don't think it would be the same. Besides"—he led her into the living room—"I set up a cozy spot in here for us."

"Yes, you have," she said sitting on the overstuffed couch. The lights were dim. Music played softly in the background and a fire in the fireplace was doing its best to warm the room. He must have raced around like crazy when he got home from work, Kate thought, impressed with the array of chips and dips and nibbles that he had managed to assemble on the coffee table.

He had just handed Kate a drink when a sharp jab at the doorbell startled her. "Are we expecting anyone?" she asked.

"Just the pizza delivery man with a double cheese vegetarian," he said, going to the door.

The very thought of strings of warm melted cheese wrapped around tangy onions and tomatoes and biting into the crisp crust made Kate realize how long it had been since she had eaten.

They were both on their second piece of pizza and Jack had just poured another cold beer before either of them spoke. Leaning her head back against the sofa, Kate sighed. "Sitting here like this with you," she said, "it is hard to believe that so much awful stuff goes on out there." She bit her lip to keep it from trembling. "After today, I'd like to stay here in my little cocoon with you and John."

Jack reached over and squeezed her hand but said nothing.

She needed to talk. She knew he sensed it, but that he also knew she needed to do it on her own terms. All day long she had kept her emotions in a straitjacket. She had to let go.

"This case is driving me crazy," she said, knowing there was no need to explain which case. "I wish I'd checked on Moran this morning," she said.

Her husband looked at her quizzically. "What do you mean?"

"When I noticed that he wasn't at the funeral, I should have gone to the tattoo parlor and looked for him. I might have surprised his killer and saved his life."

Jack shook his head. "Geez, Kate, did you ever think you might have surprised the killer and he'd have killed you, too? That right now we might be looking for the killer of three cops instead of two?"

Kate looked doubtful. "Somehow they are all linked together in a way," she was thinking aloud. "And I'm not sure I want to find out how."

"You mean Sarah Spencer and Tim Moran?" Jack asked.

"Those two and Junior Johnson," she said. "I know there is a connection."

"What makes you so sure?"

"It's more a feeling, really," she said. "Even Gallagher admits he has a bad feeling about this one. And today Sister Mary Helen named it. For some reason, the homeless women at her center claim that the police are looking the other way when it comes to a certain brothel in the area."

"So why would Sarah Spencer be killed? Did she stumble on it?"

Slowly Kate nodded. "She must have. She was undercover, but she was young. Probably no one expected her to discover it."

"You mean she put her findings in her report and the wrong somebody read them?" Jack asked.

"According to Wong, her paperwork is missing," Kate said.

"So, where is it? Did Moran have it? How does he figure in?"

Kate shrugged. "I don't know. Was he involved? Did he kill her to cover up something? If so, who killed him?"

"I still don't see how Junior Johnson fits in," Jack said.

"Neither do I," Kate said, "except that he's a real brassy thug. I wouldn't put it past him to try putting the screws on whoever was using this brothel."

"Blackmail, you think?"

"Could be. And that could be what got him shot."

"But who shot Moran?"

Kate shrugged again. "I don't know," she said. "Someone who has enough at stake to kill three people, and two of them police officers."

"Let's see," Jack frowned. "It has to be someone whose life or career would be ruined if it were known that he or she is in the brothel business."

"If the brothel is what they're trying to cover up," Kate said.

"The mayor, the chief of police"—Jack was on a roll—"the archbishop."

"Now you're getting nuts." Kate reached for another slice of pizza. "Before he died, Moran scribbled on the linoleum. It means something."

Jack hesitated before he picked up the last piece. "Any ideas?" he asked.

"None whatsoever." Even she heard the frustration in her voice as she went to the hall closet and dug into her coat pocket. Pulling out the scrap of paper on which she had copied Tim Moran's markings, she sat down again beside her husband. "I thought if I looked at this enough, something might come clear," she said. "Like those puzzles where you stare and stare, and suddenly the young woman's face becomes a witch's head. Do you know what I mean?"

Jack nodded. "Sometimes with a puzzle, when you're not thinking about it, the solution comes to you," he said.

"You're right." Kate leaned her head against the sofa. She ached all over. Although she wasn't sure if a brain could ache, she thought hers did.

"You look exhausted," Jack said.

She nodded, too tired even to answer.

"Let me get you some dessert," he said, picking up the empty cardboard pizza box. "We have chocolate ice cream and cookies. How does that sound?"

"Delicious," Kate muttered.

When Jack returned with the two bowls, Kate had dozed off. Gently sitting beside her, he ate his ice cream and studied the scrap of paper that had fallen from her hand. *Poor guy*, Jack thought, turning the paper this way and that. It was Tim Moran's final attempt to finger his killer. He had literally used the last bit of his strength to write it. *Kate is right. It has to mean something*, Jack thought, *something significant, but what?* Despite Tim's dying effort, as hard as he tried, Jack could make no sense of it either.

❧❧❧

Twilight was darkening into night as Officers Mark Wong and Brian Dineen crisscrossed the nearly deserted streets of the Tenderloin. Ordinarily, the streets would be beginning to swell with pimps and pushers and prostitutes spilling out of the rundown buildings. But not tonight. Tonight the area looked like London after the Blitz.

"Hey, partner, what was it you were going to tell me?" Dineen asked as Wong slowly cruised the neighborhood.

Wong hesitated. Maybe it was best not to say anymore. Had he made a mistake by talking to Kate Murphy? He didn't know.

"What's the matter, Tiger?" Dineen asked, a slight edge in his voice. "You seemed pretty anxious to tell me back at the Hall."

"Nothing's the matter," Wong said, pulling over beside the curb and shifting into park. He turned to face Dineen. For the first time since they had started working together, Wong really looked at his partner. How much did he actually know about this enormous, redheaded man with bloodshot eyes? Only what Dineen told him about his family and his feelings. Nothing more.

Wong squirmed in his seat. Was he getting paranoid? If you couldn't trust your partner, then whom could you trust? "Nobody," was the obvious answer. With some hesitation, he told Dineen about Susie Chang making the phone call for Donaldson.

Feeling as though a boulder had been lifted from his chest, Wong once again pulled into the street. "What do you make of that?" he asked,

The big man was silent. "I don't know what to think," he said after a few tense seconds that seemed to Wong like

191

minutes. "I sure as hell hope that nobody from the force is involved in this."

Me, too, Wong thought silently.

"Are you thinking someone is?" Dineen asked, again with that edge in his voice.

"Like you said, I don't know what to think," Wong answered.

They rode for several blocks in silence.

"Where have all the flowers gone?" Dineen joked, pointing to a corner usually crowded with prostitutes parading their wares.

"The word must be out about Moran's death," Wong turned a corner. "The neighborhood is afraid of another sweep. Anyone who can be is off the streets. Or as far off as they can get." He pointed to a couple of makeshift cardboard shelters where homeless people had already crawled in and covered the entrances with old blankets.

"Can't blame them," Dineen said, craning his neck to see down an alley. Nobody. "Doesn't look like we'll have much business tonight," he said.

Grunting in agreement, Wong slowly cruised the empty streets. He was just about to suggest a coffee break when a scream pierced the darkness. Speeding up, Wong followed the sound to an alley behind a small convenience store. As they drove in, the alley suddenly became deadly quiet. The only sound was the eerie squeak of an air conditioner.

Wong flashed the spotlight into the blackness. Two rats scurried behind a dumpster. A heap of discarded clothes were scattered along one wall.

"See anybody?" Dineen asked.

Wong was about to say no, when the spotlight framed a small, middle-aged, white woman cowering against the wall. She was trembling and her face was the color of cement. Small dark eyes stared at them, unblinking.

"Are you all right, ma'am?" Dineen asked.

The women, breathing shallowly, did not answer.

"Ma'am, are you okay?" Wong repeated.

Her eyes bounced from one officer to the other. Slowly she nodded, looking as if she might bolt at the first chance she had.

"Was it you we heard screaming?" Wong asked, trying to move a little closer without frightening her.

She nodded again.

"Can you tell us your name?"

Still nodding, she whispered, "Alice. They call me Crazy Alice, but I'm not crazy."

"Yes, ma'am," Wong said. "What is your last name, Alice?" he asked, but she pressed her lips together.

"Why were you screaming, Alice?" Dineen asked. "Was someone hurting you?"

With eyes wild, Alice searched the alley. "I saw him," she said breathlessly. "He's after me. He's going to shoot me, too." Without warning, her voice changed to a childlike singsong *"Fe, fi, fo, fum! I smell the blood of a police a-man,"* she giggled. *"Be he alive or be him dead, he'll grind my bones to make his bread."*

Dineen glanced over the woman's head at Wong. He mouthed, "5150."

Alice must have sensed that they were thinking of taking her to the mental ward. She began to tremble again. "Please take me home," she pleaded. "He can get me at the hospital."

"Who?" Dineen asked.

"Him! You know him." She was nearly hysterical.

"All right, Alice," Dineen said calmly. "We'll take you home. Just tell us where you live."

Although Alice wouldn't tell them, she agreed to show them the way. Once they had seen her safely inside a tenement, Dineen suggested their coffee break.

Wong readily agreed. Crazy Alice had given him the willies. "What about that *Fe, fi, fo fum* business?" he asked while they waited to be served.

"Like. *One flew east, one flew west, one flew over the cuckoo's nest*," Dineen joked.

It didn't strike Wong as funny. The woman was deadly afraid of someone she thought they knew. But who? And for what possible reason would he be after her?

Back in the car patrolling the near-empty streets, the questions plagued him while the answers continued to elude him. His partner didn't seem to be doing any better.

Wong was almost glad when a domestic violence call came in. At least it would get his mind off the homicides of his two fellow police officers. For the time being, anyway.

Little did he realize that Crazy Alice was watching them from her window, just in case.

❧❧

Sister Mary Helen shut off her bedroom light and stared into the blackness. A branch from a nearby tree rubbed against her window screen making a strange scraping sound. *A fitting end,* she thought, *to a very strange day.* What had started out as a day set aside to bury an undercover policewoman had ended up with her finding a second officer, also undercover, murdered. Both had died of a single bullet shot to the head—much too much of a coincidence to actually be one.

Again, the wind scraped the branch against the screen. Like the branch at the scene of Junior Johnson's murder—the branch covered with bits of his brain matter. She shuddered and she felt the goose bumps run up her arms. That sight alone would have been enough horror to last her a lifetime.

And Junior, too, had been killed by a single shot. Sarah—Junior—Tim. Again, too much of a coincidence. Three people dead. What was the single thread that joined them? There had to be one.

She turned on her side, fluffed her pillow, and closed her eyes.

Her whole body felt heavy. From somewhere down the hall, she heard the central heating click off. Soon the temperature would drop. Time to go to sleep before her feet got cold.

She knew from years of experience that this staying awake fretting business, rolling the questions over and over in her mind, wouldn't do anything but make her feel punchy tomorrow. But she couldn't seem to help it. What were the chances of stumbling across Sarah Spencer right after she had been shot and hearing her final word? Or discovering the body of Junior Johnson? Or walking into the tattoo parlor only to discover the body of Tim Moran and find his bloody scribble on the floor? Things like that didn't happen without a reason, she knew.

In her mind's eye, she saw those scratches again. *Imagine the heroic effort it must have taken the man to draw them.* She was certain that they had to be the key to solving his murder.

A small D, a 1 or an I, something that looked like a candle in a candle holder, a wobbly stick figure or maybe an upside down Y.

She replayed all the possibilities she could think of—*dicandle stickman . . . stick deholder . . . man distick . . . dicandly?* No combination seemed to make any sense. She must be overlooking something or confusing something. Something obvious, she was certain.

At this moment, her whole world seemed in a state of confusion. *Topsy-turvy.* She smiled, thinking of how much old Donata had enjoyed looking up the etymology of that word for her, finding the answer. *One never got too old to enjoy finding an answer*, Mary Helen thought, and wondered crazily if that saying would make a good bumper sticker. It was true and surely as good as, "Old Age Is Not For Sissies," which she had seen on somebody's car.

Topsy-turvy. Everything was upside down. She couldn't argue with that. Police officers were being shot; the refugees were blaming the police for committing crimes; a small-time crook had been murdered in the same way as those trying to catch him.

Now Anne and she were going to shut down the Refuge for a few days because of the danger. In a perfect world, if there were danger, they would open additional space to keep the women safe. But you didn't need to look very far to know that this was not a perfect world and it should come as no surprise. The fact was that it hadn't been since Adam and Eve were escorted out of the Garden of Paradise and their son Cain killed his brother Abel.

It had been imperfect when Norbert, today's Saint, if she remembered correctly, had helped reform the Church of the Middle Ages. And, she guessed that it probably wouldn't be perfect until Gabriel blew his final horn.

Mary Helen took a deep breath and let it out slowly. In spite of it all, she thought, God continues to love us unconditionally. This realization always comforted her.

In the last analysis, she thought, her eyes beginning to burn, the best thing was to put the whole mess in God's hands. As some wise woman had once said, "He's going to be up all night anyway."

Thursday, June 7

❧❧❧

Ninth Week of Ordinary Time

hen Sister Mary Helen woke up, her bedroom was filled with light. Blinking at its brightness, she glanced at the clock on her nightstand. The large illuminated numbers read 9:00. She couldn't believe that she had slept so long. How, in heaven's name, had she managed to miss the garbage truck making its noisy rounds, as well as all the other Sisters taking their morning showers?

Despite sleeping so soundly, her body felt heavy and her eyes burned. She wondered what time she had finally fallen asleep. After midnight, she had not checked the clock on the assumption that what you don't know won't hurt you.

She closed her eyes again as the ache of the last few days rushed in and she wondered for a moment, if she'd ever be able to reopen them—ever be able to get up and face today. *A good strong cup of coffee and a hot shower and I'll be better*, she thought, willing herself to try to put one foot on the floor.

She had not yet succeeded when she heard a light tap on her bedroom door. *Who in the world?* she thought, clearing her throat. Should she pretend to be asleep and hope whoever it was would go away?

She was still trying to decide when her visitor tapped again and cracked open the door. "Sister Mary Helen?" a voice whispered.

It was Anne. Mary Helen could smell the rich, eye-opening aroma of the cup of French roast coffee she was carrying. "Come in," she said, sitting up in bed. "What's the matter?"

"Nothing," Anne said sheepishly.

Then what possessed you to knock on my door? Mary Helen wanted to say but bit back the words.

"I just wanted to let you know that I am on my way to the Refuge. I'll put a notice on the front door for the ladies saying we'll be closed until Monday." Anne placed the steaming cup on Mary Helen's nightstand. "It shouldn't take me long."

"Do you want me to go with you?" Mary Helen asked.

Without a second's hesitation, Anne said, "No," and closed the door softly behind her.

Finally awake now, Mary Helen reached for her cup of coffee. Next to it were her bifocals. She slipped them on, then reached, once again, for the slip of paper on which she had copied Tim Moran's scribbles.

She placed the paper on her lap and studied it hoping that it would somehow make more sense this morning. *Topsy-turvy*, she had thought last night. Everything was upside down. She took a deep breath, then a sip of hot coffee.

She closed her eyes. Maybe this was upside down, too! Was that the answer? Was it that simple? Had she been too tired or too upset to see it?

Bolting from her bed, she sat at her desk. Ignoring her cold feet, she copied the letters, deliberately turning each one upside down. "P," she wrote. "I." Upside down, the candlestick became a "T" and the wobbly stick figure a "Y." PITY! The word she had written was "pity"!

Her heart beat suffocatingly against her ribs. That was the word Sarah Spencer had whispered with her last breath. Mary Helen had thought it was her prayer. But would two police officers have chosen that same word with their dying breath? Hardly! Her pulse was racing. That was too much of a coincidence. There was some meaning to the word. Some meaning that both of them knew and of which she had no clue. The realization crept in like the chill. *But somebody might*, she thought, shaking it off.

Quickly slipping into her bathrobe and slippers, she hurried down the deserted convent hall to the telephone and dialed. This was a job for her friend Kate Murphy. If anyone would know, Kate would.

Mary Helen waited, anxiously counting the rings until someone finally answered. Her heart sank when the Detail secretary told her that both Inspectors Murphy and Gallagher were out in the field and that she had no idea when either of them would be back.

❧❧❧

The first thing Sister Anne saw when she turned onto Eighth Street was a small crowd of women waiting at the front door of the Refuge. Miss Bobbie, who seemed to be serving as a lookout of sorts, was perched on the curb. Peering down the busy street, she pointed the moment the convent car came into her view. "Here she come!" she hollered.

Shouts of "Where you be?" and "You be late!" and " 'Bout time, girl!" greeted Anne as she parked the car, then made her way to the front door.

Even though a weak sun was already shining, the women huddled together, looking cold. With a twinge of guilt, Anne wondered if she should open the Refuge just long enough to serve them some hot coffee.

But how would I ever get them to leave? she thought, standing in the midst of the group.

"Why you be closed?" Peanuts was the first to grasp the situation.

"They not be closed," Venus's dark eyes shifted accusingly to Anne. "She be running late!"

Anne hesitated.

"What the matter?" Miss Bobbie asked suspiciously. "The police already down the block." The scar along her right eye twitched as she nodded toward the New You Tattoo Parlor. "What really happening here?"

Anne had been so concerned with the women gathered in front of the Refuge that she hadn't even notice the activity further down the street. Sure enough, she spotted Inspector Gallagher in front of the storefront talking to the owner of the Chinese restaurant. Kate Murphy must be inside.

"I'm sorry, ladies," Anne raised her voice so that all could hear.

"Hush, girl!" Venus chided a noisy newcomer. "She be talking."

"I'm sorry," Anne repeated, "but we are going to be closed until Monday."

Someone groaned. "What for?" Peanuts demanded indignantly.

"To give things a chance to settle down," Anne said. Peanuts looked puzzled.

"There have been two murders on this block," Anne explained, trying not to sound defensive.

"There be murders all over down here," Sonia said.

Anne hesitated, wondering if Sonia thought that was supposed to make her feel better or worse.

"You hear about Crazy Alice?" Venus asked with a mean smile that showed her missing front tooth.

Anne suddenly felt hollow. *Oh, no*, she thought. *Don't tell me she's been murdered, too.*

"What 'bout her?" Miss Bobbie's eyes narrowed as they fastened on Venus. "You know something we don't know?"

"I seen her this morning," Venus raised her chin as though she were bracing for a fight. "That girl be real scared."

Peanuts laughed. "She usually be the one scare other people."

"You got that right," Venus said. "But this time she be scared. She say she be up all night watching him prowl around, afraid he might find her. Her eyes be all black around them." With her fingers, she circled her own eyes to make her point. "Yes, ma'am, and Crazy Alice be saying them rhymes, like she do, about some police man's be after her. Going to crush her bones."

"What policeman?" Anne asked. "Maybe the police officer was trying to help her."

Several women guffawed. "That'll be the day!" Miss Bobbie said. "You dream on, girl!"

"You be opening or not?" Peanuts demanded.

"Not," Anne said before she changed her mind. "Not until Monday."

Grudgingly the small crowd of women dispersed. Several looked back in case she changed her mind. When Anne was sure they had all gone, she unlocked the front door of the Refuge. Inside the darkened building, she made her way to her small office, shivering in the cold that seemed to seep from the walls. Quickly she looked through the desk drawers for a piece of typing paper and a felt tip to make her "Closed until Monday" sign.

The ragged ring of the telephone startled her. She was even more surprised when she picked up the receiver and heard Sister Mary Helen's voice. "Did you by any chance see Kate Murphy down there?" the old nun asked, a note of urgency in her words. "She may be at the tattoo parlor."

"Yes," Anne said, not liking the sound of this. "Why?"

Mary Helen ignored the question. Or to be charitable, Anne thought, perhaps she hadn't heard it.

"Is it possible for you to ask her to call me? Immediately," she added.

"If she's still there," Anne said, "but—"

"Thanks," Mary Helen said.

The dull hum of the dial tone was the only answer to Sister Anne's questions. Blinking at the receiver, she replaced it.

❧❧❧

Uh-oh! Here comes trouble, Kate Murphy thought, watching Sister Anne walk toward her on Eighth Street. Luckily there was only one of them today. She glanced over her shoulder, checking on Gallagher's whereabouts. Her partner was busy doing whatever he was doing. She guessed from the noises coming from the small office where Tim Moran's body was found as well as the frustrated expression she observed on his round, ruddy face when they passed, moments ago, in the entrance to the New You, that things were not going well. The Chinese restaurateur had probably not been much help. What he didn't need to complicate his life further were the nuns.

"Good morning, Kate," Sister Anne called.

Kate waved in reply. "What can I do for you?" she asked, fervently hoping that the answer was, "Nothing." Neither Gallagher nor she was in any mood to be polite. Some of yesterday's headlines suggested police incompetence. Others hinted at an alleged cop cover-up. Still others made innuendoes about corruption and possible scandals in the vice unit. These unfounded allegations, of course, were driving the Department to distraction.

The pressure was on to find the perp. Lieutenant Sweeney, their boss, had made this abundantly clear when they checked in this morning. They had no time to waste listening to the off-the-wall if well-intentioned theories of these two nuns.

When Sister Anne was close enough, Kate noticed an especially worried expression on her usually placid face. Her hazel eyes jumped about nervously, almost refusing to meet Kate's own.

What now? Kate thought. *They can't have found another body, can they?* She felt almost relieved when all Anne wanted was for her to call Sister Mary Helen at the convent. *That will only take a minute,* she thought. She should have known better.

Using her cell phone, Kate dialed Mount St. Francis Convent and was not surprised when the phone was picked up on the first ring.

"Kate?" Mary Helen asked without even a hello. "I have something to tell you, although I have no idea what it means," Mary Helen admitted.

When did that ever stop you? was on the tip of Kate's tongue, but she caught herself. Hearing the old nun swallow, she held her breath and listened as Mary Helen finally began to speak. With every word, Kate felt the tendrils of dread work their way up her spine. *It couldn't be,* she thought numbly, *or could it?* "Thank you," was all she could manage when the old nun finally finished.

Her face burned as they disconnected. *This is every cop's worst nightmare,* she thought, letting Sister Mary Helen's message sink in. She fervently hoped that Sister was wrong, but she had to find out. With a sense of doom, she went to find her partner. Maybe he would be able to poke some holes in the theory. Someone had to be able to. This couldn't be right.

Pulse racing, Kate found Gallagher and related her phone call from Sister Mary Helen. While she spoke, Gallagher's face might have been chiseled from stone. He seemed frozen, scarcely breathing. When she had finished, Kate waited.

All at once, his mouth twitched and he burst into a string of swear words that Kate had never heard him use in all the years they had been partners. She fought down an unreasonable urge to laugh, biting her lip to make sure she wouldn't.

"What are you waiting for, Katie girl?" he strained through clenched teeth. "Let's go get the son-of-a-b."

"Alleged son-of-a-b," Kate reminded him as he turned on the siren. The two of them sped toward the Hall of Justice.

❧❦❧

Officer Mark Wong had finished a quick snack and was preparing for bed when his telephone rang. He debated for a moment whether or not to pick it up. It had been a busy night and he was exhausted. Besides, it was probably some reporter trying to get a quote from somebody in the unit. They were as persistent as flies on fruit when they thought they were on to a juicy story about the Force. It was their job, he knew, and you really couldn't blame them, but right now he needed some sleep. He'd let the answering machine handle it. Then, if it were anyone he wanted to talk to, he'd call back.

Wong was surprised to hear a familiar voice. It took him a moment to recognize Lieutenant Donaldson, urging him to pick up if he was at home. What in the world did Donaldson want? *If it is overtime, forget it. I'm not here*, Wong thought yawning. Every muscle in his back ached.

It was the Lieutenant all right. Wong listened. He sounded funny—strained, at first, almost frenetic. Something that Wong couldn't put his finger on . . .

"I hear your girlfriend, Susie Chang, told you about our little joke," Donaldson said.

Wong bristled. He didn't like the mocking tone in Donaldson's voice when he said "girlfriend." It was almost as if he was accusing their relationship of being dirty.

"She got it all wrong," Donaldson laughed coarsely, "just like a dumb broad, huh?"

Wong could feel his muscles contract. Susie was no broad. And if she was, she surely wasn't a dumb one. Why was Donaldson so upset? Why was he being so insulting? Susie had only wondered what the joke was. Actually, he had, too. Neither of them had been able to see anything funny in sending a fellow cop on a wild goose chase. But everyone can't be expected to have the same sense of humor.

If Wong didn't know that Donaldson was a good cop and his boss, after all, he might have suspected that there were other motives—that Donaldson wanted Moran out of that tattoo parlor for some reason.

By any chance, he wondered, was that around the same time that Moran's office was ransacked? He'd heard about it from the other guys in the unit. Donaldson couldn't be involved in that. *He is a good cop*, Wong reminded himself again. Everybody said so. Not the most popular guy in the department, but a good cop.

"Call me when you get in, Wong. When you get in," Donaldson said, "and don't forget."

Wong turned the ringer on his telephone to off. Climbing into bed, he took several deep breaths trying to clear his mind. But the encounter Dineen and he had had with Alice tonight bothered him. Who did she think was after her? She indicated that it was a police officer, but the woman was crazy. What had Dineen said? *"One flew over the cuckoo's nest."* He was probably right. At least, Wong hoped so.

Carefully he placed a sleep mask over his eyes to keep out the light. He tried not to think. He didn't like what he was thinking—not at all. Maybe after a few hours sleep, this whole mess would look better. If not, at least he'd have the energy to face it.

His insides burned. He got up and popped a couple of Tums in his mouth. With luck, he'd doze off soon. As far as he was concerned, it couldn't be soon enough.

❧❧❧

Sarah's eyes haunted him the most—always those eyes. He should be at work by now but he couldn't seem to rid himself of her eyes. They followed him everywhere—watching him, accusing him, refusing to understand.

Now her eyes were somehow set in Moran's face. Moran, who had actually laughed when he pulled the gun from his windbreaker pocket. Moran's beard twitched when he laughed. That dry, mocking laugh echoed off the wall in his silent bedroom keeping him from sleeping. Even in the dark he saw her eyes and heard that laugh ringing in his ears.

Twisting and turning in his bed he couldn't get away from the staring eyes with their dreadful accusation and that derisive laugh. The sweat broke out on his forehead and ran down into his eyes. His hand trembled as he wiped his face.

They should thank him for killing Junior Johnson. He had rid the city of one more scumbag. They should give him a medal—hold a ceremony at City Hall. He was a hero. Moran's mocking laugh split through his thoughts. He covered his ears so he wouldn't hear it.

It wasn't fair. He was a good cop but he needed the money. That was what it was all about—the money. What with the alimony and the kids in college. And the pols paid well for their pleasures. All he had to do was to keep a lid on the thing. He had planned well, made sure no one stumbled on the brothel or blew the whistle on its patrons. No one had been the wiser. No one had been hurt until that stupid young broad had stumbled onto the truth.

Why didn't she know enough to leave it alone? He had done what he had to do to protect himself. Anyone could see that.

206

Now all his careful planning was tumbling like a house of cards. That big-name pol calling almost every day—worried about his damn reputation. Giving orders, taking no risks. What about me? he thought. And what about Spencer, Johnson, Moran? Now, Susie Chang was on to it. How stupid of him to trust another chick. And she had told her boyfriend Mark Wong. And that crazy woman he had seen interviewed on television. How much did she know?

His chest heaved and he was afraid his head would split. Too many to kill. Homicide was getting too close. He fought to catch his breath. His heart pounded. He couldn't live like this. He couldn't take a chance that he'd be caught. He couldn't let them put him in jail. Life in jail would be a living hell for a cop. And what would he tell his kids, his mother?

He couldn't go on like this. He could not take any more. He needed a rest. There was only one way he knew of to get it.

Suddenly calm, he pulled open his dresser drawer, cursing its squeak. He took out his revolver, the silencer still attached. The metal felt cool in his sweaty hand. Numbly he gripped it. Like a man in a stupor, he put the revolver into his mouth.

He tasted the bitter metal and felt the cold muzzle against the roof of his mouth. His knees begin to tremble. *Dear God,* he prayed, overwhelmed with his own agony, *dear God, take away my pain.* Closing his eyes for the final time, he squeezed the trigger.

❧❧❧

When Inspectors Kate Murphy and Dennis Gallagher arrived at the Hall of Justice, they discovered that Lieutenant Donaldson wasn't in nor had he called in sick.

"Maybe he's still at home," Kate said.

"We'd better check with Sweeney before we go any further," Gallagher suggested.

Kate agreed. No matter how they played this one, it was

bound to end up a sensitive case. You couldn't very well accuse a respected police lieutenant of murdering two of his fellow officers and maybe a known criminal on such flimsy evidence. All they had to go on really was Sister Mary Helen's discovery that both officers had chosen the word "pity," as their dying message. Plus the hunch that both victims were referring to the lieutenant.

As far as Kate and Gallagher were concerned, it made perfect sense—more sense than anything else so far.

Lieutenant Sweeney listened attentively as they told him about Sarah Spencer whispering "pity," and Moran scribbling the same word in his own blood.

"Too much of a coincidence," Sweeney agreed.

"The only thing that makes any sense," Kate said, nervously twisting a lock of her hair, "is that they both were trying to tell us who their killer was."

Sweeney nodded. "So far, I'm with you."

"And who do we know that both of them would refer to as 'pity'?" Gallagher asked. Obviously still angry, he stared at the lieutenant almost daring him to disagree.

Sweeney winced, his face turning the color of tomato soup. "You can't mean Donaldson!" he shouted. "You can't think that Donaldson killed those officers."

"I think it's worth investigating," Kate said softly.

"Again, how did you come to this conclusion?" Sweeney wasn't convinced.

"Actually, we didn't. Someone else pointed it out to us," Kate said, giving away as little as possible. She was afraid he might dismiss the whole thing if he knew who that someone was.

Sweeney's eyes bored into her, but he didn't ask for any more details. "Jeez, I don't know," he said, running his finger around his shirt collar as though he were being strangled. "We have no more evidence, really, than a hunch that it wasn't a coincidence."

"But if the hunch is correct?" Gallagher wasn't going to back down.

Kate knew he'd had a bad feeling about where this case would lead. At the moment, it couldn't get much worse. She watched him struggle to keep himself in control as Sweeney mulled over the facts, trying to make a decision.

"It can't hurt to talk to him," Kate said, afraid that Gallagher wouldn't last much longer.

Sweeney's eyes bounced nervously from Kate to Gallagher and back again. "Maybe I should go over to his office and sound him out."

"He's not in his office," Gallagher said, "we already checked. And he didn't call in sick."

Sweeney looked worried. He sat down behind his desk and tented his fingers, obviously trying to decide what was the best thing to do. Kate and Gallagher both knew better than to push. "You don't suppose something has happened to him, too?" he said at last.

"That's another possibility," Kate said, hoping it would get him to move.

"Maybe you better go to his house," Sweeney said as if it were his idea. Looking through his file, he wrote down Donaldson's home address. "Good luck," he said, handing them a slip of paper, "and keep me posted."

Within minutes, Kate and Gallagher were passing Mission Dolores, the oldest structure in the city. In its small cemetery were buried some of San Francisco's most noteworthy early settlers. Beside it the ornate basilica rose in striking contrast. Going south on Dolores, Kate kept a look out for Jersey Street. The neighborhood was made of a motley group of homes—Victorians, wood-shingled, stucco flats, and Edwardians. The fire of 1906 had destroyed the houses on one side of Dolores Street. As ever, Kate was fascinated by the pre-fire houses on the right and the post-fire houses on the left.

"Here it is," she said finally spotting Jersey. Turning right, they followed it. Turning right again they found Donaldson's address, a small flat on a short street on the shoulder of Twin Peaks. The sun bounced off the windows of the buildings as Gallagher parked the car. The neighborhood was so quiet that the slam of their car door echoed. No one was on the street. No dog barked. Kate didn't even see a window curtain flick. Where was everyone?

Mounting the steps, Gallagher rang the doorbell. The sound filled the silent house. "No answer," he said when he had rung it for the third time.

"What now?" Kate asked, knowing full well that Gallagher intended to get in. She just wondered how.

As he was preparing to put his shoulder to the problem, the front door of the downstairs flat swung open. A small, round woman clutching her sweater to her neck peeked out at them. "I didn't hear him leave," she whispered. "I haven't heard any noise since he dropped something. I hope he's all right."

"We hope so too, ma'am," Gallagher flashed his badge. "Have you any idea who might have an extra key?"

"I do, of course," she said crisply, "I'm his landlady."

As soon as Kate pushed the front door open, she smelled the unmistakable stench of death. Covering their noses and their mouths with clean handkerchiefs, the two inspectors moved down the hall following the odor. Kate stopped at the door of the bedroom. Gallagher pushed around her. Crumpled on the floor was a body. Bending down, Gallagher touched the shoulder then gently rolled it over.

"Jeez, Kate," he said when he had seen the face. "It's Donaldson, all right. And he's blown off the whole top of his head."

❧❧❧

Sister Mary Helen was very surprised to hear Inspector Kate Murphy's voice on the telephone. As a matter of fact, at first she didn't recognize it. Kate sounded almost as though she'd been sick or crying.

"What's wrong?" Mary Helen asked, concerned.

"I just wanted to let you know that your clue about the word was right on. 'Pity' led us to our perp."

"Imagine that," Mary Helen said, both amazed and delighted. "Can you tell me who it was, or is that confidential?"

Kate hesitated. "By tonight it will be on all the news stations," she said. "You might as well know. Our perp was one of our own, Lieutenant Don Donaldson."

Mary Helen's stomach fell. "Oh, no," she said. "I'm sorry." And she truly was. "Are you sure?"

"His nickname was 'Pity'—why is a long story. We went to his flat. He was the one. We're sure."

"Did he confess?" Mary Helen asked.

"In a way," Kate said gently. "He shot himself."

"Is he dead?" Mary Helen couldn't believe the turn of events.

"Very," Kate said. "But he left some surveillance logs in his flat. Ones he had lifted from Vice. And they indicated his motive."

Mary Helen listened anxiously while Kate explained. "He was taking money to cover up a brothel in your neighborhood. Lots of big names in town were patrons. Sarah Spencer stumbled on it. After her death, Tim Moran was suspicious and apparently, he uncovered the same things that Sarah had."

Mary Helen felt as if her breath had been knocked out. "And Junior Johnson? Did he kill Junior too?"

"Poor old Junior must have thought he could get in on the action." Kate said. "Our guess is that he realized that Donaldson was in on the cover-up and pressed him for a little money. A fatal mistake."

Kate paused. "Again, thanks," she said, "and we'll try to keep your name out of the paper."

Saddened, Mary Helen replaced the receiver. The women at

the Refuge had been right. The police were involved—at least one policeman.

The solemn tolling of the Angelus bell rang out over Mount St. Francis College—twelve o'clock. If she hurried, she'd be on time for the noon mass.

Before the day is over, I'll call Eileen, she thought, walking quickly across the campus. She'll be anxious to hear how things worked out. Recently Eileen had been suggesting that Mary Helen should come to Ireland for a little visit. Maybe she should.

Settling into a back pew of the chapel, Mary Helen rose as Father Adams entered the sanctuary and began the mass for Thursday of the Ninth Week of Ordinary Time.

This, she thought sadly, had been no ordinary Thursday and no ordinary week. After she realized that the word "pity" had some significance, everything had moved so quickly. The police officer had been responsible for the deaths of three people. Now the sad soul had committed suicide. She hated to admit that the women at the Refuge had been correct. Even at her age, although she knew better, she was still idealistic enough to hope that all policeman were honorable, all priests and nuns holy, and all parents loving. How many times did she have to remind herself that there were no perfect people?

Sitting with the congregation, the familiar words of the offertory prayers soothed her. *What did God make of it all?* she wondered, lifting up her heart. *What did He make of our whole messy human lives?*

His words to the medieval mystic, Julian of Norwich, flooded in on her. "I can make all things well and I shall make all things well and you will see yourself that every kind of thing will be well."

Sister Mary Helen exhaled a long, deep breath. She could hardly wait!